CRIMSON RIVER

USA TODAY BESTSELLING AUTHOR

DEVNEY PERRY

CRIMSON RIVER

ISBN: 978-1-957376-41-7

Editing:

Elizabeth Nover, Razor Sharp Editing

Proofreading:

Julie Deaton, Deaton Author Services

Judy Zweifel, Judy's Proofreading

Vicky Valente

Cover:

Sarah Hansen © Okay Creations

OTHER TITLES

The Edens Series

Christmas in Quincy - Prequel

Indigo Ridge

Juniper Hill

Garnet Flats

Jasper Vale

Crimson River

Sable Peak

Treasure State Wildcats Series

Coach

Blitz

Clifton Forge Series

Steel King

Riven Knight

Stone Princess

Noble Prince

Fallen Jester

Tin Queen

Jamison Valley Series

The Coppersmith Farmhouse

The Clover Chapel

The Lucky Heart

The Outpost

The Bitterroot Inn

The Candle Palace

Maysen Jar Series

The Birthday List

Letters to Molly

The Dandelion Diary

Lark Cove Series

Tattered

Timid

Tragic

Tinsel

Timeless

Runaway Series

Runaway Road

Wild Highway

Quarter Miles

Forsaken Trail

Dotted Lines

Calamity Montana Series

The Bribe

The Bluff

The Brazen

The Bully

The Brawl

The Brood

Standalones

Ivy

Rifts and Refrains

A Little Too Wild

Holiday Brothers

The Naughty, The Nice and The Nanny

Three Bells, Two Bows and One Brother's Best Friend

A Partridge and a Pregnancy

CONTENTS

CHAPTER ONE

LYLA

"I'm staging an intervention."

Not exactly the greeting I'd expected from my sister when she and her husband had walked into Eden Coffee a minute ago. "Huh?"

"I'm kicking you out."

I blinked.

"Of here." Eloise pointed a finger at the counter that separated us. "Right now. You have to leave."

Leave? I was working. There would be no kicking me out. The last time I checked, this was my coffee shop. I stared at her for a long moment, then looked to Jasper standing at her side. "Is she drunk?"

"I'm staying out of this. Good luck, Lyla." He kissed Eloise's hair, then walked to a table against the wall, taking a seat.

"You've worked one hundred days in a row," Eloise said.

A hundred? No way. That couldn't be right. I opened my mouth to argue but she cut me off.

"Yes, I counted. You haven't taken a day off since that Sunday in April when you went to Missoula to get your hair cut."

I scoffed. "I've taken other days off since then."

"Oh, really?" Eloise arched an eyebrow. "When?"

Uh . . . Well, it was September. And the last time I'd gone to Missoula had been April—my hair was in dire straits and in desperate need of another trip to the salon. But I'd taken time off this summer, hadn't I? Maybe not a full day, but there were days when I'd ducked out early. That was practically the same as a vacation, right?

Okay, so technically I'd come to the coffee shop for the past hundred days. Who cared if I worked a lot?

I huffed. "What are you, the work police? Who are you to talk, anyway? You're always at the hotel." If she wasn't at home with Jasper, then she was running The Eloise Inn across Main Street. "Go away. I'm busy."

"Nope." She planted her hands on her hips, and if she had been able to physically dig her heels in, I'd have had two dents in my hardwood floor. There was a stubborn set to Eloise's pretty chin that meant she was not letting this go.

My sister was amazing and exasperating all at the same time.

"One afternoon," she said. "That's all I'm asking for. You leave here for one afternoon and do something non-work related."

"Why?" Couldn't I just be left alone to work in peace?

The sad smile she gave me made me feel both loved and pathetic. "Because I'm worried about you. I don't want you to burn yourself out."

I sighed. "I won't."

"But you might." She clasped her hands together. "Please? Just take the rest of the day off so I can stop worrying."

"I can't just leave, Eloise." This business was my everything. My *only* thing.

"Why not?" She waved to Crystal, my barista, as she came out of the kitchen carrying a fresh tray of scones. "Crystal is here. Jasper and I will hang out and help close."

Jasper might be able to handle it, but Eloise? Never. She was utterly hopeless when it came to cooking, and I wouldn't trust her to steam milk if my life depended on it.

But once again, the second I opened my mouth to object, she talked over me.

"Go home. Relax."

"I can't go home," I said. "If I do, I'll think of everything that needs to get done, and I'll come right back."

If anyone could relate, it should be Eloise. She knew exactly the commitment it took to run a business in downtown Quincy, Montana. Before she'd married Jasper, she'd probably put in her own consecutive hundred days at the hotel.

But now that Eloise had found love, her priorities had shifted, and she was shoving this *balanced lifestyle* down my throat.

This was arguably worse than my twin sister, Talia, who was a doctor at the hospital and kept trying to set me up on a blind date with an X-ray tech. Or my sister-in-law, Memphis, who thought the local UPS driver was cute—even in a brown uniform—and dropped not-so-subtle hints that I should ask him out the next time he brought a delivery to the shop.

It wasn't that I didn't want to date. I *had* dated. For years,

I'd gone on blind dates. I'd let people set me up with their other single friends. I'd even tried a dating app—two matches and two horrible first dates and I'd never ventured down that road again.

I was just . . . over it. Completely, emphatically over it.

Was my devotion to Eden Coffee such a bad thing? Couldn't everyone just leave me and my single, workaholic life alone?

My only ally was Mateo. Just yesterday, my youngest brother had come in griping. Apparently, I wasn't the only Eden being constantly pimped out for dates.

"You could go to a movie," Eloise suggested.

Meh. Did I mind going to the theater alone? No. I'd just rather stay at work. "I don't feel like popcorn. Last time I was there I ate too much and it gave me a stomachache."

"Then don't get popcorn."

"Then what's the fun in going to a movie?"

"You're exhausting." She rolled her eyes. "Go for a hike then. You love hiking, and I know you hardly went this summer. It's a beautiful day. Get some fresh air. Disconnect. Do anything. Just leave this building until tomorrow morning."

"Why?" I whined. "I like it here. Let me stay. I'll make you something yummy. Chocolate croissants?"

"Tempting. But no." She shook her head. "This job is becoming your personality."

What? No, it wasn't. I scrunched up my nose. "Harsh."

"You came into the hotel on Monday and asked if you could get me anything else. In my building."

Was making sure my sister had a coffee or cookie while she worked a damn crime?

"You serve and wait on people every day," she said. "Just . . . for one afternoon, do something for you."

This job *was* for me. I liked watching people come into my coffee shop and unwind. I liked that I'd created an atmosphere where friends could meet to chat. Where people could treat themselves to a pastry or dessert or fancy latte.

But there was no arguing with Eloise. Not today. She had that determined look on her face, one she'd inherited from Dad.

I groaned. "You're not going to leave me alone until I agree, are you?"

"Nope."

"Fine. I'll go for a hike or whatever."

"Yay. Thank you." She failed to hide a victorious smile. "Maybe you'll meet your dream guy while you're out hiking."

Uh-huh, sure. Because Montana hiking trails were teeming with eligible, handsome men who'd worship the ground I walked on.

I untied my apron. "I'm starting to think my dream guy doesn't exist." And maybe that was okay. Maybe this coffee shop, my family, was all I needed. "You'll call me if something goes wrong."

"Yes," she promised.

I locked my blue eyes with hers. "There's plenty of food in the kitchen, but if for any reason cooking is required—"

She held up a hand. "I promise not to go anywhere near an oven. That's why I brought Jasper. Or I'll ask Crystal."

Damn it, this was stupid. I didn't want to go for a hike. I wanted to stay in my coffee shop, surrounded by the scents of vanilla, coffee beans and cinnamon. And the walls with their scuffed molding. And the floor that would need to be mopped tonight. And the sticky tables that would need to be wiped down.

So maybe I was a teeny-tiny bit sick of this place.

Besides, this seemed to be something Eloise needed. And after the shooting at the hotel this summer, well . . . if this would take one worry off her heart, then I could give her an afternoon.

"All right," I said. "You win. I'll go. Happy now?"

"Yep." That smug grin of hers widened.

While she gloated to Crystal, I trudged into the kitchen to collect my stuff.

With my coat slung over an arm and my purse on a shoulder, I headed for the rear exit, ignoring Eloise as she practically shoved me outside. The minute I was alone in the alley, I stuck out my tongue toward the steel door and Eloise, who was probably watching from the peephole.

"An intervention," I muttered as I climbed in my car. Weren't interventions supposed to include more than one person? Jasper didn't count, considering he'd bolted after five seconds.

"Now what?" My finger hesitated over the ignition button. I stared at the back of Eden Coffee. Couldn't I just go back inside where it was familiar? No. I sighed and started my navy-blue Honda. I'd be back tomorrow at four in the morning anyway.

I reversed out of my space and headed down the alley, taking my regular route to my house on the outskirts of Quincy.

The house was quiet. It was always quiet. The couch and TV were tempting, but what I'd told Eloise was true. If I stayed home, I'd think about work and go back. So I swapped out the tennis shoes I'd pulled on this morning for my hiking boots. Then with a warmer coat and a beanie to cover my dark hair, I returned to my car and aimed my tires at the mountains.

Montana was magnificent this time of year. The trees surrounding my small hometown were a riot of color. The bold evergreen forests were infused with limes, yellows, oranges and reds. A layer of mist and fog clung to the mountaintops.

As I made my way along the winding road that led to my favorite hiking area, I cracked the window an inch, breathing in the crisp, cool air.

My shoulders relaxed deeper into the seat. My pulse calmed. Maybe after this hike, I'd feel more like myself.

Ever since my thirtieth birthday this spring, I'd struggled to feel . . . normal. Something was going on with me, but I couldn't quite pinpoint it. Was it depression? Anxiety? Restlessness?

Quincy was home. It had always been home. The idea of moving to a new town made my stomach churn, but lately I'd been wondering . . .

What next?

I'd spent the better part of a decade establishing my business. From the day I'd graduated college and moved home, I'd poured everything into Eden Coffee. I'd proved to myself that I could be a successful entrepreneur. I wasn't just the best pastry chef in a hundred-mile radius, but I also had the intelligence and savvy to manage a profitable business. I'd used my inheritance wisely and hadn't squandered the gift from my parents.

I lived debt-free. Both the building downtown and my home were mine and mine alone. I'd made enough last year from the shop to buy this new car with cash. Beyond that financial stability, I was surrounded by family and friends. If I wanted a buzzing social life—which I didn't—I could have one.

And men, well . . . I could date if I wanted to date. But I didn't.

From the outside, my life was rock solid. So why couldn't I shake this unease? This feeling that I was missing something. This feeling that somehow, I'd failed. That I was marching in the wrong direction.

I was off-kilter and didn't know how to find steady.

It was easier to ignore those feelings at work. The shop was busy and kept my head from wandering. Was that my problem? I'd been ignoring myself for too long?

Was Eden Coffee my personality? Was I okay with that?

I didn't have an answer. So instead, I concentrated on the road, driving to a small, familiar turnout off the highway.

There wasn't an established trailhead along this particular section of the river. It was a secluded area mostly frequented by local, experienced hikers.

The tourists who flocked to Quincy every summer typically headed to Glacier to hike. Those who stayed close used the wider, maintained trails.

This spot was really nothing more than an access point to the Clark Fork River. The woods were dense, and unless you knew what to expect, it didn't exactly scream *Stop Here to Discover Montana!*

In the spring, I preferred hiking trails that led to open meadows where I could pick wildflowers. But in the fall, when the river was low and the rocky banks dry, I could meander along the water as I took in the scenery.

It was my parents who'd taught me to love the outdoors. My dad had always said that breathing in Montana's fresh air for an hour was a surefire way to cure any ailment. His preferred way to explore was on horseback. So was Talia's and Griffin's. And while I did love riding my horse, Mercury, there was something peaceful about walking through nature on my own two feet.

My hiking backpack had been sitting in the bottom of my closet for far, far too long. I zipped my keys in its front pocket, patting the side pouch that held my bear spray. Then with my empty water bottle stowed away, I donned my coat and hat before heading into the woods, breathing in the scent of earth and pine.

By the time I made it to the river, a weight had lifted off my shoulders.

I hadn't even realized how much I'd needed to get away. To ignore the stress from work and just . . . breathe.

Okay, so maybe Eloise had a point. Tomorrow, I'd have to say thank you. She'd never let me live it down.

I tugged my phone from my pocket to check the time, and to make sure I hadn't missed any calls. The screen was blank.

A few years ago, I would have been flooded with texts on a Friday afternoon. My sisters wanting to go out to dinner. My brothers wanting to meet at Willie's for a drink. Mom and Dad inviting us all to some activity in town.

But lately, it seemed like everyone had their own life.

Was that what was bothering me? That I felt left behind?

With the exception of Mateo, my siblings were married. They were all having children, growing their own families. Mom and Dad were reveling in their retirement and grandkids.

I refused to be jealous of their happiness. Refused.

It was harder to refuse the loneliness.

On a sigh, I tucked my phone away and filled my lungs with the crisp mountain air, holding it in until it burned. Then I headed off my path, following the river as I made my way deeper into the forest.

Another reason I liked this area was because it kept cell service. I had my pepper spray in case I encountered an animal, but if I ever got lost, I had my phone and GPS to find my way home. So I walked in no hurry, with no destination in mind, breathing easier and easier as my muscles warmed and loosened.

A hawk's scream pierced the sky, echoing through the river valley. The bird soared overhead, then disappeared past the treetops.

After an hour, sweat beaded at my temples and my throat was parched. I unstrapped my pack, pulling out my empty water bottle, then traversed the round, smooth rocks that bordered the river. The best part about this spot was the clean, cold water.

I twisted the lid from the bottle, crouching to fill it, but froze when a trickle of red washed past my feet like a crimson cloud floating in a stream.

Blood.

Every muscle in my body tensed, my heart climbing into my throat. *Shit.*

Slowly, I stretched an arm backward, lifting my can of pepper spray from its pocket. That blood had to be coming from a recent kill. A deer had probably come to the river for a drink, like me, and been ambushed by a predator.

Would I prefer a run-in with a mountain lion or a grizzly bear? Mountain lion. Probably. Damn it.

Please don't be a grizzly bear or a mountain lion.

I rose to my feet, barely breathing as I moved an inch at a time. Maybe if I could sneak away, whatever predator was having a snack upstream wouldn't even notice me. With a silent step, I turned, bracing as I scanned the riverbanks.

Not a grizzly bear or a mountain lion.

A hunter.

The air rushed from my lungs. Oh, thank God.

I returned my canister of pepper spray to its pocket, then twisted the lid on my water bottle.

The hunter was positioned with his back in my direction. He rested on his knees as he washed his bloody hands in the river.

Closer to the trees, I spotted his kill. Not a deer, but an elk. Its tan hide had been folded into a neat square. He must have quartered the animal already because there were hunks of meat in white game bags strapped to his pack. A bow and quiver of arrows were propped up against a nearby log. And about twenty feet from his pack was the gut pile—red and greenish gray and still steaming.

The hunter stood, shaking out his wet hands.

I opened my mouth, about to make a sound so he'd know he wasn't alone, when he turned and spotted me.

He did a double take.

I waved. "Hi. Sorry to sneak up—"

He burst into long strides, moving toward me with such intensity that I glanced over my shoulder to make sure there wasn't actually a grizzly bear behind me.

When I faced forward again, he was still marching toward me so fast that I stepped backward, stumbling on a rock. I righted myself and held up both hands, dropping my water bottle. "I'm sorry. I didn't mean to startle you. I'll leave."

He kept coming, like a bullet intent on its target. He moved too fast for me to escape. Too fast for me to make any sense of this.

Run, Lyla.

He reached me before I could run. And before I could scream or make a sound, he wrapped his large, wet hands around my neck.

Pain exploded through my throat. I tried to drag in a breath but his grip was impossibly tight. My eyes burned and tears streamed down my cheeks.

"Stop." My voice was barely a gurgle. My hands came to his wrists, tugging and pulling. Smacking and slapping.

He squeezed harder.

No. No, this wasn't happening. This was just a nightmare. I'd tripped on a stick in the woods and hit my head. This was my imagination playing tricks on me. I was really at home, asleep on the couch and having a bad dream. Because why would this man want to kill me?

No, this wasn't real.

I gasped for breath, desperate to fill my lungs. Balling my hands into fists, I bashed them against his forearms, but he was too strong. Too tall. Too big.

I kicked at his shins, but the edges of my vision were growing fuzzy. The lack of oxygen was already pulling darkness closer.

This man was going to kill me. This was where I'd die. Beside the river, in the middle of the Montana wilderness, strangled by a stranger.

Dad was on the expanded search and rescue team for the county. So was Griffin. So was Knox. So was Mateo.

Please don't let one of them find my body.

Through the tears, I took in my killer's face. He had

reddish-orange hair—a ginger. The stubble on his granite face was the same color. His eyes were a rich brown, like the brownies I'd made this morning at the coffee shop. There was a jagged scar on his face, pink and about six inches long. It ran from the corner of his eye all the way to his chin.

How did he get that scar? I guess I'd never know.

The black crept closer, faster.

Why? I mouthed the word, unable to speak.

My arms and legs were getting so heavy. I batted at his wrists again, using the last of my strength until my hands dropped to my sides and my knees buckled. My eyelids might as well have been made of lead. They drifted closed as my head began to float.

The bear spray. I reached for the pocket, my movements sluggish, but I managed to slip my index finger through the trigger's circle. But before I could even think about lifting the can, his hold on my throat loosened. The can slipped from my grip, clattering against the ground at my feet.

Then I was falling too.

My knees cracked on the rocks and pain ripped through my legs. I collapsed on a shoulder, my hands coming to my throat. It burned like he'd set it on fire, but his hands were gone.

He'd let me go.

I coughed and gagged, dragging in air through my nose, anything to fill my lungs. I clutched my stomach, curling up on the ground, gasping for a full breath. Every inhale ached. The tears kept flowing, my insides churning as my head spun in circles.

He'd let me go.

Why? I forced my eyes open, risking a glance in the distance. The backpack, the bow and the man were gone.

He was gone.

I gave myself three heartbeats. Then I shoved up to my feet.

Run, Lyla.

This time, I ran.

CHAPTER TWO

VANCE

Where the hell was my wallet? I patted my jeans pocket for the tenth time, then scanned the bedroom again. It wasn't on the nightstand. I'd put it on the nightstand. The damn thing couldn't have sprouted legs and walked away.

"For fuck's sake." I didn't have time to search for my wallet when I needed to get on the road, but before I could get on the road, I needed my fucking wallet.

"Tiff," I hollered, pinching the bridge of my nose.

She emerged from the hallway and stood in the doorway, hazel eyes still blazing from our argument. "What?"

"My wallet. Have you seen it?"

She pursed her lips.

"Tiff," I clipped. Did she really think if she kept me here long enough, I'd change my mind?

She huffed and fished my wallet from her back pocket. With a flick of her wrist, she tossed it on the bed so it landed beside my backpack and suitcase.

I gritted my teeth, holding back a snide comment. "Thanks."

"You're really going." She crossed her arms over her chest, her nostrils flaring.

"I have to go." I swept up my wallet, tucking it in my own pocket, then slung my backpack over a shoulder. The zipper's seams were stretched to the max. The same was true for my suitcase. Not having any idea how long I'd be in Montana, I'd erred on the side of too much rather than not enough.

"I mean it, Vance. I won't be here when you get back."

She'd said the same earlier after I'd told her I was going to Montana. It hadn't really surprised me, probably because I'd been expecting it for, well . . . a long time.

"You don't have anything to say?" she asked.

No. No, I didn't. And my silence only heightened her frustration.

She threw a hand in the air. "When are you going to give this up?"

"Never," I whispered.

Until my dying day, I would never give up this search. Everyone else had stopped looking for Cormac. Everyone else had abandoned Norah and the girls. They deserved justice. They deserved vengeance.

There was no giving up.

"You won't find him," she said.

"I might."

"He's. Gone." She punched each word, like volume alone would make me believe them.

He wasn't gone. That son of a bitch didn't get to be gone.

Maybe this lead would turn into nothing, just like every other lead I'd followed in the past four years. But if there was even the slightest chance I could catch Cormac's trail, then I'd take it.

I hefted my suitcase off the mattress, moving for the door, but Tiff shifted and blocked my path.

"I can't do this anymore." Her chin began to quiver. "I can't stay here and wait while you chase your demons."

"Then don't."

When we'd first gotten together, Tiff had encouraged me to go. But at some point in the past three years, she'd become just like everyone else. She wanted me to let it go and move on with my life.

I couldn't move on. I *wouldn't.* And if she didn't understand that, well . . .

"Leave the keys on the counter." We were over. We'd been over. It was time to stop pretending like we had a future together.

"That's it?" Her eyes flooded. "I tell you I'm moving out and you ask me to leave the keys on the counter?"

Yes. "I need to go," I said, jerking my chin for her to get out of the way.

She shifted, just enough for me to slide past, then followed me down the hallway. "You never would have done this before the shooting."

My jaw clenched. "This has nothing to do with the shooting."

"Vance."

I sighed, turning to face her. "What?"

"Please don't go." Tears glistened in her eyes. "Stay. Stay with me."

This was why we were over.

If she truly loved me, she'd never ask me to stay.

I set my suitcase and backpack on the floor, then put my hands on her shoulders. "I'm sorry."

I was sorry that I wasn't the man she needed. I was sorry that I couldn't be the man she'd expected. I was sorry that I didn't love her too.

"I love you." A tear fell down her cheek.

I didn't catch it.

"Bye, Tiff." I stepped away as a sob escaped her mouth. Then I collected my bags and, without a backward glance, walked to the garage. My gun was already loaded in the glove box of my truck, so with my things in the back seat, I climbed behind the wheel and took off.

Maybe I should have hurt, knowing that Tiff would be gone when I got home. Instead, I felt . . . relieved.

Tiff was a good woman who'd helped me through a hard period in my life. She'd filled a void, for a time. She'd made me laugh when I'd thought it impossible. But she deserved a man who loved her entirely.

That man wasn't me.

Maybe she was right. Maybe this endless search for Cormac was ruining my life. It sure as hell had taken a toll on my job. But I wasn't going to stop. So I put Coeur d'Alene in my rearview mirror and raced along the interstate toward Montana.

It was a three-hour trip to Quincy, meaning if I hurried, I'd arrive before dark with time to poke around town and get my bearings. I'd already called ahead for a hotel room, booking it for a week. With any luck, I'd pick up Cormac's trail by then.

This lead was the closest I'd ever been to finding that slippery bastard. It had been two days since the APB had been issued, and while two days was plenty for him to disappear, maybe he'd gotten complacent. Maybe he wouldn't feel the need to rush. Or maybe he hadn't left Montana at all.

I'd spent four years chasing Cormac Gallagher. From Washington to Utah to Oregon to Colorado, the man had proved impossible to find. He'd beaten me at every turn. But this time around, something felt different.

How long had he been in Montana? Why had he come so close to Idaho? Had he been hiding right under my nose for months? Years?

Or would this turn out to be another dead end?

Three years ago, I'd followed a lead to Colorado. Police had reported a man matching Cormac's description. Red hair. Brown eyes. Same build and height. But that man hadn't had a scarred cheek, and when I'd found him hiding in a ramshackle house in the mountains outside of Fort Collins, I'd turned him over to the authorities, then come home and drowned myself in a bottle of cheap whiskey.

Six months later, I'd followed a lead to Utah. Another bust. Four months later, I'd been in Washington. Three months after that, Oregon. I'd spent four years traipsing around the Pacific Northwest, following any lead.

Chances were, my trip to Montana would be another wasted trip. Except the all-points bulletin from Quincy had clearly described a man with a scar. None of the others had given that much detail.

This time, it would be different. It had to be different.

I pulled out my phone to call Dad. The minute it started ringing through the truck's speakers, my grip tightened on the wheel. *Go to voicemail.*

"Hello," he answered.

I sighed. "Hey, Dad."

"Hold on a sec." There was a rustling noise in the background. Then came the sound of a door opening and closing. "What's going on?"

There was an echo, like he'd closed himself in the garage.

That was usually how it sounded when we'd talk. Either he'd disappear to the garage or he'd go outside so he could talk to me where Mom wouldn't overhear.

How had it come to this? How had I become the villain?

"I'm heading to Montana. Might be gone a week or two," I told him, knowing he wouldn't ask why or how long I'd be gone.

Asking too many questions might cross that invisible line drawn between me and my family. Besides, Dad knew why I left town. And like Tiff, he thought I should have moved on years ago.

"All right," he murmured.

"I left in a hurry. Would you mind taking the trash to the curb on Wednesday?"

"What about Tiff?"

"She's moving out."

"Oh." He paused. "Okay."

"And would you mind grabbing my mail every few days? Just so it doesn't pile up."

"Sure."

"Thanks, Dad."

"Yep." He ended the call.

These stinted, abrupt conversations had become normal. And somehow, that was my fault.

Next time I left, I'd call a friend to check on the house.

I set my phone aside and focused on the road, taking in the landscape along the way. Plenty of mountains. Dense evergreen forests. This part of Montana wasn't all that different from Idaho. Maybe that was why Cormac had returned. He'd wanted a taste of home.

The only thing he deserved to taste was three squares a day from a prison cafeteria.

Fuck, but I hoped this lead was something real. Hope was a dangerous game for a man like me, especially where Cormac was concerned. But with every passing mile, it stirred, building and swelling in my very bones.

By the time I arrived in Quincy, my muscles were jittery. My fingers drummed on the steering wheel as the highway slowed, turning into Main Street. As I eased down the road, I soaked in the small town like a sponge.

The Eloise Inn, the hotel where I'd booked a room, was the tallest building in sight, interrupting the jagged mountain horizon in the distance. Businesses, restaurants and a couple of bars filled the downtown area.

The lampposts that lit the sidewalks were wrapped in twinkle lights. Store windows were decked out in autumn décor, pumpkins and potted mums and vibrant leaves.

As I passed a hardware store, I made a mental note to stop by and pick up a map of the local area. Digital maps and GPS worked for some, but I'd always preferred paper.

My mentor had taught me that.

He'd also taught me that time was critical. If a suspect had too much of a head start, catching up became impossible. The APB had been posted Friday afternoon. Unfortunately, it was Sunday. But two days was faster than any of the other leads I'd found.

Maybe Cormac thought that after four years, the world had forgotten about his crimes. Maybe he'd gotten comfortable wherever it was he was hiding. Maybe if he'd built a shelter, settled into the area, he might not be as quick to leave.

A string of maybes. That was all I had.

It would have to be enough.

I parked on Main, taking my bags from the back of my silver Dodge and hauling them into The Eloise Inn. The desk clerk checked me in efficiently, sending me to my room on the fourth floor with two keys and restaurant recommendations for dinner.

I was too anxious to eat much, so rather than stop by Knuckles, the hotel's restaurant, I dropped my bags in my room, then headed outside.

"Howdy." A man nodded as I passed him on the sidewalk outside the hotel.

"Evening." I dipped my chin, already liking Quincy's friendly atmosphere and the fact that here, I was a nameless, faceless stranger.

I'd hardly left the house in the past two weeks because of the recent media attention. The one time I'd gone to the grocery store, I'd gotten plenty of sideways glances. The cashier had flat-out asked me if I was *that cop*.

Until that shitstorm died down, I was more than happy to spend my days in Montana.

Ironic, that I'd started my career to stand apart. To be one of the heroes. To wear my gleaming badge with pride. These days, the last thing I wanted was attention. And my badge had a tarnish that no amount of polishing seemed to erase.

Exactly why I'd left it behind.

I crossed Main, heading for the coffee shop. The small green building had a sandwich board out front advertising today's specials. *Mocha latte. Ham, apple and swiss panini.*

Pumpkin chocolate chip cookies. The words were written in chunky block letters, each adorned with swirly flowers.

The shop's large, black-paned windows consumed most of the street-facing wall, giving patrons a clear view of the sidewalk and street. In the evening light, they acted like a mirror, reflecting the cars that passed as well as people walking by, me included.

Goddamn, I looked like shit. I dragged a hand through my hair, attempting to tame the dark strands. It needed a cut, and I hadn't shaved in a few days. The stubble on my jaw was thick. Maybe I'd leave it, grow a beard.

Tiff hated beards.

That didn't matter anymore. And a beard might distract from the dark circles beneath my eyes. Sleep had been light since, well . . . I couldn't remember the last time I'd slept for more than four or five hours in a row.

I finger combed my hair one more time, but the effort was futile, so I straightened the collar of my plaid jacket before reaching the coffee shop's door.

Eden Coffee was written on its face in gold lettering. I pulled it open and breathed in the scent of coffee and food. Good food. My stomach growled. Guess I was hungry.

I'd been in the middle of lunch with my laptop when I'd come across the Quincy Police Department's APB. That meal had been abandoned in the trash, and I hadn't stopped again once I'd hit the road.

The shop's walls were the same deep green as the exterior, giving it a warm, inviting feel. Wooden tables and chairs filled the space on either side of the aisle that led to a counter at the back of the café.

The glass display case overflowed with pastries and desserts. The espresso machine's hiss dulled the conversation from the occupied tables. My boots thudded on the hardwood floor as I made my way to the counter.

The barista wore a pine-green apron. Her jet-black hair was pulled into a short ponytail at the nape of her neck. She had thick, winged eyeliner and her lips were stained purple. Not plum or wine, purple, like a grape jellybean.

She held up a finger as she finished steaming her jug of milk. "Give me one minute."

"Sure." I nodded, scanning the large chalkboard menu mounted to the wall behind the counter.

A table in the far corner beside the glass windows would give me an open view of Main and also provide a decent workspace. Better than the cramped desk in my hotel room.

"What can I get you?" the barista asked.

"Ham and swiss panini, please. And a, uh . . ." I peered into the display case. "What's your favorite thing in there?"

"It's all good, but I think Lyla is just finishing a batch of her cowboy cookies. Highly recommend." She pinched her fingers together and did a chef's kiss.

"Sold." I dug out my wallet, handing over a twenty just as a woman emerged from the hallway that led deeper into the building.

She carried a tray of cookies, her hands covered in tangerine oven mitts. Her apron was the same pine-green shade as the barista's. A dusting of flour covered her heart and there was a one-inch streak on her forehead, above her delicate right eyebrow.

Her cheeks were flushed the same pretty shade of pink as her soft pout. A tendril of dark hair had escaped the messy knot on the top of her head and swept across her temple.

My hand lifted, acting on its own, either to tuck that lock of hair behind an ear or wipe away the flour streak.

Her sapphire-blue eyes darted to me as she set the tray on the counter, then pulled off the oven mitts.

Even with the two black eyes she'd tried her best to cover with makeup, she was breathtaking.

She offered me a small smile before dropping her chin into the chunky scarf wrapped around her neck as she began adding cookies to the display case. That scarf was thick, but the bruises on the long column of her throat seemed determined to make an appearance. They peeked out beneath her dainty jaw.

Black eyes. Bruised throat. Clear signs that someone had wrapped their hands around her neck.

The APB from the local authorities had described Cormac perfectly. Better than any previous report. The bulletin had stated that he was a suspect in an attempted murder but hadn't listed a means.

Strangulation, maybe? That was fitting. And according to the APB, this crime had occurred outside of Quincy, in the wilderness. Cormac's playground.

There was a chance this woman had nothing to do with him. That I was simply desperate. But I'd listened to my gut for a long, long time. And it was shouting that she was the one who'd crossed Cormac's path.

"Here you go." The barista set a plate on the counter with my sandwich, some chips, a pickle and one of those fresh cookies. "Anything to drink?"

"Water. Please."

"You got it." She nodded, then put her hand on the other woman's shoulder. "I can finish with the cookies, Lyla."

She nodded as the barista walked to the sink against the back to fill me a glass of water. But she didn't abandon those cookies. She kept putting them in the display case.

Lyla. Beautiful name. Beautiful woman. Too beautiful to be covered in bruises.

It was just another sin that Cormac would suffer for. I'd make that bastard pay for what he'd done to the girls. To Norah. And to Lyla.

She noticed me staring. That flush in her cheeks brightened. "Can I help you?"

Her voice was raspy. Raw. Barely a whisper.

"Yeah." I nodded. "I think you can."

CHAPTER THREE

LYLA

There was something in the way this man spoke, the way he stared, that made me stand a little straighter. That made me stop trying to hide my face. It was like . . . he knew.

Impossible.

He was arguably the most ruggedly handsome man I'd ever seen in my life. His was not a face I'd forget, which meant he was likely just visiting Quincy. The only people who knew what had happened along the river on Friday were locals—gossip was galloping through town like a stampede of wild stallions.

Rumor was, my near-death incident would make the *Quincy Gazette*'s front page on Wednesday's weekly edition.

I would not be reading the paper this week.

This guy was probably staring because of the shitty attempt I'd made to conceal my black eyes. Most of the makeup I'd put on at three this morning had faded after a long day. Or he was staring because of this freaking scarf. It was thick and heavy, and despite my best efforts, the chunky material wouldn't stay tight enough beneath my chin to hide the bruises.

"Can we talk for a moment?" He jerked his chin toward the tables.

Talk about what? How I looked like someone's personal punching bag? *Fun.*

"Please," he begged.

There it was again. The feeling that he knew. Who was he? Only one way to find out. I pointed to his sandwich. "I'll let you eat, then join you in a moment."

"All right." He picked up his plate, waiting until Crystal set a glass of ice water on the counter, then swept it up too. "I'll be fast."

"No rush."

His gaze darted to my throat, then he turned and crossed the room. He had a confident stride. Long legs covered in faded jeans. Scuffed boots. Stubbled jaw. Broad shoulders and disheveled hair. Tall. Very tall. *Great* ass.

Exactly my type.

Of course the universe would deliver me a sexy, beautiful man when the very last thing I wanted was to be touched. When I couldn't even flirt because of my fucking voice.

I sounded like I'd been a lifelong smoker, and every hoarse, hitched syllable ached.

The pain had continually worsened over the weekend. Probably because I kept talking. Talia had told me the quickest way to recover was to rest, but I refused to stay at home and hide. I wouldn't cower and give that son of a bitch who'd tried to kill me the satisfaction of my defeat.

So here I was, working. Yesterday morning, when my mother and Crystal had shown up at five to open Eden

Coffee, I'd already been here for an hour. Their every attempt to shoo me out the door had been thwarted with an adamant *no*.

Dad and Griffin had come in this morning to try and convince me to spend a week at the ranch recuperating. But I'd held up my chin and marched into the kitchen to make cranberry-orange scones.

If I had just stayed at work on Friday, none of this would have happened in the first place. Not that I blamed Eloise—though she was determined to carry the blame regardless. She'd been so upset this morning when she and Jasper had come in to check on me that I'd had to practically shake her to listen as I'd choked out how this wasn't her fault.

There was one and only one person to blame. That motherfucking hunter.

Still, I'd be damned if anyone would run me out of my own building again.

This was where I wanted to be, so I was staying.

"Crystal." I lowered my voice. It didn't hurt as much when I whispered.

"Yeah?" She appeared at my side in a snap, abandoning the coffee she'd been making. She'd been a trooper, hovering close, ready to do whatever I asked. Crystal was the only person who hadn't tried to get me to leave. I loved her for that.

"Do you know who that is?" I nodded toward the man. He'd taken the far table beside the windows and was inhaling his sandwich.

"No. I've never seen him before."

I nodded, then touched her forearm before getting a coffee mug from the stack and filling it with hot water. Whatever that man wanted, I'd need something to drink if we were going to talk, so I made myself a tea, letting it steep while he demolished his meal.

The busy summer tourist season was over. It was too early for holiday visitors. This time of year, Quincy saw an influx of hunters, and while this guy's rough edge and outdoorsy vibe fit that image, my intuition said that wasn't why he'd come to town.

Why? No idea. Something about him just felt . . . different.

Maybe my near-death experience had given me some sixth sense—or delusions. For all I knew, I'd go to that table and he'd deliver some cheesy pickup line. Though with a face like his, he probably just crooked a finger and women hopped into his bed.

I took a sip of my tea, letting the warmth soothe my throat. Then I carried it across the shop.

When he saw me coming, the man wiped his lips with a napkin, then balled it up and set it on his now empty plate as I took the chair across from his.

"Vance Sutter." He stretched a hand across the table.

My hand was dwarfed by his as I returned his shake. His grip was rough but warm. "Lyla Eden."

"Eden." His gray-blue eyes flicked to the door at my back.

"This is my coffee shop."

He nodded, studying my face. Once more, his gaze darted to my scarf. "I'll cut to the chase. I'm looking for a man."

I sat taller, my heart beginning to race. Oh my God, I knew it. I freaking knew it. *He* knew it. How?

"Who?" I croaked.

"I'm guessing the man who did that to you." He pointed

to my throat, then opened one side of his jacket, pulling out a piece of paper that had been folded into quarters. He splayed it open, flattening it on the table. "Came across this APB from your local police station."

I'd never read or seen an APB before. As he spun it around to face me, *armed and dangerous* practically leapt off the page. There was a description of the man from the river, and even reading the words made me shiver. Red hair. Brown eyes. Six-inch scar running across his cheek, from eye to chin.

I wrapped my arms around my waist as my stomach knotted.

If I closed my eyes, I saw his face. At night, when I tried to sleep, I felt his hands on my throat. I felt them squeeze. I felt them release.

Friday, after that man had let me go, I picked myself up off the riverbank and made my way back to my car. The trek was harrowing. I stumbled and tripped, struggling to breathe.

Panic fueled my every step. I was sure that man was following me. That maybe it was some sick and twisted game to let me go, only to capture me once more and finish the job the second time around.

Thankfully, it was only paranoia and fear. I made it to my car, and the moment I slid into the driver's seat and locked my doors, my body collapsed against the steering wheel.

Crying had never hurt so badly in my life. The sobs were so painful that I forced myself to stop. And when I pulled myself together enough to quell the shaking, I called Dad.

When life got hard, Dad was always my first call.

Help. That was all I said. All I could say.

A split-second later, his recliner closed with an audible

snap. Then came a door opening and closing along with the jingle of keys.

He asked me if I was hurt. *Yes.*

He asked if I could drive. *Yes.*

Get to the hospital, Lyla. I'd been stuck before that, locked in my quiet car. That command from my father snapped me into action.

While I drove into town, so did Dad. He stayed on the line with me until I reached Quincy. Then he hung up to call my sister.

Talia was waiting in the parking lot when I pulled into Quincy Memorial. Dad arrived thirty seconds later, having broken every speed limit from the ranch to town.

They took a single look at my face and neck and rushed me into the emergency room. While Talia did her exam, Dad held my hand.

She promised there wasn't any permanent damage to my windpipe. The swelling and bruising would get worse before it got better. My bloodshot eyes would return to normal. The black eyes would fade. She gave me a painkiller to get me through the worst of it.

It wasn't until the exam was over that Dad broke. We both broke.

His shoulder had always been my favorite to cry on, so the moment he pulled me into his arms, I fell apart. Totally. The crying jag destroyed my already wrecked throat.

Dad called Winn. Winn called Mom. Mom called Griffin. An hour later, my entire family was crowded around my hospital bed to listen while I recounted the entire ordeal to Winn, my sister-in-law, Quincy's chief of police.

It had taken me longer to explain how I'd nearly been strangled to death than the actual strangling had taken. That hunter had choked me for less than twenty seconds, yet every time I replayed it in my mind, it felt like he'd had my throat in his grip for an eternity before he'd let me go.

Why had he let me go?

Vance cleared his throat.

I shook myself out of my head. It wasn't the first time I'd gotten lost in my own thoughts today. "Sorry."

"Don't be." He took his wallet from his jeans pocket, rifling through the leather billfold. Then he slipped out an old photograph and handed it over. "Is this him?"

I gulped. My heart climbed into my throat as I reached for the photo, bringing it closer. My hands trembled as I stared at the man who'd almost murdered me.

Red hair. Brown eyes. Scarred face.

He was smiling in the picture. His happiness was jarring, like this had been taken of a different man in a different lifetime. But there was no mistake. It was the motherfucker.

"Yes."

Vance's entire frame relaxed, like he'd hoped that would be my answer but had braced himself for disappointment.

The photo's edges were tattered. Its colors faded. How many times had Vance handed this picture to someone? Or had it been his own fingers that had traced the corners until they were rounded and soft?

"Has he hurt people before?" I asked.

Vance nodded.

I dropped the picture like it was aflame. "You're here to find him."

"I am." His deep, gravelly voice was infused with confidence. That surety was a sharp contrast to the hopelessness I'd felt all day after Winn's update last night.

After she'd taken my statement at the hospital, she'd

sprung into action. Within an hour, she'd issued the APB with the description I'd provided. She'd engaged with the county sheriff's department, who had activated the search and rescue team to scour the mountains.

My dad and brothers had been part of that effort. Over twenty people and three dogs had combed over the area where I'd been attacked.

They'd stayed out late Friday night, well past dark, and had finally returned to town empty-handed. Yesterday, more of the same. If there was a trail to find, it had been lost.

That asshole had escaped.

Winn would likely be here soon with another update. I didn't expect a different outcome.

"The local authorities haven't found him," I told Vance. "What makes you think you can?" Maybe it was my ragged voice, but I wasn't sure I'd ever sounded more cynical. Maybe all it took was one horrid experience to crush a person's positive spirit.

"I've been searching for Cormac for years."

I shuddered. "That's his name?"

"Cormac Gallagher." Vance nodded, taking the photo from the table and returning it to his wallet.

"Who are you?" I locked my gaze with his.

I wasn't the type of person who could spot lies. Trusting people just felt . . . normal. The default. Except I'd immediately given my trust to that man—Cormac—by the river. I'd assumed he was good.

So maybe it was time I learned to spot untruths. To be wary of those who came into this shop, Vance Sutter included.

"I'm a cop from Coeur d'Alene. Cormac is the main suspect in a murder investigation."

"Oh."

Cop. Cormac. Murder. My head was spinning.

"Who did he kill?" Was it another innocent woman out for a hike? How many people had he killed? Had they been strangled?

Vance's gaze flicked to the table. He stayed quiet.

I knew without asking he wouldn't answer. Was that better or worse than a lie to my face?

Better.

Except Vance still hadn't answered my previous question. Why did he think he'd have different luck than Winn, the sheriff and a team of people trained to search this area for missing hikers or hunters? People like my dad and brothers who'd lived here their entire lives?

"What makes you so sure you can find him?"

"I'm not sure." Honesty coated that baritone voice. "I've spent four years following dead-end leads. This might be another. Chances are, he's long gone. But what if he's not? That what-if is worth it for me to be here. You're the first person in years who can confirm Cormac's whereabouts."

"Lucky me," I muttered.

Vance offered a kind smile. "I'm sorry. For what he did, I'm sorry."

Everyone was sorry. I didn't need pity. What I needed was that son of a bitch rotting in a prison cell.

"Of all the people I've shown that photo, no one could tell me definitely yes or no. A few times, I went after a suspect with a similar description but it turned out to be someone else. I'm here because I know Cormac better than anyone alive. And I'd like him to be punished for what he's done."

It was like Vance could read my thoughts. The anger

burning in my chest gave his voice a razor-sharp edge. "Me too."

"Look." He leaned his forearms on the table, those gray-blue irises brightening with intensity. They were so light they were almost clear. Mesmerizing. "I understand if you'd rather not go through it again. You've been through enough. But I'd like to hear from you what happened. Ask a few questions if you're up for it."

Was I up for it? I took a sip of my tea, the warm liquid easing some of the discomfort in my throat.

Before I'd even made the conscious decision to trust Vance, my mouth opened and the story came pouring out. From Eloise encouraging me to go on a hike, to my panic-fueled drive to the hospital, I gave Vance as many details as I'd given Winn.

My voice was steady. Cold. It was like I was reading a report, not retelling an event in my life. Apparently two days was all it had taken for me to detach from the trauma. Was that good or bad?

When I was finished, silence descended upon the table. A crease formed between Vance's eyebrows, like he was taking my story and piecing it together with whatever history he had with this Cormac.

"Why did he let me go?" I whispered.

Vance's gaze snapped to mine. He looked as unsure as I felt. "I don't know."

If he really was running from the police, if he really did intend to escape, leaving me alive made no sense. Now I was a witness.

"I have no right to ask this, but I'm going to ask anyway," he said. "Would you go with me? Show me where this happened?"

My heart seized. "Why?"

"Cormac is not going to be easy to track. It's why he's evaded us for so long. The more help you can give me, the better chance I'll find a trail."

It should have been an easy no. Vance could sync up with Winn. He could work with the local search and rescue team to explore the area. He didn't need me as his guide.

And I sure as hell didn't need to go back there. To relive it in person. The memory was hard enough.

"Nice to meet you, Mr. Sutter." I pushed away from the table, and with my tea in hand, I walked to the counter, passing Crystal as I headed straight for the kitchen. My sanctuary.

The moment I was out of sight, I let out the breath I'd been holding. My heart raced as I planted my hands on my prep table, closing my eyes as a wave of nerves made my stomach roil. It was either from telling Vance my story or just the idea of returning to that spot.

Could I go back? Should I?

"Lyla?"

I opened my eyes at my twin sister's voice, twisting to the door as Talia rushed inside. She was dressed in blue scrubs. Her baby bump was starting to stretch her top. Not by a lot, but enough that you could tell she was pregnant with my future niece or nephew, who I planned to spoil rotten.

"Are you okay?" She tugged at my scarf, pulling it down to inspect my neck.

"Fine." I waved her off, taking the damn thing off entirely. It was too hot in the kitchen for a scarf. Tomorrow I'd suffer in a turtleneck instead.

"You pushed too hard today." Talia's eyebrows knitted

together. She wore the same concern she had since Friday. The same expression I saw on every other face in my family.

I shook my head, not wanting to speak. Talking to Vance had zapped my energy, and my throat was raw and ragged.

"Please, Lyla. Go home. You need to rest."

I shook my head again, giving her a sad smile.

Talia's shoulders slumped. The corners of her mouth turned down. Her eyes turned glassy but she didn't let a tear fall.

My sister didn't cry in front of others. At least, not often. She had this steel, this incredible strength. Whatever tragedy walked through the ER's doors at the hospital, she took it in stride.

Me? I was the blubbering mess. Show me a sappy video on social media or tell me a sad story, I'd cry a river next to the espresso machine with a crowd of customers around to watch.

Yet here I was, the dry-eyed sister in the room. Meanwhile, Talia looked like she was about to crack.

"Want to talk about it? Or write it out?" she asked. "To save your voice."

"No." I shook my head.

"Are you sure? It might help."

I shook my head again.

Normally, I harped on Talia to open up and confess her feelings. I encouraged her to talk and air her struggles—she rarely did. Strange, how we'd swapped roles.

Everything felt different. That bastard had tipped our worlds upside down and I just . . . I didn't want to cry. I didn't want to be hugged or coddled. I didn't want to talk.

I wanted justice. I wanted revenge so badly I could barely see straight. And since Winn had yet to apprehend

Cormac Gallagher, all I had to keep my sanity intact was work.

So I forced a smile and reached for Talia's hand, holding it tight when her palm touched mine. Then I let her go and walked to the fridge, taking out the ingredients for cinnamon rolls.

Talia stayed for an hour, watching me work in silence. I sent her home with a to-go container of soup so she and Foster wouldn't have to cook dinner. Then I spent the rest of the evening alternating between work and answering text messages from my other siblings and parents.

Winn came into the shop ten minutes before we closed at seven. I knew immediately by the look on her pretty face that she wasn't here to deliver good news.

"Hi." She pulled me into a tight hug. "You okay?"

"Sure," I lied. "Find anything?"

Her dark ponytail swished as she shook her head. "I'm sorry. Search and rescue did another sweep of the area with the dogs. They put them on the elk again today, having them track it. But about a mile away from the river, they lost the scent."

"Shit." I closed my eyes, disappointment settling like a thousand pounds on my shoulders.

"I'm not giving up." Winn took my hand. "I promise."

"I know you won't," I whispered.

Winn would do everything in her power for our family. But there was no missing the dark circles beneath her eyes that had been there for weeks. Ever since the shooting at the hotel.

Quincy was supposed to be a safe town. Shootings and strangulations weren't supposed to happen here. Everything was falling apart.

And Winn took so much of that on herself. Too much.

I wanted, more than anything, for Cormac to be apprehended. But if Winn couldn't bring him in, how heavy would that weigh on her already burdened heart?

My gaze flicked to the empty table where Vance had sat earlier. What if he was the answer?

"Do you want dinner?" I asked Winn.

"No, that's okay. Griff called on my way here and said he was making burgers."

Some of the stress lifted from her face at my brother's name. I had no doubt she'd go home to the ranch, to his arms and their two children, and the sparkle would return to her deep-blue gaze.

"Want to come out?" she asked. "You could spend the night."

I shook my head. "I'm going to clean up here, then go home." A hot, steamy shower might take away some of the pain. Maybe tonight I could actually get some sleep.

"You sure?"

I nodded, looping my arm with hers and walking her to the door.

"We're all worried about you."

I sighed. "I'll be fine."

"We all know that too. But we're still going to worry." Winn pulled me into a hug, then stepped outside, lifting a hand as she climbed into her vehicle.

Waiting until her taillights were two blocks down Main, I shut the door, twisting the lock. Then I shut off half the lights, leaving the others on to illuminate the space as I swept, mopped the floor and stacked chairs.

Crystal had offered to stay and close tonight, but I'd sent her home. Sunday evenings were slow, and after she'd left, not a single customer had come in, allowing me to clean the kitchen space.

It took less than thirty minutes for me to finish closing up. The shop smelled like sugar and vanilla and the citrus polish I used on the hardwoods. I was about to shut off the rest of the lights when I glanced out the front windows.

A tall figure strode down the sidewalk on the opposite side of the street, moving toward the hotel.

Vance.

He walked with his hands buried in his jacket pockets. The streetlamps lit his broad frame. He seemed in no rush, his gaze roving in every direction like he was trying to memorize Quincy. Or maybe he was hoping that if he looked close enough, he'd find a clue that would lead him to Cormac.

Was I that clue?

I flipped the lock on the front door, then I put my fingers to my lips, whistling the way Dad had taught me as a kid.

The noise split the night air.

Vance stopped. Turned.

I nodded.

When he was ready, whether I was or not, I'd take him to the river.

CHAPTER FOUR

VANCE

The bell on the coffee shop's door greeted me as I stepped inside. The jingle was light. Cheerful. The chime did nothing to stop the tornado of anticipation and dread that had been twisting my insides since I'd climbed out of bed at three this morning.

The five cups of coffee I'd guzzled hadn't helped my frazzled nerves. Pacing my hotel room had made me feel like an animal trapped in a cage, so well before dawn, I'd set out to explore Quincy, as I had last night.

The air was cold, my breath billowing as I walked. My boots left tracks in the frost that coated the sidewalks. The sun was beginning to creep toward the mountaintops, burnishing their tips in gold, but the sky was still dark. The only light in town came from streetlamps and porch lights. Nearly every building on Main was dark, save The Eloise Inn.

And Eden Coffee.

The café was empty. The tables on each side of the aisle

were lined in neat rows. The chairs were pushed in, ready to be shifted and filled.

The barista from yesterday rushed out from the back hallway, a towel in her hands. "Good morning."

"Morning," I said.

"What can I get you?"

Before I could answer, Lyla emerged from the same hallway. Her steps faltered, only slightly, when she spotted me.

I could still hear her whistle from last night. It echoed in my mind, just like the sight of her standing in the coffee shop's doorway seemed imprinted on my brain.

Beautiful. Brave, Lyla.

"Hi." Her voice was just as jagged as it had been yesterday. "I'll take care of him, Crystal."

"Okay." Crystal nodded, then hurried away.

"Hi." I came to a stop at the counter, taking in Lyla's face, searching for any sign of doubt. A hint that she'd changed her mind. But if there was any uncertainty racing through that pretty head, she didn't let it show.

We hadn't spoken last night. We hadn't traded details or phone numbers. There'd just been that whistle.

Then she'd retreated inside the coffee shop while I'd lingered outside, watching as the lights went out.

"Would you like anything before we go?" she asked.

"Coffee. Black." I reached for my wallet but she waved it off.

With practiced efficiency, she filled a paper to-go cup and fitted it with a collar and lid.

No scarf today. Lyla wore a black turtleneck sweater to cover her throat instead. It fit her frame, molding around her slender shoulders and the curve of her breasts. The collar itself climbed her jaw, concealing nearly every bruise save for those directly below her ears. But she'd kept her long, dark hair down today, the silky, chocolate strands draping nearly to her waist. The loose waves hid most of what the sweater didn't.

"Five minutes?" She set my coffee on the counter.

"Take your time." I took my coffee and walked to the front windows, sipping the scalding liquid as I peered out at the sleepy street. A single truck had rolled by in the time it took Lyla to gather her coat and pull a slouchy knit hat over her hair.

She tucked her phone in her coat pocket. If I had to guess, she'd turned on her location services. Or maybe she'd told Crystal or a friend where we were headed in fear that I was a serial killer.

"Would you like to drive?" she asked, tugging on a pair of gloves.

"Sure." I opened the door for her—earning more of that happy jingle—then I led the way to my truck, parked outside the hotel.

Lyla nodded her thanks when I opened the door for her, then she climbed in as I made my way to the driver's side.

"How are you feeling today?" I put the truck in reverse but kept my foot on the brake. "You sure about this?"

"Yes." No hesitation. The catch in her voice had nothing to do with a change of heart, just the lingering effects of her wounds. "Head north."

"All right." I let go of the brake and followed her instructions.

As we hit the edge of town and sped down the highway, my pulse quickened. I wasn't sure if it was her anxiety or mine, but the tension in the truck became so thick, so heavy, that I could hardly breathe.

This was breaking all the rules. This went against every protocol, every courtesy, that had been drilled into me since the academy. By rights, I should have checked in with the local authorities yesterday.

I'd always played by the rules. I'd always been considerate of other departments. Where had that gotten me?

Cormac was still on the lam, and I'd spent four years ducking under red tape.

Risky as it was, I was forging my own path this time. I'd make my own rules. And if I actually found Cormac, well . . . I'd pray the FBI didn't care how he was found, just grateful that he'd be one less person on their most-wanted lists.

Lyla shifted in her seat, her knees bouncing as she pointed down the road. "Take a left up here."

"'Kay." I eased off the gas. Part of me wanted to ask again if she was okay. Give her another chance to turn this truck around. But I was too desperate. Too scared she'd take the out if offered. So I took the left and drummed up some idle conversation. "How long have you lived in Quincy?"

"Other than for school, my whole life. My family founded Quincy."

"No kidding."

"You're staying at The Eloise, right?"

"I am." It was the only hotel around.

"My great-great-grandmother was Eloise. Now my younger sister, her namesake, owns it. There's an ongoing joke around town that you can't throw a rock down Main without hitting an Eden."

"Ah. Would I have met any other relatives?"

"My brother Knox owns Knuckles and is the head chef."

"I was planning on dinner there tonight. Anyone else?"

"Probably not." She cleared her throat and I expected

her to stop talking, but she kept on going, like if she stopped, her fears would win out. "My twin sister, Talia, is a doctor at the hospital. My parents live on my family's ranch. So do my other brothers. Both are on the search and rescue team along with my dad. My sister-in-law is Winslow Eden. She's the chief of police."

For fuck's sake.

So much for steering clear of the local authorities. Goddamn it. What were the chances?

I dragged a hand over my face, feeling the scrape of my whiskers against my palm.

Lyla was my only connection to Cormac, and given my typical shitty luck, she was also related to the chief of police. *Hello, red tape.*

My captain in Idaho would undoubtedly be getting a phone call. And that would lead to questions. Lots and lots of questions.

Fuck. I didn't need the mess at home infecting what I was trying to do here in Quincy.

"Listen, Lyla." I glanced over, her striking blue gaze waiting. "I haven't spoken to anyone in Quincy about this. If I was following protocol, I should have checked in with your sister-in-law already."

"Why haven't you?"

"I guess you could say I have trust issues with other cops." An understatement. In more ways than she'd ever understand. "Like I told you yesterday, I've been searching for Cormac for four years. There's never been much to go on. He disappeared and has been slippery."

Another understatement.

Lyla's attention stayed fixed on my profile as I spoke. Her hands remained clasped in her lap. For her sake, I'd spare her the details of Cormac's crimes. But for my own, I needed her to stick with me. To see this through, just for today.

"Early on, when the media was all over the story, tips and sightings poured in like a spring flood. Most of them were bogus. People claimed they'd seen him but couldn't provide any details. Still, we followed up on nearly every tip. Then the FBI got involved. The agent in charge shoved us local cops out of the way. Didn't want any input." Especially from me.

I was *too close* to the murders. Like being invested, dedicated, was a bad thing.

"I spent a year watching them chase their tails until they moved on to other cases and this one fell to the wayside."

That first year, it hadn't been easy gleaning information from the federal team, but I'd kept my ear to the ground and had done everything in my power to stay in the loop.

"Will the FBI come here?" Lyla asked.

"Maybe." There was a chance that the agent assigned to Cormac's open case would come across the APB. That they'd put the pieces together too. But I was counting on sluggish federal processes to delay their involvement. Maybe it would get overlooked entirely.

The sad truth of it was, without media attention or pressure from family members, cases were often forgotten, especially those that had been open for a significant amount of time. And when it came to Cormac, the only person who truly seemed to care about justice for the girls was me.

"After the FBI basically gave up, I started my own investigation." Not exactly legal, considering I'd been using police databases to glean information, but I hadn't been caught. Yet.

"I watched for crimes and criminals who matched Cormac's description," I told Lyla. "Most of the time, it led me on a wild goose chase. A couple years ago, a man matching his description robbed a gas station in Oregon. Eighteen months ago, there was a guy who'd stolen a truck in Wyoming with red hair and a similar build. I went to Oregon. I went to Wyoming. I talked to the local authorities. The man in Wyoming was someone else. But I'm fairly confident Cormac was in Oregon. In both cases, by the time I convinced the local cops to let me into the loop, any chance at finding Cormac was gone."

"So this time, you came straight to the source."

I nodded. "Yeah."

"How did you know it was me?"

"I didn't," I told her. "It was a guess."

"Good guess."

I kept driving, waiting for her to order me back to Quincy. Waiting for her to call her sister-in-law and blow my plan to smithereens.

"See that turnout up ahead?"

"Yeah." That was where she'd tell me to flip this truck around.

"That's where I parked. We'll walk from there."

Thank fuck. I slowed, easing into the turnout. When we were parked, I faced Lyla, about to give her one last chance to call this off. But she was already gone, opening the door to step outside.

Beneath my coat, my Glock was in its shoulder holster. I snagged my pack from the back seat, stowing my keys, then I joined Lyla outside.

She stood next to the truck, her eyes aimed at the forest ahead. "My family is protective."

"They don't know you're here with me today."

"No." She shook her head.

"Why'd you come?" When she'd left the table at the coffee shop yesterday, I'd expected that to be the last I'd hear from her. But here she was, shoulders pinned, hands fisted.

That bravery I'd seen in her last night shined as bright as the dawn.

"Winn is a good cop." She looked up at me, waiting until our gazes locked. "I'm not here because I don't have faith in her. But she has enough to worry about."

"They are protective of you. And you're protective of them."

She gave me a single nod. "I want him to rot in prison for the rest of his life."

"Are you expecting me to argue?"

"I'm expecting you to do what you came here to do. Find him."

The ferocity in her voice, the steadiness. There was no rasp. No crack. "Then let's go."

She released a breath, then marched into the trees, taking a rough path that hadn't seen much use. This trail was likely only used by locals. Fishermen. Hunters.

We walked in silence, the only sound coming from the forest itself. Birds chirping. Leaves and boughs rustling in the breeze. A twig snapped beneath Lyla's boot as she walked. My own thudded on the cool, damp earth.

In the distance, the rippling sound of the river grew louder. The rush and trickle of water over rocks soon overpowered the other noises.

Lyla turned course, stepping off the path to weave past trees. When we emerged from the forest onto the riverbank, she stopped.

Her hand came to her throat as she swallowed.

"You good?"

Lyla's face whipped to mine. She blinked, like she'd forgotten I was standing at her side.

Damn, but she had beautiful eyes. Blue. Broken.

This hike wasn't just about saving her sister-in-law some heartache, was it? It was about Lyla facing this place on her own terms.

"You can do this."

"I can do this," she whispered, her eyes falling closed. When she opened them again, the fear was gone. In its place was iron.

She walked ahead, following the river's path.

I stayed close. Alert.

The scent of rot drifted on the wind. The *caw* of a crow split the air.

Lyla stopped walking and lifted a hand, pointing to where the large black bird jumped from a rock and took flight. "That was where the gut pile was. From the elk he killed."

Scavengers had picked the area nearly clean. Larger animals, like coyotes or bears, must have dragged the rest of the carcass to a different place to feast. All that remained were a few dried bits of entrails and a circle of black-red dried blood.

"After he let you go, any idea which way he ran?"

"No." Lyla shook her head. "I was out of it."

"Do you remember hearing water splash?"

"I don't think so."

There was a chance Cormac had crossed the river. Or maybe he'd gone upstream and crossed out of sight.

"They've been searching up here for days," Lyla said. "Winn came to the coffee shop last night. She told me that the dogs lost his trail. Do you think that's because he went through the water?"

"Dogs can scent through water. But Cormac is very good at covering his tracks." He knew how search and rescue dogs were trained. And he knew how to avoid detection.

I walked to the remains of the animal Cormac had hunted. It had to be for food. Meaning there was a chance he'd built himself a shelter around here. Possibly a place he'd intended to stay during the winter.

"Did Winn say anything about search and rescue finding the remains of the elk he killed? You said he'd quartered it, right?" I asked Lyla.

"That's what it looked like. I think I came across him when he was about done. There were game bags strapped to his pack. And his bow."

An elk was a large animal. If he'd kept most of the meat, he'd have to dry it. Preserve it. Otherwise he would have gone after smaller game. Rabbits or fish were for a single meal. But an elk? That was long-term sustenance.

"How well do you know this area?" I stood, returning to Lyla. "Are there caves anywhere?"

"I don't know. My brothers might."

"I doubt they'll be as willing to talk to me without the police in the room."

She barked a dry laugh, wincing at the pain it caused. "Probably not."

"That's all right." I turned in a circle, mentally committing a few landmarks to memory so that when the carcass of that elk was well and truly gone, I'd still have a reference point. "This gives me a place to start. Let's head back."

Before the local authorities came out exploring on their own today.

Lyla turned, about to lead the way back into the forest,

but paused. She spun her own circle, slowly. Deliberately. "This used to be my favorite hiking trail."

Used to be. Cormac had stolen it from her. "I'm sorry."

"Why did he let me go?"

It was the second time she'd asked that question. The second time I couldn't give her an answer.

One moment, she was staring forward, the next she whirled so quickly that her boot caught on a rock.

My arms shot out, catching her at the waist before she could fall.

Her hands gripped my biceps as she righted her feet. But she didn't step away once she had her balance.

And I didn't let her go.

Our eyes clashed, and for a moment, I let myself drown in those sapphire irises. The inner circle was a blue, bright and striated with white. The outer ring was dark, almost navy, like the sky before a thunderstorm.

My God, she had stunning eyes. I leaned in closer, drawn to that blue. Then my gaze shifted to that rosy pink mouth.

Lyla blinked and broke away. Her breath hitched and she ducked her chin, moving past me for the trees.

Fuck. What the hell was I doing? I scrubbed a hand over my face, clearing the fog, then turned away from the river.

Lyla led the way to the Dodge without a backward glance. She climbed inside as soon as I hit the locks.

I rounded the hood, stowing my pack in the rear seat. Then I took a deep breath, ready to apologize the moment I was behind the wheel. But just as I hopped inside, a sniffle filled the cab.

A tear fell down Lyla's cheek. Without thinking, I reached out and caught it.

Her blue eyes snapped to mine.

Instead of taking my hand away, instead of obeying that invisible boundary across the console that marked her half of the truck from mine, I skimmed her smooth cheek. My fingertips forged the trail that tear would have taken. All while I let myself get sucked in by those cobalt pools once more.

What was it about this woman? What was it about those eyes I found so entirely tempting?

My heart pounded, skipping every other beat. I couldn't seem to take my hand away from her face. My God, she was beautiful.

Her skin was impossibly smooth. She had a perfect nose, straight and pretty. Her chin came to a soft point. She smelled incredible, like sugar and vanilla and cinnamon.

Her mouth parted. And this time, it was her gaze that shifted first, dropping to my mouth.

I leaned closer, drawn by the magnet that was Lyla Eden, and a hard edge dug into my rib.

The Glock.

I was wearing my gun. Because I'd brought Lyla up here to track a murderer. Her attempted murderer. And for fuck's sake, I was acting like I'd kiss her. Again.

I dropped my hand, shifting both palms to the steering wheel.

"I, um . . ." I hit the ignition. "I'll drive you home."

"The coffee shop. Please."

"Sure."

The silence on the drive to town was miserable. Neither of us spoke, about Cormac or the river or whatever the hell had happened between us.

Something. Chemistry maybe? I'd never felt anything

like that in my life. Whatever it was, one thing was certain, I didn't trust myself to stare into her blue eyes. So I kept my gaze fixed on the road, and Lyla studied whatever streaked past her passenger window.

When I parked in front of Eden Coffee, I expected her to fly out the door.

Instead, she twisted to face me. "I won't tell Winn what you're doing. Or anyone."

"I'm not asking you to keep a secret from your family." I couldn't ask that.

"We all have secrets."

Truer words had never been spoken. "Thank you."

"What will you do?"

"Spend some time scouting the area. Start with maps. Make a grid. Check the boxes, one by one."

"What makes you think he's still around?"

"He might not be," I told her, wanting to set her expectations for failure rather than success.

"But you'll look anyway?"

I nodded. "I'll look anyway."

She gave me a sad smile. "Want some breakfast?"

Breakfast. She was inviting me to breakfast, even after I'd acted like a dipshit. The tension crept from my shoulders. My spine relaxed. "Yeah. I'd like breakfast."

"Come on in."

With my backpack over a shoulder, I followed her into the coffee shop. Gone was the quiet, still café from earlier. Customers occupied over half the tables. A line three-deep had formed at the counter.

Lyla headed that direction to help out while I took a chair at the same table I'd eaten at yesterday, the one closest to the window, so I could watch out across Main. Then I dug through my bag, pulling out the area maps I'd bought yesterday at the hardware store.

Twenty minutes later, a plate appeared in front of me. On it was what looked like a cherry turnover. Next to it, a breakfast sandwich. Lyla set down a steaming mug of fresh, black coffee.

We didn't speak. To anyone else in the room, I was just another patron.

But those blue eyes found mine throughout the morning.

And in them, a flicker of hope.

Hope in me.

It had been a long time since someone had given me blind faith.

My resolve to find Cormac turned to steel. He'd pay for hurting her.

Tomorrow, I'd begin my search.

For Norah. For the girls.

For Lyla.

CHAPTER FIVE

LYLA

Whenever the bell rang at Eden Coffee, I smiled. After so many years, it was automatic.

Jingle. Smile.

I'd trained my ears to listen for that ding. Even from the kitchen, I could hear when someone came into the shop. But the way I'd listened for that bell in the past three days was nothing less than obsessive.

Whenever it rang, my attention whipped, not wandered, to the door. My breath would catch and hold, hoping it was Vance. Each time it wasn't, I'd hide my disappointment in that automatic smile. And I'd wait, greeting customer after customer, wondering when he'd finally stop by.

Until, like now, that bell chimed for Vance. And the smile I gave him was filled with relief.

The coil of anticipation that had been winding tighter and tighter as the afternoon wore on sprang loose. The stiffness in my spine melted as he strode into the café, tugging off a pair of leather gloves.

Vance's long legs made short work of the space. The

half-smile that tugged at the corner of his mouth made my heart skip. He stopped on his side of the counter, bringing with him the scent of clean soap and earth and wind. "Hey."

"Hi." Even with the rasp in my voice, it came out breathy. This man made me nervous, in a good way. "You were out in the mountains."

He nodded. "I was."

"Anything?"

"Not yet."

He'd given me the same answer for the past three days. But I liked that he said *not yet* instead of no. The subtle difference meant he still had hope.

So I'd keep some for myself too.

"Coffee?" I moved for a mug, expecting him to nod. He did. "Hungry?"

"I am." He reached for his wallet but I shook my head. Vance pulled out a twenty anyway, setting it on the counter. No matter how many times I offered to give him a meal, he insisted on paying. "Surprise me."

"All right." I bit back a smile, filling his mug. When I set it on the counter, he took it and retreated to the table by the window. The same table he sat at each day, in the same chair.

Vance's chair.

My family members didn't have a regular table, no area in the café that I considered theirs. But somehow, in less than a week, Vance had claimed that spot as his. Whenever another customer sat there, it irked me.

Luckily, every afternoon when he'd come to the shop, that chair and table had been empty.

Vance was settling into a routine. He'd eat a late lunch.

He'd drink a few cups of coffee. And he'd sit here for an hour, sometimes two, reviewing maps and notes.

We hadn't spoken much since that day we'd hiked along the river. Partially because I wasn't exactly chatty at the moment. Partially because I didn't know what to say.

Something had happened between us. First, along the river. Then, in his truck.

When we locked eyes, it was like the world around us vanished. Like there was this rope cinching us together.

The pain in my throat was gone. The fear Cormac had planted in my mind, erased. The turmoil in my heart, ancient history.

There were only his eyes the color of a winter storm.

Would he have kissed me? Would I have let him?

With everything happening in my life, the last thing I needed was some romantic attachment with a stranger. Yet I couldn't stop my pulse from quickening when he was in the room. I couldn't fight the blush of my cheeks when he gave me that crooked smile.

And no matter how many times I told myself to leave the man be, my attention wandered to his chair as automatically as the *jingle, smile.*

Vance was left-handed. Something I'd learned in the last three days. He always drank his coffee black. He seemed to like my food—I had yet to clear a plate with more than a crumb left behind.

His dark hair was unruly and a month overdue for a cut. But like today, he covered it with a beanie. After he'd warm up, usually after his first cup of coffee, he'd shrug out of his coat but the hat would stay on. His beard was filling out, the scruff becoming thicker each day. Sexier.

And whenever I met his gaze, the world tilted beneath

my feet, like my stomach was full of butterflies trying their hardest to carry me away.

Maybe I was just imagining a spark between us. Maybe I was clinging to anything that seemed normal, and crushing on an incredibly handsome man felt *normal.* Maybe I was drawn to him because he made me feel safe.

Whatever the reason, Vance was constantly on my mind.

Did he feel that tether too? More often than not, when I'd look over to his chair, his stormy gaze would be waiting.

I made Vance a sandwich—grilled chicken with avocado—and delivered it to his table with a pastry from the display case, leaving him to eat. As other tables emptied, I cleared dishes to the kitchen, working quietly. Efficiently. Feeling Vance's gaze on me each time I left the room and returned.

The bell jingled again. My smile appeared. My attention wasn't as quick to shift to the door, knowing that it wasn't Vance.

It was Winn.

Her expression was granite, her shoulders stiff. My stomach pitched. This wasn't my sister-in-law coming to check on me. This was the chief of police here to deliver an update for the victim.

Fuck, I hated that word.

Winn didn't so much as glance in Vance's direction. But over her shoulder, he tracked her every step. The badge on her belt, beside her gun, was impossible to miss today since she hadn't worn a coat.

"Hi," I said warily.

"Hey." Her face softened. "Got a minute?"

"I'm not going to like what you have to tell me, am I?"

She gave me a sad smile. "Probably not."

I sighed. "We can talk in the kitchen."

Crystal was off today. Now that my black eyes had faded enough that my concealer could do a decent job covering them up, I'd given her a day off. She'd been amazing, jumping in to help with longer than normal hours.

I was still sporting turtlenecks and scarves to hide my throat, but day by day, I was healing. The evidence of the attack was vanishing.

Winn followed me into the kitchen, standing beside the prep table with her arms crossed. "Sheriff Zalinski just came by the station."

"And?"

"They're calling off the search."

"It hasn't even been a week."

"I know," she said gently.

"Six days and he's already giving up."

"I'm sorry." Winn came closer, putting her hand on my shoulder. "I tried to talk him into another few days, but he refused."

My molars ground together as anger surged. "This is bullshit."

"Yep." Her nostrils flared. "I called the mayor but he was out, so I left a message. Maybe he'll have more luck changing Zalinski's mind."

"Fingers crossed," I deadpanned.

Sheriff Zalinski was a lazy asshole. I never should have voted for him.

Search and rescue fell under the sheriff's umbrella. The team had a few dedicated employees who served the greater county area, but the majority of search and rescue members were local volunteers. People, like my dad and brothers, who had lives of their own.

I bet Zalinski was getting pressure from some of the

volunteers to call it quits, and the spineless bastard was caving.

"Now what?" I asked.

"We've got the APB posted. Everyone at the station knows to keep an eye out for a redheaded man matching his height and build with a scar. The same goes for the sheriff's deputies."

Cormac Gallagher.

Winn didn't have a name to put with that description because she hadn't met Vance. Because he hadn't followed protocol.

Maybe it was foolish, but I kept my mouth shut.

Zalinski had given up. Winn had no control over search and rescue.

The only person actively searching for Cormac was Vance.

I wouldn't thwart his chances by sharing a secret. If he had any hope of finding Cormac, I wouldn't put an obstacle—my sister-in-law—in his path.

"Thanks for telling me."

"If search and rescue was under my control—"

"I know." I gave her a sad smile. Winn wouldn't have stopped. Of that, I had no doubt.

"Griff called me as I was driving here. He was on the afternoon team to go out today. He got the notice from the search and rescue lead that they called off the meeting. To say that he's pissed is an understatement. So is your dad, Knox and Mateo. Apparently, Knox suggested they tell Zalinski to fuck off and just search on their own, but . . ."

But it would only cause trouble for Winn. As soon as someone from the sheriff's department found out, she'd have a mess to clean up.

She'd dealt with enough messes in the past two months.

"No. They should just leave it alone."

My dad and brothers loved me, of that, I had no doubt. If I asked them to spend every day scouring those mountains, they'd sacrifice their time and do just that.

But they hadn't found Cormac either. They weren't professionals.

Vance? Maybe he had a chance.

"I'm sorry," Winn said again.

"It's not your fault."

"I feel like I've failed you." Her voice cracked. She was so determined to make this right, to be our family's hero, when she already was.

I pulled her into a hug. "You didn't fail me."

Her hands might be tied, but mine weren't.

She hugged me back, holding tight, until a jingle in the background broke us apart. "I'd better let you get back to work."

The owner of the jewelry store was waiting at the counter when we emerged from the kitchen. While I went to work on a cinnamon soy latte, Winn slipped out of the shop.

After a quick text to my dad and brothers telling them I knew about Zalinski's decision and not to make trouble for Winn, I walked to Vance's table.

"They called off the search," I said.

His eyes met mine as he reclined in that chair. The way he stared was rattling. Unnerving. I fought the urge to look away.

He stared like he could read my thoughts. No one had ever looked at me like that before. He probably made a great cop. I had the sudden urge to tell him everything.

How I was so tired and just wanted to sleep without a

nightmare. How I wavered between anger and sadness each time I looked in the mirror. How my pulse spiked whenever he was around.

Had he replayed that moment in the truck? Would he have kissed me? My gaze dropped to his mouth and those soft lips. What was wrong with me? Why couldn't I stop thinking about a kiss? Would it take the pain away?

Vance's tongue darted out, just a quick, small lick of his bottom lip, and desire coiled in my belly.

I tore my eyes away, dropping them to his empty plate. He'd devoured the sandwich and chocolate croissant I'd brought him over for lunch. His coffee mug was empty and in need of a refill.

"I'll get you more coffee."

"Lyla." He stopped me and nodded to the seat opposite his. "Sit down."

I sank into the chair.

"Are you all right?"

"I don't know," I confessed. "I'm mad."

To everyone else in my life, I'd lie through my teeth, promising I was fine. Pretending to be myself. It was easy to give Vance the truth.

"Part of me wishes they hadn't given up so soon. The other part hopes this means they're out of your way."

His expression changed. He looked almost . . . bewildered?

"What?"

"Nothing." He waved it off, then dropped his gaze to the table.

Beneath his plate was a map marred with red lines and circles. "What's this?"

He set the plate on the table beside ours, shifting his mug

out of the way too. Then he spun the map my direction, pointing to a red X beside a curved blue line. The river.

The point of attack.

From that X, he'd drawn what looked like a bike wheel, each spoke converging at the central point. Two of the segments he'd shaded in with more red.

"I've ruled out these areas. This one with the highway." He pointed to a shaded section. "And this one that surrounds Quincy. Cormac wouldn't venture that close to heavily populated areas unless he was desperate."

"What makes you think he's not desperate?"

"He's got food. Water. Everything he needs to survive in the wilderness. The only reason I'd expect him near a town or people would be for medical supplies. You didn't notice him injured, did you?"

"No. Not that I could tell."

"My plan is to start here." He pointed at the map again, this time to the area that led straight north from that red X. "It's the roughest terrain. If he's hiding his scent, it would be easiest here where the mountains are dense and steep."

"So section by section, you'll search for him."

Vance nodded. "Exactly."

"Do you really think he's out there?"

"I don't know. But if there's a chance he is, I won't stop looking."

Not just for my sake. But his. "Who is he? What did he do?"

Vance turned his face toward the window, staring out through the glass. For a moment, I didn't think he'd answer me. "He murdered his wife. And his daughters."

I gasped so loudly that the couple having coffee three tables away glanced our direction. "Oh my God. Why?"

"I don't know," Vance said, lowering his voice. "No one does."

Was that why Vance was here? Was this a quest to get answers?

He stiffened, those broad shoulders curling inward as he leaned his elbows on the table. His focus stayed firmly on the map, like he was attempting to conjure Cormac out of the paper.

"From the outside, they were the perfect, loving family. He was a model husband and father. Took his wife out on a date every Wednesday. Coached his oldest daughter's softball team. When it first happened, there were a lot of people who refused to believe he was the killer."

"I guess you never really know what happens behind closed doors."

"No. I guess not," he murmured.

"How, um . . . how did he kill them?" Did I really want to know?

His Adam's apple bobbed as he swallowed hard. "He lived on the lake. Had a dock. Boat. He drove his three daughters to the middle of the lake during a thunderstorm and threw them in the water. They drowned."

I slapped a hand over my mouth to cover my gasp this time. What kind of father would do that? Those poor girls. "And his wife?"

Vance dropped his gaze to my neck.

Strangled.

He'd strangled his wife.

My hand drifted from my mouth to the cloth covering my throat. It burned, not from what Cormac had done, but the threat of tears.

"Why did he let me go?" I'd asked that question so many

times it was beginning to crawl beneath my skin. "It makes no sense."

"Agreed," Vance muttered, rubbing at his jaw, like his beard was new and he was still testing out the feel of it beneath his palm.

"It's all blurry," I said. "I've thought about that day so many times I feel like I can't tell what was real and what I've made up in my head at this point. But I feel like there was this moment when he looked . . . scared? Sad?"

Vance's gaze shifted to the window again, letting it sink in. "I'm sorry, Lyla."

There was so much behind that apology. "It's not your fault."

"Isn't it?"

The pain in his voice, the guilt, sent me deeper into my seat. He really felt responsible, didn't he? That because Cormac had escaped years ago, it was his fault that I'd been attacked.

"How did he get away?" I asked.

Vance lifted a shoulder.

I waited, hoping he'd explain, but that shrug was all the answer he'd give. So I stood and collected his dishes. But before I left his table, I paused and took in his profile.

That granite jaw was clenched. He looked lost in an anger four years in the making as he stared through the glass.

"What will you do when you find him?" Not if, when.

"Whatever I need to do." The menace, the hatred, in his voice was unsettling.

A chill spread through my veins as I carried his dishes to the kitchen.

When I returned to the counter, Vance's chair was empty.

CHAPTER SIX

VANCE

My boot splattered a puddle as I stepped out of my truck. The water sloshed onto the already drenched hem of my jeans. The wet denim hung heavy on my legs, and my coat, just as soggy, sagged on my shoulders. I'd have to wring out my beanie in the hotel's bathroom sink and hang it to dry.

Though it would just get damp again tomorrow. But this wasn't the first time I'd spent my days getting soaked while I slogged through mountains. Given the rainy forecast for tomorrow, it wouldn't be the last.

I snagged my pack from the back seat, then slammed the truck's door closed, shoving the keys into my pocket as I walked toward the hotel.

My stomach growled. Lyla's coffee shop was like a golden beacon glowing bright on a gloomy, gray day. I could practically smell the sweet, rich scents. A sandwich, a cup of hot coffee, a few of her pastries would go a long way toward improving my mood.

But I kept moving forward, away from Eden Coffee, as I strode for the hotel.

It had been two days since I'd told Lyla about Cormac's murders. What I'd shared was just a tip of that iceberg, but even sharing part of the story had been difficult. Every time I spoke about Cormac, about what he'd done, it left me feeling shaken. Frayed.

Four years had passed, and I still couldn't wrap my head around it. What had happened that night? What had caused Cormac to snap? Was there something I could have done to stop him?

If Lyla knew the whole story, she'd ask the same questions.

So I'd avoided her and that charming coffee shop entirely. I was afraid she'd see through me. I was afraid she'd demand the details I'd omitted, and I wasn't sure I had the strength to tell her no.

Except if she knew the truth, it would shatter her illusion. That blind faith she had in me would fade.

Her confidence in me was startling. Addictive.

No one believed in me, not like that. Not my captain. Not the other deputies in the department. Not my family. Not Tiff.

These days, people seemed to expect my failure. Or maybe I was just used to disappointing myself.

But Lyla . . .

She looked at me like I was her salvation.

The reality was, I'd likely disappoint her too. And that sat like a rock in my empty gut.

I'd spent two days combing the mountains for any sign of Cormac. Each day I drove back to Quincy, it was with empty hands.

Still, I wasn't going to quit. Day by day, I was eliminating possible places where he could have built a shelter. Another day, maybe two, I'd have a section of my map to cross out.

My process wasn't foolproof, but it was how I'd been taught to search for fugitives. And the man who'd taught me was the best.

His education was either going to bite me in the ass, or maybe, for once in my damn life, I'd get lucky. Though the rain wasn't helping. With every drop, Cormac's trail was being washed away.

A steady drizzle had greeted me this morning when I'd headed into the mountains. It had finally stopped raining about an hour ago, just as the sunlight had begun to fade, a signal that my day of hiking had come to an end.

Now it was time to dry out and prepare for tomorrow.

My boots squeaked on the floor as I walked inside The Eloise Inn. There was a couple at the desk, checking in. Suitcases crowded their feet as they spoke to a smiling Eloise Vale. Sitting stoically at her side was her husband, Jasper.

I hadn't actually been introduced to Eloise or Jasper. A different desk clerk had checked me in when I'd arrived. And last night, when I'd come down to extend my reservation by two weeks, there'd been yet a different person stationed at the reception desk.

But I knew Jasper and Eloise from Quincy's local paper. From the article about the shooting from this summer.

Was that why Eloise and Jasper were always together? The times I'd seen them, they were never far apart. My guess was that Jasper stuck close to his wife's side—the man had taken a bullet for her.

I respected that devotion. In another life, I would have made it a point to introduce myself. To shake his hand.

Instead, I ducked my chin and walked with my head down, not wanting to draw any attention as I made my way to the stairwell and climbed to the fourth floor. Even after a day spent hiking, pushing my body, I wasn't ready to let up yet. The physical outlet was my only release. Maybe if I exhausted myself, I'd get some damn sleep.

Sleep was never easy, even at home in my own bed. Six hours a night was huge. Since I'd come to Quincy, it had been even more sporadic. Three or four hours was all I'd managed. I just couldn't shut down my brain.

With nothing to do but dwell on my mistakes, on the clusterfuck that was my life, I'd climb out of bed and spend hours charting my hikes. I'd pore over the maps in my pack, memorizing every inch. And when that was done, I'd spend hours reading news about Quincy.

For a small town, this community had suffered more than its fair share of trouble.

About three years ago, there'd been a murder, a young woman in the mountains. Indigo Ridge was more than twenty miles from where I was currently searching for Cormac. But had the newspaper archives not detailed the crime and how Winslow Eden had apprehended the person responsible, I would have wondered if he'd been responsible.

After that murder, there'd been an incident at a local daycare and an AMBER alert. Possibly an attempted kidnapping. Since it had involved a minor, the details hadn't been released to the press. However, I'd come across a few social media posts that speculated the child involved was none other than Knox Eden's son.

The hardships for Lyla's family hadn't stopped there.

The most recent news articles all centered around Eloise and the shooting. Lyla's sister had been working in the lobby when a kid, a former hotel employee, had come in armed with a pistol. He'd gotten off a few shots, one of which Jasper had taken for Eloise. Then Winslow, who'd been in the building, had taken the kid down.

From everything I'd read, Winn was a damn good cop. Maybe it was stupid of me not to trust her. But I'd already made the decision to fly under the radar. That meant avoiding anyone with the last name Eden.

Except Lyla.

But I guess . . . I was avoiding her too.

Because I feared she'd ask about Cormac. And, if I was being honest with myself, because of how that woman stirred my blood.

I didn't just wake up at night restless. I woke up hard and aching for release, Lyla's striking eyes haunting my dreams.

Just the thought of her beautiful face sent blood rushing to my dick.

Of all the women, why did it have to be Lyla to capture my interest? Shit was complicated enough without adding this attraction into the mix.

I jogged up the last flight of stairs to the fourth floor, taking them two at a time, needing the burn in my thighs to shove the image of her pretty mouth wrapped around my cock out of my mind. When I reached my room, I set my pack on the table and breathed in the clean scent of fresh laundry and citrus.

This was the nicest hotel I'd ever stayed in. It was airy and spacious, yet it had a comfortable, homey feel. The king-sized bed was comfortable and its white comforter plush. Housekeeping had lined the pillows against the headboard. The heavy curtains I'd left drawn this morning were now pulled away from the window. I had a perfect, unobstructed view of the fog and mist that cloaked Quincy.

I crossed the room and tugged the curtains closed. A long, hot shower was calling my name, so I stripped, letting my wet clothes plop on the floor. My jeans smelled like rain and mud. Tomorrow night, I'd have to find a place to wash a load of laundry. My suitcase in the corner was piled high with dirty clothes—today's were tossed into the heap.

I had one pair of clean, dry jeans left in the dresser drawer.

Wearing only a pair of black boxer briefs, I rounded the bed for the nightstand, snagging the two chocolate mints that the housekeeper left for me each day. I ate them both without hesitation. Maybe they'd tide me over until dinner.

Maybe I'd order room service from Knuckles again after my shower. The burgers were great. Though what I really wanted was one of Lyla's chocolate croissants. Everything that woman made was top tier, but damn those croissants.

My stomach growled, the pangs sharpening to razor blades. But before I could disappear into the bathroom and get going on my shower, my phone rang. I walked to my pack, digging it out of the front pocket.

Alec.

He and I weren't exactly friends. We were coworkers in the same department. Friendly, but not friends. I didn't have a lot of friends in the department these days—I'd learned it was best to draw that line.

"Fuck." If he was calling, it wasn't to chat. Maybe he'd heard something about the shooting. Maybe the captain had said something in their weekly meeting. Whatever the point, I braced as I accepted the call. "Hey."

"Hi, Vance. How's it going?"

"Not bad, Alec. You?"

"Can't complain."

I waited, gritting my teeth.

"I ran into Tiff at the store earlier."

Tiff and Alec had met at a few of the department's mandatory gatherings over the years. The summer barbeques. The holiday parties. They'd bonded over their mutual love of karaoke.

I bet she'd told him where I was and what I was doing. *Shit.*

"Okay," I drawled.

"She said you two broke it off."

"We did."

Alec hummed, the disapproval in his tone as thick as the blanket of clouds outside.

I didn't need this bullshit. "Listen, I'm just about to head to dinner and—"

"What are you doing, Sutter? Are you trying to get your ass fired?"

I sighed, taking a seat on the edge of the bed. "I'm on vacation."

"Right." Alec scoffed. "Tiff told me what you're doing. You're going after Gallagher. Again?"

"It's not like I'm swamped with work."

If there was ever a time in the past four years to search for Cormac, it was now, when the captain had told me to *take a break.* Until the media attention died down. Until the investigation was over.

I wasn't technically on administrative leave. Yet.

"The captain's going to flip his shit when he hears about this."

"The captain wants me gone. He's already shoving me toward the door."

"So what? You're quitting?"

"No." My captain was a raging prick. I refused to give him the satisfaction of me quitting. If he wanted me off the force, he'd have to fire me. "But this seemed like a good time to get away from Coeur d'Alene."

"You didn't do anything wrong. You shouldn't have to leave town."

"Agreed," I muttered.

But everyone was pointing fingers at the moment. Everyone was searching for a person to blame. If the captain needed a fall guy, that fall guy would be me.

"Look, I, uh . . ." Alec sighed. "I don't know what to say."

"Nothing to say."

"I'm sorry about Tiff."

Maybe I should have been sorry too, but this was best for her. For both of us. "It was time."

"Funny. That's exactly what she said."

Good. I wanted her to move on. To forget about me and find someone who made her pulse race.

"Have you found anything on Gallagher?" Alec asked.

"Not yet." In the past week, Cormac could have made his way to Canada for all I knew. Or he might have gone south for the winter like a bird.

"Think you'll find him?"

If there was ever a chance, it was here in Quincy. But I wasn't going to voice those hopes. Not to Alec. That would make them too real. "What's going on with you?"

"We're busy." Alec had known me long enough to go along with the change in subject. "We're a man down."

Me. I was that man.

Alec and I worked for the same backcountry unit in Idaho. I didn't consider him my partner. I didn't have a partner these days. But we were coworkers.

Ours was a small team with one sergeant and two deputies. We responded to calls and patrolled the backcountry areas across hundreds of thousands of acres in the national forest land surrounding Coeur d'Alene. We spent a lot of time in remote, forested areas that were only accessible by off-road vehicles or on foot.

Given the nature of our job, the diverse terrains and landscapes, we also spent time working with volunteer search and rescue teams. The same was true with marine patrol and dive rescue.

I was a cop who got to spend his days outside, not trapped in a cruiser or assigned a desk.

It was my dream job.

Maybe another man with my skill set would have aspired to join the U.S. Marshals. Lead federal manhunts or solve high-profile cases. But I'd always been content as a deputy. I didn't need flashy cases or shiny accolades.

When I returned home, would there be a job waiting? Maybe if I'd played the game, if I'd spent more time in the precinct making friends and practicing politics, I'd have more confidence in my future. I'd have a better relationship with the captain.

"Don't work too hard," I told Alec.

"Be careful." Alec knew enough about Cormac to know what I was up against.

"Bye." I ended the call and tossed my phone aside.

I appreciated Alec checking in on me. My family certainly hadn't.

But Alec wouldn't say anything, would he?

No. He'd keep it quiet. But what about Tiff? Hopefully she wouldn't bump into anyone else while I was gone and start blabbing. Hopefully she wouldn't decide to punish me by making a quick call to the captain.

The last thing I needed was him getting wind of why I was in Montana. That asshole would call Winslow Eden faster than I could blink, just for the satisfaction of fucking my plans. Then he'd talk to the FBI.

They hadn't connected the Quincy APB to Cormac . . . yet.

How long would it be until my secrets caught up to me? How long until the truth I was trying to keep out of Quincy made its appearance?

All it would take was a quick Google search and everyone would know my story. Lyla had been more willing than I'd ever hoped to keep my identity to herself. How long until her curiosity got the better of her? How long until my vague answers to her specific questions began to fester?

It was only a matter of time before everything collapsed.

"Fuck." I raked a hand through my hair.

What was I doing? I should be at home. I should be doing everything in my power to clear my name. To prove to the world I was a good cop. Tiff had told me once that this obsession with Cormac would ruin my life.

Maybe she was right.

But the idea of leaving, of walking away when I'd never been so close, was unthinkable.

I just had to push through. Keep going until someone made me stop. Cormac had to pay for what he'd done.

The simmering rage, as familiar as my own skin, swept through my veins, chasing away any doubt. I walked into the bathroom and turned on the shower, lingering under the hot water until I was clean. Then I toweled off, combing my hair with my hands.

Steam billowed from the bathroom as I walked out, a towel wrapped around my waist, about to call down for room service. But before I could lift the phone from its cradle, a knock came at the door.

I froze.

There was no reason for anyone in this town to visit my room. It was probably housekeeping. Maybe another guest had the wrong room. Or maybe it was Winslow Eden, and I was fucked.

My heart climbed into my throat as I crossed the room and checked the peephole.

The breath I'd been holding rushed out of my lungs. *Christ.* My paranoia was getting the better of me. I twisted the knob and opened the door. "Lyla."

"H-hi." Those blue eyes widened as they dropped from my face to my bare chest. Inch by inch, they traveled lower, her cheeks flushing. When her gaze reached the hem of my towel, it dropped like a rock to my bare feet. "Sorry. I, um . . . sorry. I should have called first."

I glanced past her, checking the hallway, but she was alone. "Everything okay?"

"You haven't been to the coffee shop."

No. I'd been avoiding her spectacularly.

Why was that again?

Damn, she was beautiful. I kept my arms pinned to my sides to keep from reaching for her. My heart thumped hard against my sternum, like a hammer pounding at a nail.

She was wearing an olive coat that hit midthigh on her black ripped jeans. Her scarf was the same shade as her jacket. Lyla's hair was up, the dark strands piled on top of her head in a messy knot. Some of them were damp from the rain, curling at her temples. She must have walked over from the coffee shop.

Wait. How'd she known this was my room? Had she asked Eloise or Jasper?

Like she could read my mind, Lyla glanced down the hallway, then inched closer. "No one knows I'm up here."

"How did you know this was my room?"

"I, um . . . I waited until Eloise and Jasper left, then I asked the night clerk. I told her you forgot your wallet at the coffee shop, and I'd run it up to you."

"Ah." The hotel clerk should have called up first, but Lyla's last name probably went a long way in this building. That, and she was trustworthy. I doubted anyone who looked at her pretty face expected a blatant lie.

A little rebellion. God, it was sexy.

My entire life, I'd done the right thing. Where had that gotten me? Alone, in Montana, with my career in shambles.

Even after the investigation was complete, I had no delusions about keeping my job. The captain would find a way to take my badge, either by firing me or sitting me at a desk, knowing I'd eventually get fed up and quit.

All because I'd done the right thing.

Did I regret pulling the trigger? Every fucking day. But was I guilty? No.

The only thing going in my favor was this chance at finding Cormac. So fuck the rules. At this point, I was asking for forgiveness, not permission.

"Everything okay?" I asked Lyla.

"Yeah, I just . . . I'm sorry. I'm interrupting your night. I'll leave." She twisted, about to take a step, then stopped and turned back. "I just wanted to know if you'd found anything."

"Not yet." Was it foolish giving her hope? Was it foolish keeping some for myself?

"Okay." She gave me a small smile before her gaze traveled down my chest again, lingering on my abs. Her tongue darted out to lick her lower lip, and fuck me, my cock twitched.

I sank my heels deeper into the floor, every muscle in my body locking so I wouldn't drag her across the threshold.

"You almost kissed me. In the truck. The day we went to the river." Her voice was soft, barely a whisper. Those blue eyes lifted to mine, and the grip on my control began to falter. "You almost kissed me, didn't you?"

Yes. Why was she asking when we both knew the answer?

"You should have kissed me."

Fuck. Me.

"Lyla," I warned, forcing myself to take a step back. "You should go." Before I buried my face in that long, silky hair and breathed in her sweet, vanilla scent. Before I caved and she did something she'd regret in the morning.

"I see his face. At night." She stopped me before I could close the door. "Just before I fall asleep, I see his eyes. That scar. I feel his hands on my throat."

She lifted her fingers, touching the scarf around her neck. "Once I see him, I can't shut it off. Everyone keeps telling me what I need. My parents. My sisters. My brothers. I need to rest. I need to stay home. I need to stop working so hard. I need to heal. I'm so tired of everyone telling me what I need. All I want is to forget. For just one night, I *need* to forget."

What would it be like to forget? It sounded like heaven.

Lyla wasn't the only person with nightmares.

I should have closed the door. I should have sent her on her way.

Instead, I took a step forward.

And sealed my mouth over hers.

CHAPTER SEVEN

LYLA

Good God, this man could kiss.

My entire body went up in flames as Vance's tongue slid against mine. Sparks cascaded across my skin and fire licked my veins.

Everything outside this room faded away. The thoughts I hadn't been able to shut off, the worries, the fears—vanished. Poof. Gone. All that existed was Vance and this kiss.

This erotic, consuming kiss.

When I was fifteen, I'd kissed Jason Palmer. He'd been my first. It had been awkward and exciting. Fumbled and quick. But when I'd shared the details with Talia, I'd told her that when Jason kissed me, it was like being wrapped in a rainbow. At fifteen, I'd loved rainbows.

In all the years since, finding a man who'd give me those rainbows had been impossible, no matter how much I liked a guy.

But regardless, I'd kept chasing rainbows.

Years utterly wasted. *This* was what I should have been

chasing. Sparks. Heat. Sin and sex. It was a thousand times better than any rainbow.

Vance wrapped his arms around me, hauling me into his room, the door clicking shut behind me. His tongue tangled with mine, his mouth slanting to get a deeper taste.

I melted against him, my hands sliding up that strong chest. The dusting of hair over his heart was coarse against my palms. He was so solid. Hard. Male. And damn, but I loved that he was so tall.

Even standing on the tips of my toes I wasn't tall enough to reach his mouth. It forced him to bend, that towering frame folding over and around me.

Vance's beard scraped against the smooth skin around my mouth. The smell of his skin, spicy and clean from his soap, filled my nose. He was head-to-toe rugged strength and honed muscle. The arms banded around my back were like chains, locking me in place.

A mewl came from my throat as Vance devoured me whole, exploring every corner of my mouth. A low groan rumbled deep in his chest, the sound of utter satisfaction. Of insatiable need.

Between us, his arousal pressed against my hip, hard and long.

Desire pooled in my center, my core clenching.

He tore his mouth away, dragging his wet lips across the line of my jaw to my ear. "Fuck, Lyla."

"Yes," I whispered. *Please.*

My hands dove into his hair, gripping the damp strands. They were as thick and soft as I'd imagined. The length made it possible for me to hold him to me, to clutch him close as he nipped at my earlobe.

I rolled my hips, rocking against his erection.

Vance hissed and let me go, his arms falling to his sides. With a hard swallow, he took a step away. Then another. His hands fisted, like he was holding himself back.

The space between us was like an open window. Cold air rushed in, taking with it the sparks. And like a flood, every worry, every fear, came surging back.

I was so tired of my own damn thoughts. I wanted the sparks back. I wanted to just feel.

For the first time since Cormac, I craved another person's touch. Vance's touch. That seemed like a miracle. So I reached for the scarf around my neck and tugged it free, letting it fall to the floor.

Vance's eyes stayed locked on mine. The torment, the restraint, burned in those light irises.

Fucking restraint.

I ripped off my jacket, the move violent, and threw it on the floor. Then I reached for the hem of my tee, whipping it over my head. Next came my ivory lace bra. It joined the other items on the floor.

Vance wanted me. The bulge tenting his towel was evidence enough. But he stood statue still, refusing to cross the invisible line between us.

Never in my life had I been this brazen or bold. Doubt crept its way beneath my skin, my confidence withering with every second that he still didn't move. Was he even breathing?

My heart pounded as we stared at each other. His Adam's apple bobbed, but otherwise, he might as well have been a granite statue.

All while I stood half naked, exposed, bruised and desperate.

What the hell was wrong with me?

I was just about to swipe my clothing from the floor and scurry out of this room when Vance moved.

With a flick of his wrist, his towel was gone, pooled at his bare feet. His cock, hard and thick, sprang free, jutting between us.

I gulped. *Oh sweet lord.* Every part of this man was massive.

With a single step, he crossed the space between us, his mouth claiming mine once more.

If the first kiss had been sparks and fire, this was an inferno of blue flame. My pulse boomed in my ears as his tongue twisted with mine. There was nothing gentle about this kiss. Nothing slow. It was a kiss that echoed with a single word.

Fuck.

We were going to fuck.

Just like before, he wiped my mind clean.

Vance reached between us, flicking open the button on my jeans and ripping down the zipper. He shoved them off my hips so fast that I stumbled. But before I could fall, he caught me at the ribs, hoisting me into the air. Then he threw me.

I yelped as I landed on the mattress with a bounce.

No man had ever craved me so desperately he'd tossed me around a bedroom.

My laugh was wild, the sound as hysterical as my movements as I kicked my shoes to the floor.

Vance moved just as frantically, tearing away my jeans. Then with a fist he gripped my lace panties and shredded them from my body. The torn fabric went sailing over his shoulder as he sank into the cradle of my hips.

His mouth crashed onto mine. His tongue plundered

and stroked as he lined up at my entrance. We didn't waste time with foreplay. Neither of us needed it. I was drenched from the kiss alone.

With one thrust, he drove in to the hilt.

I gasped down his throat, my eyes squeezing closed as I adjusted to his size. To the delicious stretch of my body around his.

Vance stilled, tearing his mouth away. "So fucking tight," he gritted out.

My breath came in labored pants. "Move."

He thrust forward, making my back arch off the mattress.

"Vance," I cried. No man had ever gone so deep.

"Take it, Lyla. Take the whole fucking thing."

I whimpered at his dirty mouth. *Yes.* My fingertips dug into his skin, clutching his shoulders as he eased out.

He slammed inside again, hard enough to shake the bed and earn another cry. "You feel . . ."

"So good," I panted.

As he rocked into me, I wrapped my legs around his bulky thighs, matching his rhythm. Then I lifted my head from the pillow, putting my mouth at his ear. "Fuck me, Vance."

He groaned, easing out to slam inside again. He set a fast, hard pace as our bodies slapped together.

It wasn't graceful. It wasn't sweet or gentle. But God, it was good. *So, so good.*

The hair on his chest brushed against my pebbled nipples, turning them to stone. The feel of him was like no other, and my insides turned to liquid as I held on for the ride.

Vance dipped his lips, trailing them along my throat. He kissed every mark, every bruise, all while his hips pistoned, his cock sinking inside my body. He kept me pinned to the bed, dwarfed by his large frame.

Never in my life had I felt so craved. Worshiped. Protected.

My orgasm built with a fierce power, my inner walls fluttering.

Vance drove me to the edge, stroke after stroke, until my legs began to tremble. Until my toes curled and it was impossible to fill my lungs. Heat bloomed across my skin, my breath caught in my throat.

"Let go," he commanded. "Come for me."

I shattered. Every muscle in my body pulsed as I came on a cry. My limbs shook. Stars broke across my vision, my mind blissfully blank.

Vance didn't stop. He fucked me, harder. Faster. Chasing his own release. "Fucking hell." He let out a roar before pouring inside of me.

I clung to him, holding tight until the aftershocks began to fade and I floated back to reality. Our bodies were slick with sweat and my hair was everywhere, the knot in it having worked loose. My heart raced like I'd just run ten miles.

Vance collapsed on top of me, his weight crushing for a split second as he wrapped me tight. Then he rolled off, his chest heaving like my own as he worked to regain his breath. "Fuck."

I hummed. "Yes, we did."

The corner of his mouth turned up.

A giggle escaped, and I fought the urge to pinch myself. I'd come to his room for answers, not sex. Two days without a word from Vance and my fears had gotten the best of me. Somehow, in just days, having him in my coffee shop had become an anchor. My hope was tied directly to his presence.

Then he'd disappeared.

On the walk over to the hotel, I'd convinced myself that he was gone. That he'd already checked out and there'd be no chance of finding Cormac Gallagher. But I'd had to know.

So I'd lied to the desk clerk about Vance leaving his wallet at the shop.

I wasn't a good liar. But apparently that had changed in the past week because she hadn't even blinked twice before looking up his room number.

My ability to tell a fib wasn't the only change. Two years ago, I'd forbidden myself one-night stands. Bad, drunk sex with a stranger I'd met at a bar had been the catalyst. Hookups always left me feeling cheap and empty.

Yet here I was, naked in Vance's bed with no delusions that this was anything more than one night.

Oh my God, we'd had sex. Crazed, reckless sex. The evidence was dripping down my slit.

"We didn't use a condom," I whispered, more to myself than Vance. "I'm on birth control."

He lifted a hand, dragging it over his beard. "Sorry. Got caught up."

"Me too." I sighed. "I haven't been with anyone in a while."

"I just got out of a relationship. We were exclusive for three years."

I was a rebound then.

A year, a month, a week ago, that would have sent me into a tailspin. I was a woman who loved relationships and commitment. After witnessing my parents live their lives madly in love, they had become the gold standard.

Maybe, for me, that standard was just too high.

At the moment, I felt too fragile to enforce my own rules. To insist any man I take to bed be husband material.

So I let it go. All of it.

Vance was a visitor in Quincy, like most guests in this hotel. He'd be gone sooner rather than later. If all he had to give me was an orgasm, then I'd be the rebound. I'd be the hookup.

I'd be the easy one-night stand.

Shifting to sit up, I threw my legs over the edge of the bed, about to get up and dress. But before my feet could touch the floor, Vance's hand wrapped around my elbow.

"Wait." He let me go, climbed out of bed and walked toward my pile of clothes, bending to snag my torn panties on the way.

His body was truly a work of art. Perfect, sculpted muscle. Male power and virility. The globes of his ass were mouthwatering, round and hard. If this were more than one night, I'd spend hours licking along his narrow waist and tracing the dimples at the base of his spine.

Vance's shoulders were covered with tiny crescent moons. My nails. Had I ever marked a man before? *No*. But I liked it. A smile tugged at the corner of my mouth.

Definitely not myself lately.

He collected my clothes and brought them over. But as I reached for them, he pulled them back, his gaze raking down my naked body. A muscle in his jaw feathered. The same conflicted expression he'd had earlier marred his handsome face.

I held out a hand for my bra.

Vance shook his head. Then my ball of clothes went flying across the room, crashing into the dresser beneath the TV.

"What—"

He bent and crushed his mouth to mine, silencing any protest. His hands drifted down my ribs, trailing over my hips. With a quick lift, he hauled me to my feet and swept me off my toes before carrying me to the shower.

Then Vance showed me just how good one night could be.

MY BREATH BILLOWED in a white cloud as I hurried along the sidewalk toward the coffee shop.

A fog had settled over Quincy last night while I'd been asleep in Vance's bed. The streetlamps cast halos into the thick mist.

I glanced over my shoulder at The Eloise.

The same clerk from last night was still stationed at the front desk. I'd snuck out the back alley door this morning, wanting to avoid being seen. It was dawn, long before Eloise and Jasper would arrive for work, but I didn't want to risk questions.

Above the lobby and first floor, the only light visible was one in the upper corner on the fourth floor. Vance stood in the window of his room, his hands braced on its top sill as he watched me walk past the coffee shop, heading for the alley where my car had been parked since yesterday.

The windshield was covered in frost, so I unlocked the doors, settled into the cold seat and started the engine, letting the defrost blast while I replayed last night.

My body ached. My muscles hadn't worked that hard in years. My nipples were sensitive against my bra and the flesh between my legs was tender. I flipped down the visor, inspecting my swollen lips in the mirror.

Vance and I had gone at it hard last night. Every time I'd thought he was spent, he'd reached for me. We'd alternated sex and sleep. I should have been exhausted, but I had more energy now than I'd had in days.

Damn, what a night.

A year, a month, a week ago, it would have bothered me knowing I was just a fling. A tryst. A distraction.

Vance had secrets. He'd dodged too many of my questions during our conversations at the coffee shop.

Maybe he'd confide in me, give me the whole story. Maybe not.

At this point, I didn't care. Last night was the first time since the river that I'd been able to shut my mind off. I'd been able to sleep without Cormac's face invading my dreams.

A year, a month, a week ago, I would have wanted more from Vance. I would have wanted a relationship. A boyfriend.

And he likely would have become my next ex-boyfriend. The next man to break my heart.

Now . . . he was a means to an end. He was my chance at justice. And he was leaving.

Vance wouldn't be here long enough to hurt me.

So I put my car in reverse and backed away from the coffee shop.

And when I passed by The Eloise on my way home, I didn't let myself look up at the fourth-floor window to see if Vance was still there watching.

CHAPTER EIGHT

VANCE

A rush of nerves hit as I opened the coffee shop's door.

Fuck, but I hoped last night with Lyla hadn't been a mistake.

The door's bell jingled. The warmth of the room seeped through my damp coat. The comforting, sweet scents filled my nose and made my stomach growl. The granola bar I'd scarfed on the drive to town hadn't been enough to satisfy my hunger.

Behind the counter, Lyla's gaze flicked my direction. She wore a smile. It didn't drop when she saw me. It didn't widen either. It was just . . . her pretty smile. A kind smile for a customer or a friend. It was the same smile she'd given me before last night.

Sex was always more complicated than casual, at least in my experience. No matter how many times a woman said she didn't need a commitment—hell, even if I *made* a commitment—she usually ended up hurt.

For her sake, I hoped Lyla would prove to be the exception. The sex had been. Hands down, last night had been the best time I'd ever had with a woman. Maybe we'd be able to keep having a good time while I was here. That smile of hers gave me hope.

The breath lodged in my throat loosened, working free as I crossed the room.

She picked up a white ceramic mug, filling it with black coffee. "You look like you could use this."

"Yeah." I nodded, taking the mug as she handed it over and letting my hands soak in its heat.

I'd had another long day in the mountains getting rained on. The chill that had settled deep in my bones would only go away after a hot shower. Though the steaming coffee would help. I took a sip, letting it warm my insides.

"Thanks, Blue."

Lyla's head cocked to the side. "Blue?"

I winked.

"Oh." Her cheeks flushed. And those striking blue eyes—eyes worthy of a nickname—sparkled. "Hungry?"

"Starved."

"What would you like?"

I took another sip of coffee. "Surprise me."

"All right." She smiled, wider this time.

I fought the urge to reach for her, to kiss her like I'd done before she'd slipped out of my hotel room this morning.

It had taken an effort to focus while I'd been out hiking today. Too often I'd let myself picture her face, imagine those eyes darkening while I moved inside her. At one point, I'd tripped on a stick because I'd been too busy picturing her dripping wet in my shower.

This woman was enchanting, the chemistry between us palpable. Never in my life had a woman's body come alive under my touch like Lyla's. She'd pulsed and clenched around my cock like a fucking vise, and I'd practically blacked out from the pleasure.

My pulse quickened, my dick stirring behind my zipper.

Lyla pulled her bottom lip between her teeth, her gaze dropping like she'd been thinking about last night too. After a quick, sexy clear of her throat, she went to work on my surprise, spinning away to grab a plate and open the display case.

I retreated to my regular table beside the window, glad to see it empty, and set my backpack on the floor. With my coat hanging on the back of a spare chair, I took my seat and sipped my coffee until Lyla appeared with a plate in one hand and a coffee pot in the other.

Today she'd brought me a grilled chicken sandwich with some sort of pesto. Beside it was a brownie with fudge frosting.

My mouth watered. For the food. For the woman.

She topped off my mug. "Anything else?"

"No, this is great. Thanks."

"Sure." She glanced over her shoulder, checking to make sure no one was paying us any attention. "You were out today."

"I was."

"Anything?"

I shook my head, hating the flash of disappointment in her gaze. One day, I wanted to give her a different report. But my search in the mountains had been fruitless.

Cormac wasn't going to make this easy. The motherfucker.

"Flag me down if you want another refill," Lyla said, then returned to the counter.

A strange feeling pinched as she left. I didn't like that she seemed so . . . normal.

The last thing I needed was a clingy woman. Other than orgasms, I had very little to offer Lyla. She seemed perfectly happy to have casual sex and not discuss it the next day.

This was exactly what I wanted. So why did it bother me so much to see her walk away?

You're losing it, Sutter.

I shook the feeling away and dove into my meal, inhaling the food. I was draining the last dregs of my coffee when the shop's door opened and Winslow Eden walked inside, carrying a cute little girl. Her daughter?

The girl had dark hair, like her mother's, and it was curled into wisps beside her ears. She was cute as a button and couldn't have been much older than one. When Winslow set her down to walk, it took a moment for the girl to get her balance.

"Emma!" Lyla darted around the counter.

The girl gave Lyla a drooly smile as she took off, trying to run. She stumbled, falling forward, but caught herself and pushed back up right before Lyla swept her into a hug.

"How's my girl?" Lyla kissed her cheek.

"Fussy," Winn answered. "She's getting a new tooth. Griff took Hudson to do a few things on the ranch after lunch, so we decided to come to town for a treat."

"How about a brownie?" Lyla tickled Emma's side. "And a triple-shot latte for your mom?"

"Yes, please." Winn yawned, following Lyla to the counter.

Emma toddled around, leaving fingerprints on the display case, while Winn and Lyla talked. I was too far away to make out their conversation, but Lyla was in the middle of making the latte when her expression hardened.

Winn must have given her an update on the case. Likely, no update at all.

Lyla nodded, forcing a smile that didn't reach her eyes. Then she finished with the coffee and put half a brownie on a plate.

The three of them sat together at a table, the women watching as Emma made a mess with her treat. Then after cleaning up her daughter's chocolatey face, Winn hugged Lyla goodbye and headed for the door.

I pretended to be intrigued by the blank screen on my phone until she was out the door.

When I looked for Lyla, she was already walking my direction.

"You okay?" I asked.

She lifted a shoulder and pulled out the chair across from mine, slumping into the seat. "I asked if she'd heard anything and she said no. It's what I expected."

Expected, but still disappointing. How much longer did I have until she felt disappointed in my visits too?

"Winn said they're just keeping a close watch around town," Lyla murmured, her voice low. "And you said there was no reason for him to come to town."

"Not likely."

She turned her gaze to the glass, giving me a moment to study that beautiful profile. I'd done the same last night, in the muted light of midnight. I'd lain at her side and traced the line of her face, from her smooth forehead, down the straight bridge of her nose, over those soft lips to her graceful chin, then down the column of her slender neck.

The scarf she wore today was hunter green. It would

look great on the floor of my hotel room. So would her black Eden Coffee T-shirt and those fitted jeans. Heat washed through my veins.

"How did he get his scar?" Her question might as well have been a bucket of ice water dumped over my head.

The more she wanted to know about Cormac, the more it opened me up to questions that I couldn't—*wouldn't*—answer.

"Was it from his wife? The night he, um . . ." Strangled her. "Did she fight back?"

I wished I could tell her yes. But the truth was, given that there hadn't been any evidence of a struggle, it was assumed that Cormac had taken Norah off guard. That she'd been as shocked at his actions as everyone else.

Maybe she'd tried to fight back, but he'd been too big, too strong. Her blood toxicity report had shown she'd been drinking, probably a few glasses of wine with dinner. She'd likely been too shocked and muddled to respond, and for him to choke her to death would only have taken mere seconds.

"He got the scar from a car accident." Of Lyla's questions, this one seemed to be the easiest to answer. "He was in his twenties, I believe. He was out running one day through a neighborhood. There was a kid playing basketball in his driveway. The ball got away from him and rolled into the street. The kid chased after it, not seeing there was an oncoming car. Cormac was close. Saw what was about to happen. Ran into the street and managed to shove the kid out of the way. Earned that scar when the car's bumper hit him instead."

"Oh." Lyla's eyebrows came together, confusion contorting her face. "That's not at all what I was expecting you to say."

"Yeah."

She probably thought I'd tell her a story about a hardened criminal in a knife fight.

It was hard to reconcile a hero and a villain who shared the same scarred face.

Lyla shook the confusion away, then shifted her attention to my empty plate. She stood quickly, collecting it and my wadded-up napkin. "Can I bring you more coffee?"

"No, thanks. I'll probably take off."

"Okay." She gave me a nod, then headed for the opposite end of the coffee shop.

Once again, walking away like I was just any other patron, not the man who'd fucked her four times last night.

Another day, I'd sit here and study my maps. I'd mark out the country that I'd traversed today and chart tomorrow's plan.

But at the moment, her normalcy was digging beneath my skin. So I collected my things and slipped out the coffee shop's door, making my way to where I'd parked my truck outside the hotel.

Instead of going inside and taking a hot shower, I climbed behind the wheel and drove down Main, following the road as it turned into the highway that led out of town.

I'd told Lyla that Cormac wouldn't come to Quincy. I still doubted he'd show his face in any town, though especially the closest one to where his encounter with her had occurred. But I wanted a better idea of the area, so I drove to the neighboring town, fifty miles away.

It was no more than a blip with a few businesses, including a gas station, bar and small hotel. It was the kind of place where Cormac and that scar would stand out like a neon sign. Not a place he'd go unless it was an emergency.

The biggest town in the area was Missoula, but it was hours away by car. Days on foot. Maybe he'd hiked the backcountry to get to that larger town. Maybe not.

Where was he? Where would he go?

I had no idea why, but my gut told me to stick to Quincy. So I turned around and headed back, bypassing the hotel once more to stop at the grocery store.

My stash of breakfast and hiking snacks was dwindling. So I walked through the store's double doors, tugged a basket from the stack and wandered down the aisles. I was studying my options for protein bars when a woman passed the end of the aisle.

She disappeared with a flash of red hair.

My heartbeat stuttered. My muscles tensed. The response was involuntary.

Red hair reminded me of Cormac. Of the girls. In my mind, I knew there was no possible way he was in this grocery store. That one of the girls was out shopping for ice cream or Lucky Charms.

Still, part of me wanted to follow that woman. See her face. Rule it out. Wouldn't be the first time I'd followed a redheaded stranger.

But it was just red hair.

I dragged a hand over my face, shaking it off. How many years would it take before I could see a redhead and not do a double take?

If I didn't find Cormac, maybe forever.

He was the ghost haunting my everyday life. He was the past I couldn't let go. Until he was found, there'd be no peace.

So I grabbed five boxes of granola bars, enough to last me this week, and returned to the hotel.

My shower was long and hot. I let the steam work the tension from my shoulders and thighs. I'd covered some rough terrain today that would have been steep on a good day, but with all the rain, it had been slippery, adding to the challenge.

My energy was waning, but if Lyla came over, I'd find a second wind.

By the time I finally shut off the water, my skin was raw and red. I stood at the sink, my ears trained for the door, hoping for a repeat of last night. For Lyla's soft knock. But there were no sounds beyond this room, so I dried my hair with the towel and tugged on a pair of sweats.

With nothing else to do, I grabbed the TV remote, about to turn on a game or something.

And there it was.

The knock.

My dick swelled as I crossed the room, not bothering to check the peephole as I whipped open the door.

Lyla stood in the hallway, out of breath. Her cheeks were flushed like she'd just raced up the stairs. It was a Sunday. Eloise and Jasper hadn't been here today, but Lyla had still likely tried to escape notice from the front desk clerk.

"The coffee shop is closed," she said. "I don't want to go home."

"Then don't." I opened the door wider.

She stepped inside. "I—"

I sealed my lips over hers, stopping whatever it was she was going to say. My tongue stroked the seam of her lips, savoring her sweet taste.

She parted for me and I swept her inside, devouring every inch of her mouth. Then I did exactly as I'd planned earlier. I took off her scarf and dropped it on my floor.

Her hands trailed up my chest, her nails digging into my flesh. This woman liked to leave her mark, and I fucking loved it. If she came at me with her nails like she had last night, my shoulders would be shredded by morning. I didn't give a damn.

I stripped her out of her clothes while she shoved my sweats off my hips. Then I picked her up and pinned her against the closest wall. "Are you wet for me?"

"Yes," she panted as I licked her throat. Her legs wrapped around my waist.

I pressed against her center, feeling that slick heat against the crown of my cock. Another night, I would have tasted her sweet pussy, but I was too impatient. So I lined up with her entrance and thrust home. "Fuck."

"Vance." With one arm, she clung to my shoulders as she stretched around my length. Her other hand dove into my hair, her short nails scraping my scalp and tugging at the roots. "Fuck me."

"Say please."

Her head lolled to the side, her eyelids fluttering closed. "Please fuck me."

I pulled out and slammed inside. Hard.

Lyla cried out, her inner walls already beginning to pulse.

"Give me that blue."

It took her a moment but I waited, buried to the hilt, until she opened her eyes, locking them with mine.

I kept her firmly against the wall, holding her jeweled gaze as I fucked her. Stroke after stroke, I lost myself in her lithe body.

"Oh God." She came faster than I'd expected, a gasp escaping her lips like it had surprised us both. The grip on my hair tightened and there was a real chance she'd have a clump torn from my scalp by the time we were done.

I savored the sting, the pain, and kept driving into her tight heat as she pulsed around my shaft. That delicious squeeze triggered the build at the base of my spine. Then I was coming on a roar.

"Fuck, Blue." My release quaked through my bones. My vision blanked, and all I felt was her.

When I finally came down, Lyla had collapsed against my shoulder, her body still pulsing around me as she clung to my frame, boneless.

I peeled her off the wall and carried her to bed, ripping the covers back and setting her on the sheets. Then I went to the bathroom for a warm cloth to clean her up.

Her eyes opened as I pressed the washcloth between her legs. "You make me forget."

"You make me forget too."

Forgetting wasn't an option, not with what I'd come to Quincy to do. But that didn't stop me from hitting the lights and climbing into bed.

Or from spending the rest of the night making sure we both forgot.

CHAPTER NINE

LYLA

The Eloise Inn had been in my family for generations. As a kid, I'd played in the lobby while Mom attended to the desk, greeting and helping guests. As a teen, I'd spent my summers here as a housekeeper, cleaning rooms for clothes and gas money.

But it hadn't been until this past week that, for the first time, I truly understood the charm of this hotel. Because for the past week, I'd basically been a guest.

Each night after work, I'd slip up the stairwell to Vance's room on the fourth floor. We'd spend hours in the plush bed, wearing each other to exhaustion. We'd take a hot shower together in the middle of the night, then dry off with soft towels that smelled like spring rain. Then I'd crash, sleeping like the dead until my alarm blared at four. I'd wake early to sneak out of the building and head to my coffee shop across the street.

This hotel had become a sanctuary. Or maybe that was just Vance.

"Are you going to work or home?" he asked.

Dressed only in his familiar gray sweatpants, his hair askew from my fingers, he opened the door, leaning out to check the hallway. When he confirmed it was empty, he stood against its face, propping it wide.

"Work." I kept my voice low from my seat on the edge of the bed, bent to tie my tennis shoes.

The longest tendrils of my hair were still damp from last night's shower, so I'd twisted it into a knot. My skin smelled like Vance, a heady mixture of soap and spice and earth. And, other than the clean panties I'd stashed in my purse, I was wearing yesterday's clothes. A tee and a pair of jeans were waiting for me in my office.

I'd sneak to the shop and change, no one the wiser that I hadn't slept in my own bed for a week.

The secrecy was a rush. So far, I'd managed to avoid my family by coming to The Eloise each night and leaving before dawn each morning. In a way, I felt like a teenager, infatuated with a boy for the first time in her life.

Not that Vance could ever be mistaken for a boy. Not with that six-foot-five frame.

His biceps flexed as he crossed his arms over his chest, relaxing against that door. The dusting of hair over his pecs only made him seem broader. Stronger. Last night, I'd traced every inch of his washboard abs with my tongue.

"Are you going out today?" I glanced over my shoulder to the windows. We'd been so caught up in each other last night, from the moment he'd pulled me into the room, we'd barely broken apart. And when we'd finally crashed, neither of us had mustered the energy to close the curtains.

Beyond the glass, only the muted lights from Main illuminated the outline of roofs and buildings.

"Yeah," Vance said. "I'll head up before first light."

"Watch out for grizzly bears." I stood, crossing the space between us.

Vance framed my face in his hands, bending to brush a kiss to my lips. His tongue flicked out, licking my bottom lip.

A shiver raced down my spine, and as I shivered, he deepened the kiss, his tongue sliding inside and stroking mine with a lazy swirl. When I rose up on my toes, seeking more, he wrapped his arms around me, hauling me into the hard plane of his chest.

Then he kissed me. God, the way this man kissed me.

It was like I was his air. His reason for breathing. Silly, considering we were just fooling around while he was in town. Still, I sank into the kiss as a pulse bloomed in my center. Desire coiled in my lower belly.

But before I could shove those sweats off his narrow hips, he pulled away. "If we don't stop now . . ."

We wouldn't stop for hours. And while I hadn't needed to mention to Vance that I was sneaking in and out, doing my very best to go unnoticed, he knew. If people saw us together, it would only lead to questions.

We weren't answering questions, not even each other's.

Vance hadn't told me much about his life in Idaho. He hadn't offered more details about Cormac. Pillow talk this past week had centered around a safe topic—me.

We'd talked about my family. About life growing up in Quincy. How my mom had taught me to cook and bake. Last night, he'd asked me question after question about the coffee shop, so I'd told him how I'd used my inheritance to start the business and some of the hurdles I'd jumped over along the way—employees and expenses.

He'd listened with rapt attention. Maybe I should have been flattered. No man before Vance had ever taken such an avid interest in my life. Most guys I'd dated had seen Eden Coffee as competition for attention.

Vance's genuine curiosity was refreshing. Still, something about his interest bothered me. Maybe because it was too strong.

Because if we were talking about me, then we *weren't* talking about him.

He hadn't shared one tidbit of personal information. Not one scrap that I could cling to.

This was just sex. Incredible, mind-blowing, toe-curling sex. Before Vance, I hadn't even known what an orgasm should feel like. My body came apart under his hands. I found myself becoming bolder, taking the pleasure I craved. And Vance delivered, time and time again.

Another woman might have been okay drawing that line. She'd simply be grateful that she was getting fucked by an Adonis every night.

Yet I yearned for more. Was that my problem? That I always wanted more?

I wanted what this man couldn't give me.

Was I okay with that? *Maybe. Maybe not.*

"Did you decide how long you were staying?" I asked, grabbing my coat from where it had landed on the floor last night. "Do you need to get back to work?"

"Not sure yet," he said. "I'll let you know."

Would he though? Or would I come to this room one night and find him gone?

That was a question I didn't want answered, so I snagged my purse, looping it over a shoulder, then went to him for a chaste kiss. "See ya."

"Bye, Blue."

That nickname, like the coffee shop's bell, always made

me smile. My cheeks warmed as I stepped into the hallway, doing my own check to ensure I was alone. Then I hurried for the stairwell, looking back for a brief moment before ducking through the door.

Vance was gone.

I hurried downstairs, taking the exit that led to the alley and parking lot behind The Eloise. Then I zipped up my coat, tucking my hands into the pockets to keep them warm as I rounded the building and jogged across Main.

When I reached the sidewalk outside the coffee shop, I looked up to the hotel, searching for Vance in the window. His frame filled the glass.

I didn't wave. Just in case someone saw me out on the street, I didn't want to risk that exposure. I simply turned and walked to the coffee shop, digging my keys from my purse to unlock the front door.

The stillness in the shop settled my racing heart. Necessity was the reason I'd started coming to the shop at four o'clock in the morning. While the rest of Quincy was asleep, I could work in silence without distraction.

So after quickly changing my clothes, I busied myself in the kitchen. Today, I felt like a slice of homemade whole wheat toast with salted butter and apricot preserves for breakfast, so I got to work.

The scent of yeast and flour was normally as comforting as any hug, but as I left the dough to rise, I waited for the tension to slip from my shoulders. I waited for the peace I normally found in these quiet, early hours.

It never came. There'd been something *off* about my mornings for weeks. Ever since the river.

Instead of enjoying a latte before I flipped on the rest of

the shop's lights and opened for the public, I found myself sitting in Vance's chair, staring out at the street.

His truck was still parked outside the hotel.

The light in his room was off.

My hand came to my throat, feeling my skin. I was tired of scarves, so I hadn't brought one to wear today.

The bruises were fading, day by day, and besides, it wasn't like everyone in town didn't know what had happened by now. Gossip traveled faster than a bullet in Quincy, Montana.

Was that why I wanted to know all about Vance? Because I'd been trained by this small town to feed my curiosity? That secrets weren't sacred, they were a challenge?

Or maybe I was just a woman who wanted to know about the man she'd let inside her body.

I shook off the thought. It was the first Monday in October. Mondays were usually slow, especially this time of year, when we had few tourists in town.

On a day like this, I'd usually let Crystal make coffee and serve customers while I spent hours decorating these windows, hand-painting white spiderwebs in the corners of the glass. I'd have spooky cookies in the oven and a jar of candy corn on the counter for decoration.

I looked forward to Halloween each and every year. But just the thought of finding my paintbrush and decorating the windows made my lip curl.

God, what was wrong with me? When was I going to start feeling like myself again? It had been weeks since the river. When would it stop weighing so heavily on my soul?

"Lyla."

"Ah!" I jumped, practically leaping out of my chair as

Crystal's hand touched my shoulder. "Oh my God. You scared me."

"I'm so sorry. I thought you heard me come in the back door."

"It's fine." I waved it off, then took a breath, willing my heart to climb out of my throat.

"What are you doing?" she asked. "Just sitting in the dark?"

"Oh, I was just, um . . . trying to figure out how I could paint spiderwebs and then turn them into snowflakes after Thanksgiving," I lied.

"Good idea. I'd offer to help, but I'm hopeless with art projects." She gave me an exaggerated frown.

Her lipstick was orange today, the color of carrots. Crystal had a different color lipstick for each day of the month, ranging from blue to red to green.

Her quirky nature was part of why I'd hired her. She didn't care that some of the grumpy old men in town gave her strange looks when she wore purple lipstick. She was confident in her style and herself.

I usually felt the same. Just, not lately. Not since the river.

Was it the bruises? Would I feel like me again once they were completely gone?

My gaze shifted to the windows again. "What if there were no webs this year? What if we skipped the snowflakes?"

"What do you mean?" Crystal asked. "Like do something else? Spiders or whatever?"

Or whatever.

"I'll come up with something," I said, giving her a forced smile. Then I followed her to the counter and helped prep for the day.

I pretended that everything was normal. I smiled like I meant it.

Not ten minutes after Crystal had unlocked the front door at six, the bell jingled and I looked up from where I'd been making that latte for myself.

Vance crossed the shop, stopping at the counter. "Hi."

"Good morning." I'd assumed he'd be long gone for the mountains by now, but with Crystal here, I didn't ask.

His beanie covered his unruly hair. His coat molded to those broad shoulders. Those bright, clear eyes raked over my body, head to toe. "Coffee."

"They didn't have any at the hotel?"

"Yours is better."

Yes, it was. "To go?"

He nodded. "Please."

Please. Last night, Vance had made me say please each time I'd wanted to come. He'd made me beg, and it had made the release so much sweeter. My cheeks flushed as I filled his paper cup.

The timer I'd brought out from the kitchen dinged, signaling the bread was done.

"I'll get it," Crystal said, leaving us alone.

"You like that, don't you?" Vance's voice was a deep murmur. "Me, saying please."

"Yes. But I like to be the one to say please too," I whispered.

"Noted." The corner of his mouth turned up. "I'll make you say it later."

"You're on, Sutter." I handed over his coffee, shaking my head when he tried to pay. "It's on me."

Vance reached for his wallet, taking out a five-dollar bill. He winked as he set it on the counter. "See ya, Blue."

He walked away, coffee in hand. He was escaping to the mountains.

An odd feeling came over me as he headed for the door. It felt a lot like . . . envy.

For the first time in my life, the last place I wanted to be was within these walls. I didn't want to bake and serve and smile.

"Vance?" I called, stopping him.

He stopped. "Yeah?"

"Can I go with you today?" What was I even asking? I needed to work. Didn't I?

"Sure," he agreed without hesitation.

My heart galloped. Spontaneity was not, well . . . me. But the idea of ditching work felt so right. "I need to take my car home. Meet me in the alley in five minutes?"

"'Kay."

I rushed away from the counter so fast I nearly tripped on my own feet. Then I hustled to the kitchen, where Crystal was putting my bread loaves on cooling racks. "Hey, would you care if I took off for today?"

She blinked, like that question had shocked her into silence. "You're not supposed to work Mondays."

"Huh?"

"When you hired me, you said you were going to take Mondays off."

"Oh." Yet I never let her work alone.

It had nothing to do with her. And everything to do with me.

"Well, if you're okay with it, I'll take off today."

"Of course." She smiled, standing taller. Her brown eyes sparkled. "I can handle it."

"I know you can," I told her, then hurried to my office to collect my coat and yesterday's clothes.

With them shoved into my purse so Crystal wouldn't notice, I headed for my car. Like it had been every morning, the windows were coated in frost. I tossed my things inside and quickly scraped the glass, finishing just as Vance pulled his truck into the alley.

I climbed in the car and led the way to my house.

There weren't a lot of brand-new homes in Quincy, but along with buying and renovating the building on Main for Eden Coffee, I'd used my inheritance to build my dream house about two miles from town.

It was farmhouse style, with pretty white siding and a quaint porch. The black shutters matched the shade of the tin roof. There were three bedrooms, a spacious kitchen and an office. The other houses in the neighborhood were home to growing families. That was what I'd envisioned for this house. A family.

As I eased into the driveway and parked in the garage, taking in my charming home, a heaviness settled in my chest.

What if there was no family? What if it was only me?

The slam of Vance's truck door snapped me out of that thought, and I shut off my car and got out, joining him in the driveway so we could go in through the front door.

"Nice place." He took it all in, top to bottom, just like he usually did with me.

That was his way, wasn't it? He scanned. Assessed.

"I just want to change into something warmer," I said.

"Take your time." He followed me inside, closing the door behind us while I rushed down the hall for my bedroom.

It only took minutes to pull on a thick sweatshirt and

hiking boots. Then I grabbed a coat, hat and gloves, carrying them out to the living room, where I found Vance leaning in to study a framed picture hanging on the wall.

"This is your family?" he asked, not tearing his eyes from the photo.

"It is. Those are my parents and my brothers and sisters." I came to stand by his side, taking in the dated photo. Strange how I passed this picture every day but hadn't really looked at it in a while.

"That was Knox's senior year in high school," I said. "Mom was saying the other day how we needed to get a new photo taken now that our family has grown so much."

Husbands. Wives. Children.

Mateo and I would be paired together, no doubt, as the only two single people in our family.

"Do you have a big family?"

Vance straightened, turning from the picture. Not a word escaped his lips.

Apparently his family, along with every other personal topic, was off-limits.

"Right," I muttered. "Too personal. You can fuck me senseless every night, but that's where it ends."

"Lyla—"

"It's fine." I flicked my wrist. It wasn't fine. Nothing right now was fine. If I was being honest with myself, that outburst had more to do with me than it did Vance.

I pulled off the hat I'd just put on, feeling too hot. The sweatshirt was suddenly suffocating. "Actually, I think I'm going to just stay home today. You go without me."

Vance's face was unreadable. Maybe he was relieved. Maybe he was sorry. Maybe he was annoyed. Fuck if I knew.

"Rain check." He gave me a single nod, then walked down the entryway and out the door.

I didn't stop him. Instead I reached for the hem of my sweatshirt and ripped it from my torso, throwing it on the floor. "Gah!"

What was wrong with me? I didn't want to be at work. I didn't want to be at home—I didn't want to be anywhere. I'd been sleeping with Vance and knew nothing about him.

Everything was *wrong*.

And I didn't know how to make it right.

I unglued my feet, about to go to the kitchen. Maybe my favorite room in the house would make me feel more like myself. But then my own reflection caught my eye in the decorative mirror I'd hung on one of the living room walls.

It stopped me cold.

My throat was a wash of greenish yellow. But there were a few circles still black and blue. I stepped closer to the mirror, taking in those circles.

Fingertips. They were from Cormac's fingertips.

The motherfucker.

"Cormac."

It was the first time I'd said his name out loud.

"Cormac." My voice was stronger. Firmer. Angrier.

I knew his name. I knew his crimes. I knew because of Vance. Because I'd believed every word he'd given me about my attacker.

Meanwhile, he didn't speak of his family. His friends. His job. His life. All he'd ever really shared was about Cormac.

The hairs on the back of my neck stood on end.

Who was Vance? What if I was wrong? He'd told me he

was a cop, but he'd never shown me a badge. I'd never asked to see one.

Winn never went anywhere without hers. Even when she went to Mom and Dad's house for a family dinner at the ranch, she brought along her badge.

I'd spent a week sleeping in Vance's hotel room with no badge in sight.

"Oh my God." I wrapped my arms around my waist, my head spinning.

Everything he'd told me I'd kept from Winn. He'd asked me to keep it quiet and I'd agreed. What if I'd made a huge mistake?

The day I'd found Cormac on that river, I'd assumed he'd say hello. I'd assumed we'd talk about the weather before going our separate ways. I'd assumed he could be trusted.

And I'd trusted Vance.

I'd blindly believed Vance because he'd told me everything I'd wanted to hear. My stomach pitched.

"You're such a fucking idiot," I snapped at my reflection, then I bolted, grabbing my keys before I sprinted for the garage.

And while I drove to the police station, I pretended that I wasn't betraying Vance.

CHAPTER TEN

VANCE

The moment I stepped across the threshold at the hotel, I felt a prickle of awareness. Of wrongness. There'd been a knot in my gut ever since I'd left Lyla's house this morning.

It untied.

Not because I didn't have to worry. But because I could stop dreading the inevitable.

Winslow Eden stood next to the mahogany reception desk, her eyes trained on me as I walked across the space.

Beside her, Eloise sat taller, her eyes narrowing. Jasper's face was granite, his frame locked and hands fisted. He looked ready to leap in front of his wife and shield her from danger. Again.

Wasn't that a fucking shame? That these people thought *I* was a threat?

When I was ten feet away from the desk, Winn pushed off its edge, closing the distance between us. Wearing a black button-down and a pair of jeans, her dark hair unbound and falling over her shoulders, she shouldn't have been imposing. But her badge was unmistakable. And that gun.

This was a woman who was not afraid to use it.

We stopped three feet apart. She tilted up her chin to keep my gaze.

"Chief Eden." I dipped my chin.

"Officer Sutter." Her voice was cool. Calm. Lethal.

So she knew I was a cop. It didn't come as a surprise but it still fucking sucked. *Shit.*

"I think we'd better have a conversation," Winn said.

I glanced longingly to the lobby's fireplace and the leather couches arranged around a coffee table. Not a chance we'd be having that conversation here, would we?

"Your car? Or mine?"

TWO HOURS after I'd arrived at the Quincy police station, I stood from the chair that had been my captor and extended a hand across Winslow's desk.

"Appreciate you hearing me out," I said.

She stood too, shaking my hand with a nod. "Lyla was upset when she came down earlier. She deserves the truth."

"She does. If it's all right, I'd like to be the one to tell her."

"Tonight." Winn arched an eyebrow, a silent threat. If I wanted to be the one to tell Lyla the truth, the clock was ticking.

"Tonight." I took my coat from the back of the chair and tugged it on. Then I strapped on the backpack I'd taken hiking with me.

Winn hadn't let me drop it off in the room. Instead, she'd

hauled me directly to the station in her unmarked rig. I'd expected her to sit my ass in an interrogation room, but she'd shown me no mercy and chosen her office for this conversation instead.

Only cops understood that a chief's or captain's office was worse than an interrogation room.

A file with my name on it had been sitting on her desk when we'd walked in, left out in plain sight for me to see. But she hadn't touched it since we'd come in here. Probably because we both knew what was inside.

My demons.

Cormac. The shooting.

Rather than tell me what she knew, she'd asked for my story, then she'd listened. When I was done, she'd delivered the ass chewing of all ass chewings.

I'd always thought my captain was the best at cutting a man down, but damn, Winn could give him lessons.

She'd lectured me for not contacting her in regard to Cormac. For not sharing information about a criminal. For potentially contaminating a crime scene. She'd put me in my damn place and hadn't minced words in the process.

The fucking hell of it was, I liked her. Still. I liked her. That ass chewing had been done with respect. Poise.

I admired the hell out of her for that. I bet the cops working in the bullpen outside her office admired the hell out of her too. They'd be fools otherwise.

"I should make a phone call to your captain," Winn said. "Then tell you to get the hell out of my town."

"You should." But would she?

"My jurisdiction is Quincy," she said. "The sheriff has county as well as search and rescue."

Meaning beyond the town's limits, her hands were tied.

Mine were not.

Winn smirked as she shrugged a shoulder. "I can't stop people from going hiking."

And if I was her only resource at the moment for tracking down the man who'd harmed Lyla, she wasn't going to stand in my way.

"What about the FBI?" I asked.

Her eyebrows came together as she thought about it for a long moment. "I'll pass the APB along to a local agent. If they choose to investigate, then I won't stand in their way."

Well, fuck.

I guess it would have been too good to be true for me to be left alone. But she couldn't exactly lecture me on following proper channels while she ignored them too.

"All right." I nodded, then opened the door and strode out of her office.

I felt eyes on me as I walked toward the exit, but I kept my gaze forward until I was outside the station.

The second the cool October air hit my face, I realized I didn't have a vehicle. "Son of a bitch."

Winter was coming and the days were growing shorter and shorter. It was only six but the sun had already set behind the mountains. Darkness had fallen over Quincy, and though I'd already spent most of the day hiking, I put one foot in front of the other and trudged downtown to the hotel. But instead of going inside, I dug my keys from my coat pocket and headed straight for my truck.

The lights at Lyla's were on, glowing gold and bright from the abundance of windows. I parked in her driveway but couldn't bring myself to shut off the engine.

Maybe I should have been angry with her for going to Winn. Maybe I should have felt betrayed.

But this was on me.

There were just too many fucking secrets.

How long had I kept them all to myself? Not even Tiff knew the full truth. We'd started dating after Cormac had disappeared, and while she'd gotten bits and pieces of the story, she'd never heard it all.

If I got out of this truck, if I knocked on Lyla's front door, she'd understand why Cormac was so important.

Was she ready for that? Was I?

It had been four years, and fuck, I was tired of carrying this alone. I was tired of failing. I was tired of sleepless nights.

The best sleep I'd had in years had been this past week. Lyla and I had spent plenty of hours having sex, but when we'd exhausted each other, I'd crashed, not waking until her alarm went off at four.

Winn had told me to get my ass over here, but the real reason I was staring at this farmhouse was because I wasn't ready to lose Lyla.

That would come soon enough. That would come when I returned home.

Or tonight, when she slammed the door in my face.

I shut off my truck and climbed out, tucking my hands in my pockets as I climbed the stairs to her porch. Then I pressed the doorbell and held my breath.

Footsteps sounded inside. Her face appeared in the glass insert of the door as she rose up on her toes to see who was outside. The moment she spotted me, her beautiful face hardened.

It looked strange on her lovely face. Out of place. And fuck me for being the asshole who'd made her smile disappear.

I was just as bad as Cormac for that.

Lyla hesitated, standing on her side of the door unmoving.

It felt like hours that I stood there, my shallow breaths white in the cold night air. Then finally, she flipped the dead bolt.

Thank fuck. The air rushed from my lungs as she stood in the threshold. Her feet were bare. Her toes would get cold. But I didn't ask to come inside.

She wouldn't let me anyway.

"Are you really a cop?" she asked.

My forehead furrowed. If that was her first question, it meant that she was questioning everything. That she thought I'd been lying to her from the start. *Damn.*

"Yes," I said. "I'm a cop. I'm a deputy with the Kootenai County Sheriff's Office, in the Back Country Unit. I don't have my badge. It would be useless in Montana, so I left it behind."

It was more or less the truth.

Some secrets weren't for tonight.

"I grew up in Coeur d'Alene. I've always loved the outdoors. Hiking. Fishing. Hunting. But I also wanted to be a cop. I guess you could say my job is the best of both worlds."

Though maybe I should have just become a guide. Maybe I should have gone to work for an outfitting company, pandering to the wealthy tourists who came to the Pacific Northwest in search of a wilderness adventure.

Hell, maybe I shouldn't rule that out yet. Depending on the outcome of the investigation, that might be my fallback option.

"How can I believe you?" A flash of guilt crossed her

face, like she hated to even ask. Like a month ago, she wouldn't have had to ask.

But then she'd met Cormac.

And I knew firsthand how he could destroy a person's ability to trust.

I fished my phone from my jeans pocket, quickly pulling up a newspaper article. "This spring, two sixteen-year-old kids went hiking. A thunderstorm blew in fast and they got lost. I went out and found them."

The paper had called me a hero. Ironic that just months later, I'd become the bad guy.

I scrolled down the article to the photo they'd taken of both Alec and me after the rescue. The two of us were dressed in tan canvas hiking pants and matching button-down shirts. My badge glinted under the summer sun as brightly as Alec's bald head.

Handing the phone to Lyla, I waited as she scanned the article and inspected the picture. Her shoulders slumped as she reached the end.

"Thanks." She returned my phone, then crossed her arms. "I told Winn who you are."

"I just came from the station."

Another flash of guilt crossed her face.

"It's okay," I told her.

Lyla glanced past my shoulder, staring into the darkness. She looked anywhere but at my face.

"Are your toes cold?"

She dropped her gaze, like she'd forgotten her own feet. "Yes."

"Grab some socks. I'll wait."

With a nod, she turned, partially closing the door. She

returned a minute later, her feet covered in thick wool socks. She'd pulled on a sweater too.

She'd bundled herself from the cold because I was not invited into her house.

Damn.

At least I could give her the truth she deserved, then leave her alone to find her peace with it.

"Alec is the guy in the photo with me, from that article," I said. "The backcountry unit is a small part of the sheriff's department, so most of the time, I work alone. But in a sense, you could consider him my partner. He's only been around for four years. Before that, my partner was a guy from Alaska."

Lyla shifted, leaning against the door's frame as she listened, like this day had worn her out so entirely that she needed the support.

"His love for the outdoors was tenfold mine. He was into survivalist stuff. He talked about applying to be on that show *Alone*. Have you seen it?"

"Yes," she murmured.

"He had a lot of skills. He taught me a lot. More than I'd ever learned as an Eagle Scout."

"You were an Eagle Scout?"

"Yeah." I nodded. "Other guys did basketball or football in high school. I was a Boy Scout."

Literally. Figuratively.

No one was surprised when I'd decided to go into law enforcement.

"That man from Alaska was Cormac. He was my partner."

Lyla's gasp rang loud in the still night.

"Not just my partner. He was my best friend. My mentor."

Her gaze snapped to mine. "That's how you know so much about him."

"He was a good man. I looked up to him. I learned from him. In a way, he was who I wanted to become."

"Vance . . ."

"It doesn't make sense. The Cormac I knew adored his wife. He doted on his children and treated his family like they were his entire world. He was a good man." Or so I'd thought. "It's been four years. How did I not see the monster he became? How did I miss that? How could I be so wrong?"

Those bright blue eyes were so sincere. So honest. "I'm sorry."

"Me too." I gave her a sad smile. "If I don't find him, no one will. He's too good. Too careful. But I have to know what happened that night. I have to know why he . . ." *Murdered them.*

Lyla's face softened as desperation cracked my voice. "Did I ruin everything today? Going to Winn?"

"No." I shook my head. "I should have gone to her from the start."

"What did she say?"

"She said she couldn't stop a guy from hiking."

A ghost of a smile crossed Lyla's lips. "Really?"

"She wants Cormac found for what he did to you. I'm her best chance."

"And mine." She closed her eyes, drawing in a long breath. Then as she exhaled, she stood tall. "Thanks for telling me."

"Sorry I didn't sooner."

"It's probably not the easiest thing to relive."

Of course she'd understand why I'd kept it to myself. There was something uniquely special about Lyla Eden. *Her heart.*

She was the woman waiting in the coffee shop with a kind smile. The woman so steady, so constant, that *not* telling her everything had taken effort.

"Good night." I turned to leave. My boots thudded on the porch boards, but before I could jog down the stairs, Lyla called my name.

"Vance?"

I twisted. Those pretty eyes waited.

She took a step back into the house, then opened the door wide. "Come inside."

"You sure?"

"Please."

The corner of my mouth turned up.

It felt like a lifetime ago, but it had just been this morning when I'd promised to make her say please.

Time to make good on that promise.

So I crossed the porch and walked inside, closing the door. Then, right there in the entryway, I sealed my lips over hers and stripped her out of that sweater and those socks. The rest of her clothes came off too.

And when she was pressed against the wall, my cock buried inside her, I bent my lips to her ear. "Say please if you want to come."

A shiver rolled over her shoulders as her pussy fluttered around my length. "Please."

CHAPTER ELEVEN

LYLA

"You're taking the day off?" Crystal's eyebrows shot up, practically skimming her hairline. "Again?"

"Um, I don't have to." I wanted to blow off work today but wouldn't if it made her uncomfortable. "I can stay."

"No!" She shook her head and waved her arms in the air. "I was just surprised. Go."

"Are you sur—"

"See ya."

A smidge of guilt prickled, but I shoved the feeling away as I took one last glance around the kitchen. I'd been here baking since four this morning. The display case and walk-in were both stocked. Most of the prep work was done and every dish and coffee cup was clean.

For the second day in a row, I was leaving Eden Coffee in Crystal's hands. If today was anything like yesterday, I had nothing to worry about.

When I'd come in this morning, the shop had been spotless and the kitchen gleaming beneath the bright florescent lights. Crystal had reorganized the shelves beside the dishwasher, swapping the bowls and plates, moving the latter down. We used the plates twice as often as the bowls and now they were easier to grab.

It was a little change, one I hadn't even thought to make myself. Now it was glaringly obvious that we should have done it ages ago. What else was I missing because I'd refused to step away?

"Thank you," I told Crystal, making a mental note to give her a raise.

"Of course." She smiled, her lime-green lips splitting wide.

She'd be fine on her own today, but maybe it was time I hired another barista. Someone to help her out if I was gone. A part-time employee to work weekends or days like this, when I had somewhere else I wanted to be.

Vance and I were going to the mountains today, on the hike I hadn't gone on yesterday. I'd left him in my bed earlier, his hair tousled and wild as he'd hugged a white pillow. Before I'd slipped out of the bedroom, he'd woken just enough to ask if I wanted to go along on his search.

After his confession about Cormac last night, saying yes had been easy.

But first, I'd needed to ensure Crystal was happy to take charge. More than happy, judging by the smile on her face.

"The cutest brunette ever came in yesterday," she said. "We flirted a little bit. I'm really hoping she comes back today."

"Ooh." I laughed. "I hope she comes back too."

It wouldn't be the first time she'd dated a man or a woman she'd met at the shop. Crystal was as sweet as the apple turnovers I'd just pulled from the oven, and part of why I'd hired her was because she was so friendly and open.

But she had a tendency to gossip with customers, so I always made sure that if there was something private to discuss, I did it where she couldn't eavesdrop.

"What are you going to do today?" she asked as I pulled on my coat.

"Clean my house," I lied. I adored Crystal, but my tryst with Vance would be all over Quincy if I let it slip. "Maybe go out to the ranch. We'll see."

"Well, don't worry about the shop."

"I won't." I actually believed that too. What was the worst that could happen? The building burning down? Once upon a time, that would have been the end of my world. Now . . . I'd be sad. But I'd pick myself back up.

Just like I had weeks ago along the riverbank.

"I'm glad you're taking a day for yourself," Crystal said.

"Me too." With a quick wave, I left her to finish opening the shop, ducked out the back door to the alley and drove home.

Vance's truck was in the driveway but parked closer to the garage door than it had been when I'd left this morning. I eased into the garage and went inside.

In the kitchen, he was dressed in yesterday's clothes—a pair of thick, canvas Carhartt pants, a long-sleeved gray thermal and his usual soft flannel coat. The beanie I'd become accustomed to pulling off his hair was fixed in place.

He was scrolling through his phone as he sipped coffee from a paper cup covered in a black lid. Those weren't the to-go cups from the hotel, but the gas station.

That coffee tasted like tar.

"We don't drink that burnt sludge in this house," I said.

Vance glanced up, those gray-blue eyes dancing as he tucked his phone away and set the cup aside. "You left me no choice but to get this from the gas station. You weren't open when I drove to town."

"I would have brought you coffee." I closed the distance between us, rising up on my toes, but I couldn't quite reach his lips, so I tugged on his collar, pulling him closer to kiss the corner of his mouth.

He bent over me, folding around me, and tucked his hands in the back pockets of my jeans, giving my ass a playful squeeze. "Get ready."

I trailed my lips to the underside of his jaw. "Are we in a hurry?"

He kneaded my curves, but before I could reach for the button on his jeans, he had his hands on my shoulders, spinning me around. With a quick swat on the butt, he sent me toward my room.

"Prude," I muttered.

His deep chuckle followed me down the hall as I hurried to change clothes.

The bed was made, the white quilt smooth. Like the exterior of the house, most of the rooms were painted white or cream. I liked bright and open spaces with wooden accents and different textures to add warmth.

The plethora of pillows were neatly arranged against my beige tufted headboard. He'd even done the karate chop, creasing them at the top. No man in my life knew about the karate chop.

Had Vance's ex taught him to make the bed like that?

Jealousy swirled, but I shoved it away, ducking into my walk-in closet to pull on a sweater and warmer socks.

Vance wasn't mine. I had no claim on his heart or body. While he was here, this was just sex. Incredible, addictive sex. And every night we'd shared a bed, either his or mine, I'd slept without a nightmare.

That had to be enough. Sex and sleep.

And today, searching for Cormac.

So I finished getting dressed and collected the same coat, hat and gloves I'd planned to wear yesterday. Then with a water bottle tucked in the crook of my arm, I followed Vance outside and climbed into his silver Dodge truck.

The drive toward the mountains was quiet, oddly reminiscent of the drive we'd taken together two weeks ago toward the river. Had it really only been two weeks? There were moments when it felt like I'd known him for years.

In reality, we were just strangers. Lovers, for a time. Would he go back to his ex after he left Montana? That jealousy surged again, harder to shrug off this time.

When was he leaving? After he found Cormac?

What if we found him today? His face flashed in my mind, causing my insides to twist. How was it that I hadn't thought of this yet? Today wasn't some leisurely hike in the mountains with Vance. We were after a killer.

Vance stretched across the cab and put his hand on my thigh. "Lyla."

"Yeah?"

His thumb stroked my kneecap.

My knees were bouncing. I hadn't even noticed.

"I'm okay."

"You can do this." He'd said the same thing weeks ago.

"I can do this."

Vance kept his hand on my knee, a firm yet soft grip, until he needed both hands to turn into the gravel lot where we'd be leaving his truck.

The moment I stepped outside and breathed in the cool,

mountain air, a bit of my nerves eased. These were my mountains. This was my home. Cormac Gallagher didn't get to steal that from me.

Vance stowed my water bottle in his pack, strapping it to both shoulders, then, without a word, started for the trail.

I fell in step behind him as we traversed the path for about a mile.

"Have you been here before?" Vance's question startled me, and I nearly tripped over a rock.

We'd been walking so quietly, I'd assumed it was because he wanted to keep some level of stealth. But he spoke in his normal voice, his boot stepping on a branch that snapped under his weight.

"Yes," I whispered. "But not in ages."

He glanced back. "Cormac isn't anywhere around here."

"How do you know?" The trees bordering the path were thick. Some had to be over a hundred years old, their trunks wide enough to hide a man.

"He won't come near an established trail."

"Oh." My forehead furrowed. "Then why are we searching on a trail?"

Vance stopped, shifting to slide one strap of his pack off a shoulder. He unzipped the largest pocket, pulling out a map. With practiced ease, he unfolded and refolded it to show me a section. Part of it was marked out with a series of red, parallel lines.

"This is where we parked." He pointed to the map, his finger trailing along the paper as he spoke. "This is the trailhead. Yesterday, I hiked around this area."

The area shaded with the red lines.

"Today, we'll hike through here." Vance drew an imaginary circle on the map, directly above where he'd been yesterday. "Quickest way there is the trailhead. Once we make it up another mile, we'll veer off the path."

"Ah, okay." It was impressive that he was so comfortable in the wilderness. And attractive. He was a rugged, mountain-man fantasy come to life. "So once we get off the trail, what are we looking for?"

Vance shrugged, returning the map to his pack. "Anything."

With it secure, he kept walking, his strides easy, probably so I could keep up. No way he'd searched all of the area he had yesterday at this slow of a pace.

"I'm looking for what doesn't belong," he said.

"Like a footprint?" I turned, inspecting the path behind us. In some of the soft spots, the indent from his boot had imprinted the earth. "It's muddy. That's probably a good thing, right?"

"Good and bad," he said. "A footprint would at least be a sign someone was in the area. Maybe from Cormac. Maybe not. Chances are, I'd be chasing someone else. Cormac would stick to the heavily forested areas, where the needles offer good cushion and camouflage on the ground."

"Interesting." I'd spent most of my youth exploring the ranch. Hiking as a teen. Horseback riding with my parents and siblings. Not once had I thought about the traces I'd left behind. Or how to mask them.

We continued along the trail, walking in silence as the terrain steepened. When Vance stopped, digging out my water, sweat was beading at my temples beneath my hat.

Meanwhile, he barely looked winded. Was this how he kept that magnificent body in shape? How he had such stamina to play with mine for hours and hours each night? *Hooray for hiking.*

"Let's take a break." He walked to a fallen tree, using his boot to kick off a piece of decaying bark. Beneath it, the wood was smooth and tan.

"I can keep going."

"Sit," he ordered. "I need you to save some energy for later."

"Why? What's later?" I turned in a circle. A rock cliff loomed in the distance. We weren't climbing that today, were we?

"Later, I'm fucking you on that fancy couch in your living room."

"Oh." My face flamed. "*Later.*"

Vance winked. It was so playfully sexy my heart tumbled, so I took my seat, catching my breath as he leaned against a neighboring tree trunk.

"Hungry?" he asked.

I lifted a shoulder.

He rifled through his pack, taking out two granola bars, tossing one to me before he tore at the wrapper of his own. He didn't wolf it down or seem to be in any hurry to move along.

Today wasn't really about the search, was it?

Today, he was humoring me. Bringing me out here because maybe he knew I needed a break from the coffee shop. Or maybe he knew I needed more days in these mountains to reclaim them for myself.

"How long were you and Cormac partners?" I asked.

"Seven years." The lightness in Vance's eyes faded.

"We don't have to talk about him."

"No, it's all right." He stared into the forest, his gaze losing focus. "I haven't talked about him in a long time. Kind of made it a point not to."

"We really don't need to."

He balled up his now-empty wrapper and leaned deeper into the tree. "After the academy, I spent a couple years as a deputy doing fairly routine work. Mostly putting my time in, proving myself. I met Cormac at a department holiday party. We got to talking, and I told him I was interested in working for the backcountry unit. He took me out hiking the next week. Snow to our waists. Cold as hell. He pushed me to the extreme, but I kept pace with him to the summit. Views for days. Worth the work."

His voice quieted as he spoke, almost like he was tiptoeing around those memories, careful not to disturb them.

"I didn't realize until we got back to town it was a test," he said. "Cormac pulled some strings, and by that summer, I'd been transferred. He became my mentor. Partner. Friend."

Until Cormac had snapped and murdered his family.

"I spent a lot of time with him and his family," Vance said. "I told you he was the coach for his daughter's softball team?"

"Yeah."

"I was the assistant coach. I taught his twins how to whittle wooden spoons. When Cormac was working, I'd shuttle his oldest to swim team practice. Those girls were the closest thing to my own daughters as I've ever had."

And he'd lost them. My heart cracked. "I'm sorry."

"He was a good dad." Vance shook his head, his eyebrows coming together. "He was a great dad. He *loved* those girls."

Then why? Why had he killed them? Unless . . .

"Do you think he really did it?" I hated even asking that

question. After what Cormac had done to me, I had no trouble thinking of him as a murderer. But the doubt written on Vance's face crept into my mind.

"In my head"—he tapped his temple—"he killed them. He strangled Norah."

Norah. A pretty name. I pitied her already for the way she'd died. I hoped, for her sake, that she hadn't known that he'd killed their children.

"There's no question," Vance continued. "I've gone through the evidence countless times. It all points to Cormac. And the fact that he ran."

"Innocent men don't run."

"No, they don't." He sighed. "In my head, all the pieces fit. But in my heart, I can't make sense of it."

Because to Vance, Cormac had been a friend and mentor too. Not a cold-blooded killer. "That's why you need to find him. You want answers."

Vance went quiet again, his gaze roving the nearby trees. "Starting to think I might not get them."

"I hope you do."

"So do I," he murmured, swallowing hard.

I stood from my seat, brushing off the seat of my jeans. Then I handed Vance my bottle to put in his backpack with my own granola bar wrapper. "Okay, we're looking for footprints but we're not looking for footprints. What else?"

"Cormac was out hunting when you found him. Not for sport, but food. Which means he probably has a shelter in the area. I found no signs of him around the river, so he's probably been careful to hunt far away from where he's camped."

"Then why did he come to the river that day?" That

place wasn't close to the road, but it wasn't exactly secluded either.

"Hunting season. Maybe he thought he'd blend in as just another bow hunter. Maybe he was tracking the elk and that's where she led him."

I guess when you lived off the wilderness for food, you took the opportunities given. "How much distance would he put between his camp and where he was hunting?"

Vance shrugged. "Ten miles? Twenty? Maybe more."

"Twenty miles?" A mental circle extended in my head, its edge stretching farther and farther into the forest. Twenty miles on a smooth, flat highway would take at least five hours to walk. But through these woods? Days.

The magnitude of this search, the improbability of it being successful, rolled over me like the dense fog clinging to the jagged mountain peaks.

Was this hopeless?

Like he'd plucked the question from my thoughts, Vance reached out, his palm cupping my cheek. In that clear gaze, I saw the truth he'd been hiding for weeks.

This was hopeless, wasn't it? Yet he was still here, combing through this forest day in and day out.

He hadn't given up, not yet. So neither would I.

"What else do you look for?"

"Animal snares." His thumb stroked my skin before he dropped his hand and adjusted his backpack. "Tree stumps that look like they've been cut down, not broken. And he'd stay relatively close to a water supply."

"But not the river?"

"Probably not. There are plenty of mountain streams around. He'll use one of them as his source instead."

A stream. Or . . . a waterfall.

I spun in a slow circle, trying to get my bearings. "There are two waterfalls off this trailhead."

"Two?" Vance asked. "According to the local guidebooks, there's only one. Are you sure?"

"Positive. This trail leads to the main one." Hence the reason there was even a trail to begin with and a parking lot at the base. "But there's another waterfall up here too. There's just no trail leading to it. I don't know how far we've walked and it's been forever since I came up this way. But I want to say five miles, maybe? I *think* I'll recognize the way to get there? Fingers crossed."

"All right. Lead the way."

"Promise not to be mad at me if I get us lost?"

He stepped close and brushed a kiss against my forehead. "You get us lost. I'll get us found."

CHAPTER TWELVE

VANCE

"How do you know about this waterfall?" I asked Lyla as she weaved a path through the trees.

"I came up here a couple times in high school." She slowed, looking to her left, then right, before continuing straight.

From how often she stopped to spin in a slow circle, I was fairly certain she was lost. But I had a good idea of where we were—countless hours studying local maps had been time well spent.

If she got turned around, I'd be able to find our way back to the truck. So I let her keep going, my gaze alternating between the forest and her sweet, delicious ass.

I'd been fighting a hard-on ever since she'd taken the lead. Not exactly what I should be focused on today. But Lyla needed this hike. She hadn't said anything, I just had a hunch.

Today was more about her getting a piece of herself back than tracking Cormac.

More time well spent.

"I had this boyfriend my junior year who loved to hike. He was a year older and spent a lot of time hiking in these mountains. He found this waterfall and brought me along." She glanced over her shoulder, a shy smile on her mouth as she dramatically pressed her hand to her heart. "I thought it was so romantic, him discovering this waterfall just for me."

So this was a hookup spot. A spear of jealousy shot through my chest, in one side and out the other.

Lyla faced forward before she could see my jaw clench.

For fuck's sake.

Jealous of a high school boyfriend. What the hell was happening to me? I couldn't remember the last time I'd been jealous. None of Tiff's past lovers had irritated me. Hell, she worked with an ex, and I hadn't cared—maybe they'd get back together now. Good for them.

So why did just the mention of Lyla's former flame make me want to punch a tree?

There was no reason to get jealous. No reason to get attached. This would end soon.

With either me finding Cormac. Or me leaving empty-handed.

Until then, Lyla was a lovely distraction, a balm over a wound I doubted would ever heal. A woman who needed an escape as much as I needed to forget. She was a miracle, really.

When she was in bed with me, I'd even managed a few decent nights of sleep.

This morning, it had been all too easy to drift back to sleep after she'd left for Eden Coffee, her scent lingering on the pillows.

When was the last time I'd slept past five? *Years*. Four, to be exact. Back when the world made sense, before everything got so fucked up, I used to love sleeping in.

That was before the dead haunted me in my dreams.

"What else happened with Winn yesterday?" Lyla's question snapped me out of my head.

"What I told you last night. She basically said that I fucked up by coming here and not making her station my first stop."

Lyla shot me an exaggerated frown over her shoulder. "Ouch."

"She's not wrong. I broke protocol. She had a right to be pissed."

"But you're still here."

"I'm still here." For another day. Another week. Maybe another month.

Lyla had only asked once how long I'd be in Quincy. I hadn't answered because I wasn't sure. I'd stay as long as possible, nothing more.

"Winn's a good cop," I said. "She'll follow the rules. She's a good sister-in-law too. Her hands are tied, mine aren't. So I get to keep searching with the understanding that if I fuck up this investigation, she'll castrate me."

Lyla's giggle filled the air. God, that sound. I hadn't heard her laugh enough while I'd been in Quincy.

"I read about what Winn has done as chief in the newspaper," I said.

Lyla stopped, turning to face me. "Did you read about the shooting?"

"I did. I'm sorry. That had to be hard on your family."

"It was, especially Eloise. Winn too. I worry about her after what she had to do." Lyla's shoulders slumped. "Have you ever had to shoot someone?"

"Twice."

"Did they die?"

"Once."

Lyla's eyes locked with mine, the sympathy in them so deep it made my chest feel too tight. She closed the distance between us, her hand splaying across my heart. "I'm sorry."

"Me too." I cupped her cheek, my thumb tracing the smooth line of her cheekbone.

Strange, but I hadn't thought about that time in a while. I used to replay it daily.

Years ago, a hunter had called in a tip that he'd stumbled across a meth house in the mountains. I'd only been working with Cormac for about a year, and in those days, we'd done everything together. True partners. Friends. So the two of us had gone scouting to see if we could find the cabin. The plan had just been to scope it out, then call in for the local drug task force to take it down.

We'd found the place easily enough. It had been a shitty old hut, miles from any road or house. We'd stopped about fifty yards away, close enough for Cormac to pinpoint the place on GPS and take some photos.

He'd just dug his phone from a pocket when we'd heard a branch snap. Then everything had happened in slow motion.

The guy who'd lived in that cabin had been out in the woods, doing whatever it was that meth addicts do. He'd seen us approach and had planned on killing us to keep his hideaway a secret. At least, that was what I assumed.

Had he not stepped on a branch, I'd probably be dead. Instead, that had given me enough warning to draw my gun and shoot him four times in the chest.

Cormac had been closer. He would have gotten hit first. But I'd saved his life.

Maybe that was where it had all gone wrong. Had I known what would happen, maybe I would have let that addict kill us both.

"Vance." Lyla's voice pulled me from the memory. She leaned her cheek into my palm.

I cleared my throat as I dropped my hand. "Winn seems solid. I don't think you have cause to worry, but you should just ask her if she's okay. Chances are, she'll say yes. Whether she means it or not. But just keep asking."

"Is that what someone did for you? Kept asking if you were okay?"

"Yes."

"Who? Your family?"

No, not my family.

Cormac.

And *that* was how he'd become my family.

But Lyla wouldn't want that answer. It made Cormac too likable. Too good. So I did what I did best—changed the damn subject.

"Winn knows that we're sleeping together, doesn't she?"

Lyla blinked, taken off guard for a moment. But in our short time together, she'd already picked up that when I was done with a topic, I was done. So she nodded. "Yes, but I asked her to keep it between us."

A secret. That had been my idea. So why did I hate it so much?

"I've never kept a man secret before," Lyla said. "It's strange."

"I'm not asking you to keep a secret."

"You're leaving. I know the stakes here."

The stakes. The fucking stakes. Yeah, I knew them too.

"I won't lie to my family. Honestly, someone will figure it out anyway. I'm surprised they haven't yet."

"Why do you say that?"

"I have this habit of wearing my feelings like jewelry, bright and sparkly for the world to see. I trust people just because people can trust me. That's how I was raised. That's who I am. Lately, I just . . ." She let her gaze slide away, unfocused past my shoulder. "Don't feel like myself."

Of course she wouldn't feel like herself.

"Hey." I hooked my finger beneath her chin, tilting it up until her eyes came back to mine. "Are you okay?"

Tears filled her eyes. "Not really."

My heart squeezed. Fucking Cormac. This was on him. These tears were on him. "What can I do?"

She sniffled, reaching up to dab the corner of her eyes. "Help me find this waterfall."

If a waterfall was what she needed, then a waterfall was what we'd find.

I took her by the shoulders, turning her around. Then I smacked her ass. Hard. "Lead the way, Blue."

It didn't earn me a laugh, but I'd keep trying to make her smile.

We hiked for another hour, mostly in silence. But whatever heaviness weighed on Lyla seemed to fade while her frustration mounted.

She stopped walking so quickly that I nearly plowed her over.

"What?" I asked.

She huffed and tossed up her hands. "I'm lost."

Was she? There was a faint noise in the distance. I'd heard it for the past few minutes, just assuming she had too.

"Shh," I said.

She tensed. "Why?"

"Listen."

"To what?"

This woman. I clamped my hand over her mouth, earning a growl. Then with my free hand, I pulled off her beanie so she had nothing over her ears.

The moment she heard it, her gaze tipped up over her shoulder to meet mine. Those blue eyes lit up like stars.

Water.

She raced toward the sound, leaping over a fallen log as she jogged.

I chuckled, shaking my head as I hurried to catch up.

Not a hundred feet away, past a cluster of bushes, the forest floor gave way to wet, black rocks, some spotted with moss. A stream trickled from a small pool fed from a gentle waterfall.

The current was slow. The cold weather was moving farther and farther down the mountains, and soon, this would be frozen. The waterfall itself was only four or five feet tall, but it was enough to fill the air with a steady rush of noise.

Lyla made her way along the slick rocks, her arms held out wide and ready to catch herself if her foot slipped.

I stayed back, watching as she navigated her way, inch by inch, around the pool's perimeter. Then when she was close enough, she took off a glove, stretched out a hand and let it disappear into the waterfall.

There was the smile. White and wide, illuminating her whole face.

Fuck, but she was gorgeous. I couldn't tear my eyes away, not even in a place like this, where nature was showing off.

The cool, clear water. The vivid green forest. It was a beautiful place, worthy of paintings or photographs.

But I couldn't take my eyes off Lyla.

She moved her fingers in and out of the water, letting it dance across her knuckles. Then she yanked it free, probably when the cold got to be too much, and after drying her hand on her jeans, she hurried to put her glove back on. As carefully as she'd moved to the water, she walked away.

"I found it." Her smile was breathtaking as she stopped by my side.

"You found it."

The smile vanished. Lyla's eyes flooded again, and like before, she dabbed at the corners, stopping any tears before they could fall.

"You okay?" I'd keep asking that question. While I was here, I'd ask every day.

She looked around, her gaze leaving nothing untouched. "Being here feels almost like stepping into a different lifetime. And I feel like an entirely different person than the girl I was when I came here all those years ago."

I couldn't even remember who I'd been at that age. Too much had happened. Too much had changed.

"I'm glad we came here," she whispered.

"But . . ."

She sighed. "But it's a hard truth to face that the life you're living, the life you built day after day after day because of the dreams you had when you were young, might not be the life you want. In a way, it feels like the girl who came here so long ago got it wrong."

"Did she?"

Lyla shrugged. "I don't know. Maybe. Partially. She'd

probably argue with me. I miss the confidence I had. I miss the faith that it would all just . . . work out."

The mental picture of seventeen-year-old Lyla was clear as day. Bright blue eyes, full of dreams.

I'd known another seventeen-year-old girl just like that once.

"I'm thirty," Lyla said. "Somewhere along the way, I lost that girl. You're good at finding people, right? Maybe after you catch Cormac, you could teach me your tricks."

I stepped closer, so close that not even a breath of wind could come between us. Then I laid my hand on the center of her chest. "You don't need me to find her. She's right here. Where she's always been."

Lyla's eyes searched mine like she couldn't quite believe me. Then she fell forward, into my arms, burying her face in my chest. "Thanks."

"Welcome." I dropped a kiss to her hair, then let her go.

She took a few steps away, turning to face the waterfall again.

This was my chance to memorize this hidden paradise. To soak it all in. But again, all I could do was look at Lyla.

We were two sides to the same coin. Two people trying to find their way back to center.

Maybe it was too late for me to go back. But for Lyla, I wanted her to find a glimpse of that seventeen-year-old girl. To find the spark.

"We'd better get going," I said. "I don't want to get stuck out here in the dark."

"Neither do I. And I'm starving."

"Want another granola bar?"

She held up a hand, stopping me from digging one from

my backpack. "We're getting cheeseburgers. Double cheeseburgers."

I chuckled. "Double cheeseburgers. With fries."

"Obviously." She smiled, and when I offered her a hand, she held it tight, letting me guide her down the slippery rocks and back to the forest floor.

"We'll follow the stream down for a bit," I told her. "I'm guessing that will be faster. Then we'll work our way back toward the trail."

"Okay," she said, staying close as we hiked.

It was always harder on the trip back, your muscles straining to keep balance with gravity working against you. I cut my normal stride in half, making sure she didn't feel rushed.

Beside us, the stream trickled, growing wider, deeper the farther we worked down the mountain.

It wasn't a river, not something you'd find on a map. But it was larger than I'd expected to find today. Maybe a good place for me to start tomorrow.

I was about to change course, head toward the trees and hike until we reached the path that would take us to the trailhead, when a yelp echoed behind me. I spun just in time to see Lyla's feet sweep into the air.

And her land in the dirt with a thud.

"Lyla," I gasped, rushing to her side and crouching down, my hands roaming over her body, searching for injury. "Are you hurt?"

"Ouch. No. I'm fine." She tipped her head to the sky, drawing in a long breath, then surveyed the damage. "Shit."

One side of her jeans was coated in the mud she'd slipped on.

She wiped at it but the only way that was coming out was in the wash. "I hate mud."

"I've got a blanket in the truck. We'll get back and peel you out of those wet jeans."

"Why, Mr. Sutter." Lyla fluttered her lashes. "Are you flirting with me?"

I chuckled, my heart sinking back down my throat.

It felt good to laugh, and Lyla had a way of coaxing it free. I'd laughed more in Quincy than I had in, well . . . four years.

I stood, offering her a hand to help her to her feet. "Come on."

When she was standing, Lyla twisted to inspect the seat of her jeans—also coated in mud—then let out a string of curses that would make most guys on the force blush. When she looked to my face, she cocked her head to the side. "What?"

Except I wasn't looking at her.

I was staring at the stream, just over her shoulder.

"Vance?" She followed my gaze to the water. "What? What are we looking at?"

"Stay here." I passed her, taking slow, deliberate steps toward the water. I made sure every step was on a rock so my footprints wouldn't show. Then I dropped to my haunches, peering through the clear stream.

And there, in its center, was a woven cone of willow branches.

A fish trap.

"Fuck me." I looked around, scanning the trees. My pulse thudded in my ears.

Not a fish trap anyone would buy, but one made.

"Vance?" Lyla's voice wobbled.

"Don't move, Blue."

"Is it a bear?"

"You see that?" I pointed to the water. "It's a fish trap."

The outer cone had a wide end that tapered to a smaller hole. At the wide opening, another cone fit inside, shorter, with the same smaller hole. Fish could swim inside the cone —I couldn't tell if there was bait inside without pulling it from the water—and once they were in the cone, they'd get trapped, unable to find their way out of the smaller holes.

It was empty at the moment. Either because there weren't any fish in this stream, or because someone had stopped by recently to put it in place.

"Son of a bitch," I muttered, then stood and stepped away, taking as much care as I had earlier to step only on rocks as I made my way to Lyla.

There were footprints everywhere around where she'd slipped. *Damn.*

"Do you think Cormac made that trap?" Lyla asked.

"Maybe." I turned, looking up the mountain from where we'd come.

Part of me didn't want to hope. The other part didn't want to even consider this could be possible.

But that trap . . .

It had Cormac's name written all over it. Whenever we'd go camping, he'd spend a night by the fire, weaving branches and reeds together for fun while the girls would roast marshmallows and make s'mores.

Maybe he had made this trap. Maybe he hadn't left the area yet.

Maybe I'd find that bastard after all.

CHAPTER THIRTEEN

LYLA

My heart seized as Vance walked into the coffee shop, his face unreadable.

"Hi," I breathed when he reached the counter.

"Hey." He'd spent the past two days in the mountains, searching for signs of whoever had made that fish trap.

As much as I'd wanted to go with him, Crystal was off and I needed to be at the shop. That, and I'd only slow Vance down.

Except left behind, I'd had nothing to do but worry and wait. Today, I'd been so rattled that I'd dropped a coffee mug. The shattered ceramic remains were now in the trash can beside my feet. But one lost cup was better than my mishap yesterday—an entire double batch of cookie dough had gone splat on the kitchen floor when I'd been so distracted that I'd knocked over my mixing bowl.

"Are you hungry?" It took everything in my power not to ask him the question I was dying to voice.

Did you find Cormac?

I guess him being here was answer enough. If Vance had

found Cormac, he'd likely be at the police station. Or possibly packing his hotel room.

"Yes," he said. "I pushed hard today. Scarfed a granola bar on the drive back to town, but if you had a sandwich or something, that would be great."

"I'll bring it over." I nodded, already going to work on a plate.

Vance headed toward the window, taking his usual seat. He hadn't brought in his backpack today. Was that a good thing?

He pulled off his beanie, his hair disheveled, much like it had been this morning when I'd left him in my bed to come to work at four.

I usually chased after guys who styled their hair with combs, not fingers. I'd never, ever be able to look at a nice, clean-cut man again without wishing he had Vance's messy hair.

Thick and soft, nothing had ever felt better threaded in my grip.

How many days, how many nights, did we have left?

Two days and everything had changed. It was like we'd started this, whatever this was, at a slow, unhurried pace. Like the way my dad drove through pastures at the ranch, slow enough to feel each bump in the dirt lanes.

Now the pedal was to the floor and we were driving a hundred miles per hour, headed straight for a brick wall.

The end was coming.

With every passing day, Vance was one step closer to leaving Quincy.

When?

I wanted him to find Cormac. More than anything, I

wanted Vance to get his answers. To gain closure. To put his demons to rest. At the same time . . .

I didn't want him to find Cormac.

How ridiculous was that? That asshole was a criminal. He'd turned me inside out and deserved to spend the rest of his life rotting in prison, not just for what he'd done to me but to his family.

Vance *had* to find Cormac.

But when this mess was over, Vance would return to Idaho. And me?

Maybe I'd go back to normal.

Normal sounded . . . horrible.

I poured Vance a cup of steaming coffee, taking it and a turkey sandwich to his table. "Here you go."

"Thanks." His smile was weak. Weary.

More than anything, I wanted to slide into his lap, wrap my arms around those broad shoulders and bury my nose in the crook of his neck.

That would have to wait until tonight when we were safe behind my closed doors.

There weren't many customers in the shop at the moment, but Emily Nelsen was across the room and five tables away.

She was a reporter at the *Quincy Gazette,* the local newspaper owned by her parents. Emily and I had graduated high school together, and besides a few incidents of minor teen-girl drama, we'd mostly gotten along.

She used to come in and kiss my ass because of her crush on Griffin. But since he'd married Winn, the ass-kissing had stopped. Now she came into the shop because she loved gossip. And Eden Coffee was one of her regular stops for fodder.

Emily's blond hair was pulled up, revealing the white earbuds she'd put in earlier when she'd started working on her laptop. Maybe she was listening to music or a podcast. Maybe it was a ruse to make people think she wasn't eavesdropping.

So I stayed on my feet. If Emily was watching, I was simply making nice with a customer.

"How'd it go today?" I asked, keeping my voice low.

"Nothing." He frowned, then took a bite of his sandwich, his strong jaw flexing as he chewed. When he swallowed, his shoulders sagged, like his body was finally relaxing now that he was giving it some decent food.

"Do you think he saw our footprints?"

"Maybe," he murmured.

We'd done our best to conceal them, taking a few branches to scratch them from the mud and dirt. Vance had hoped that with the fall rain we'd been getting each night, our tracks would wash away. But there was no guarantee.

"Or maybe it's not him." Vance sighed.

"It's him." It had to be him.

"I set up a few game cameras today in the area. One is aimed right at the stream."

"Smart."

"We'll see." His voice was so flat. Two days ago, he'd been keyed up after finding that trap. But the roller coaster that was Cormac Gallagher was now at the bottom of the track, along with Vance's spirits.

Up and down. Down and up.

He ate another bite of his sandwich, doing what Vance did when the topic was getting too heavy. He changed the subject. "This is really good."

"Thank you."

He winked, forcing a half smile. "How's your day going?"

"Other than the broken mug in the trash can, it's been fine."

"You okay?"

"Are you?"

"I asked you first, Blue."

"I'm okay." I nodded, and today, it was the truth. I was more worried about him than myself. And maybe what I'd needed all along was to talk. To let it out. He'd given me that outlet at the waterfall.

No one knew those feelings. Not my parents. Not my siblings.

But there was something about Vance that had made me confess it all. Maybe because it seemed like he'd understand.

"Will you keep searching?" I asked. "Or just rely on the game cameras?"

"I'll keep going." His coat was hung on the back of his chair. He reached into an interior pocket, taking out the same map he'd shown me while we'd been hiking. It was folded differently now, reduced to the area around that stream. "Until it snows."

What? My heart dropped to the floor. Until it snowed. That was it?

It could snow any day now. My eyes shot to the windows and the sky above Main. The late afternoon light had mostly faded as the days got shorter and shorter.

The sky was clear for a change. The rain clouds had blown away while Vance had been hiking. The stars would put on a show tonight, but this reprieve wouldn't last. Especially in the mountains.

Snow was coming.

I wasn't ready to let him go. Not yet.

"Why the snow?" I asked, hoping he couldn't hear the sadness in my voice.

"Just too hard to hide tracks."

"Right." Of course. Like the mud, any tracks would help find Cormac. But they'd also alert Cormac to someone in the area.

What if there was another way? "My brother, Mateo, is a pilot. If it snows, wouldn't Cormac need a fire or something to stay warm? What if you searched by plane instead?"

"Maybe. Though that could spook him."

"But I'm sure wherever he's been hiding, he's heard planes fly around."

Vance hummed. "I'll think about it."

If he was anything like my father, *I'll think about it* meant *no.*

The bell dinged behind me, the door opening, and with it, a gust of cold air swept inside.

Mom walked in, her cheeks flushed and smile bright. "Hi."

"Hey, Mom."

"How's it going?" She walked over, pulling me into a hug. "I was just coming to say hi and see if you needed an extra set of hands in the kitchen. I feel like baking but your father told me that he wanted to lose five pounds, so I wasn't allowed to make a pie. I give it a week."

I laughed. "Me too."

"So . . . need free labor?"

"Sure." I glanced at Vance.

He nodded to Mom, a silent hello as he chewed more of that sandwich.

"Hi," Mom said, looking between the two of us. "Oh, sorry. Am I interrupting?"

"No, it's fine. We were just chatting." I looked at Vance. "I'll let you eat."

He nodded again, and as I headed for the counter, Mom at my side, I felt his eyes on me.

"Honey." Mom leaned in close to whisper. "Who is that?"

"Just a customer."

She scoffed. "And I'm twenty-nine years old."

Being close with your mom was wonderful. Most of the time. But she'd always had this uncanny ability to know when I was lying.

Of her three daughters, why was I the one she could read like her favorite book? Eloise had been married to Jasper for a month before any of us had found out. And the few times Talia and I had broken curfew in high school, it wasn't my twin Mom had interrogated. It was me.

Busted. Every damn time.

Winn was the only person in my family who knew about Vance, and she'd kept it quiet simply because I'd asked. Griffin probably knew, but he'd always been more concerned about Eloise's choice in men, not mine.

To be fair, before Jasper, Eloise had picked some disasters as boyfriends. I guess I could take it as a point of pride that my oldest brother trusted me to be a good judge of character.

"What's his name?" Mom asked.

I checked over my shoulder as we passed the counter, making sure Emily Nelsen was out of earshot. Then I nodded for Mom to follow me into the kitchen.

"Vance," I told her when we were alone.

"He's . . . wow." Mom fanned her face. "*Wow*. Different from most of the men you've dated. Very rugged and he seems tall. Is he tall? Is he new in town? Tell me he just moved here."

"Yes, he's tall. No, he's just visiting."

"From where?" Mom asked, unzipping her coat. "Missoula?"

"Idaho."

"Oh." Mom's face scrunched up. "That's farther than Missoula."

"It's fine." I lifted a shoulder. "We're just . . . it's fine."

"Oh, honey. It's not fine. You like him."

So, so much. But diving into the details about why he was here and when Vance would leave would only lead to questions I wasn't going to answer.

"I was thinking about making pumpkin bread with a cream cheese swirl for tomorrow," I said. If Vance had taught me anything besides just how good sex could be, it was how to change the subject when the current topic was headed down a dangerous road. "Want to take the lead?"

Mom gave me a flat look.

"Or we could do chocolate chips instead of the cream cheese."

"Lyla." Mom wouldn't drop this.

I sighed. "Yes, I like him. But he's leaving. It's nothing serious. And right now, I need that. He's an escape."

Her eyes drifted to my throat. No matter how many years passed, she'd always see those bruises, wouldn't she?

"Chocolate chips or cream cheese?" I asked.

"Cream cheese." She gave me a sad smile, then walked to the rack tucked in the back corner of the kitchen, trading her coat for a green apron.

I pulled dry ingredients from my shelves, setting them on the prep table, while Mom went to the walk-in, getting eggs and butter and cream. "Okay, I'm going to go check on things out there and leave you to it."

"I'm going to invite him to family dinner at the ranch on Friday."

"Oka—" *Huh.* "What?"

"Dinner at the ranch Friday. If he's visiting, that means he's eating out for every meal. Wouldn't it be nice to have something homemade?"

"First, I won't take offense to that statement, considering the majority of his meals have been here. Second, no. Just . . . no, Mom."

"Do you think it would be weird if I went out there and invited him?"

"Beyond weird."

"You're probably right. I could ambush him in the hotel lobby."

"That's called stalking. Hard no."

"It's just dinner."

"Mother," I warned.

"Fine." She waved it off. "I'll butt out."

"Thank you."

She came closer, tucking a lock of my dark hair behind an ear. "I'm worried about you. I love you."

Two statements that meant the same thing. "I love you too."

"Here's an idea." She bopped my nose with a finger, then turned to the table. "What if we topped this pumpkin bread with some toasted sunflower seeds? Give it a little hint of salt."

"Yum. Do I have sunflower seeds?"

"You go back to the counter. I'll dig around the pantry."

"Okay." I left her to her task, knowing that her pumpkin bread creation would be a marvel.

Emily was gone when I returned to the counter, her empty mug and plate left behind, so I quickly cleared them away and wiped down the table before wandering back to Vance's corner.

His plate was empty too.

"Can I get you anything else?"

"I'm good." He pointed toward the kitchen. "You and your mom look alike."

"We are alike. She's in the back, baking." Now that Emily was gone, I pulled out the chair across from his and took a seat. "She taught me how to cook. Knox too."

I had countless memories from my childhood of spending hours and hours with Mom in the kitchen. At the time, I hadn't realized just how much I was learning from her while she'd been standing at the stove.

She'd taught me about hard work. About the pride that came with accomplishment. She'd taught me patience. Grace.

And through every meal, Mom had taught us all about love.

"Eden Coffee was my dream job come true," I told Vance. "In a way, I think it was for Mom too."

Vance leaned his elbows on the table, not speaking, just listening. His gray-blue eyes locked on mine.

The more time I spent around him, the more I was learning to read those striking eyes. They unfocused whenever he was lost in memory. They darkened each night before he fucked me to sleep. And when he was interested in a story, soaking up every word like he was now, they had a brightness that made his irises almost iridescent.

If only we had more time together.

I'd learn every color of Vance Sutter's eyes.

"While my dad was working on the ranch and running the family businesses, Mom managed the hotel," I told him. "She loves The Eloise. Not the way Eloise loves The Eloise, but Mom enjoyed working there until she retired. But I think if she could do it all over again, she'd have a restaurant. Maybe not like Knox has with Knuckles, but something smaller. Something like this."

"It's good of you to let her come here."

"It's no hardship. Trust me. She's an incredible cook. Better than me."

Vance scoffed. "Doubt it."

His reaction was so swift, so confident, that I forgot whatever I'd been about to say.

He liked my food. Why did that surprise me? He ate whatever I put on his plate. He never left so much as a crumb behind. Still, it was nice to hear.

I hadn't realized until now how much I wanted him to like my food. To like me. They were one and the same.

The door opened, stealing Vance's attention as he looked over my shoulder.

That freaking bell. I was starting to resent the jingle.

With a sigh, I twisted in my seat, smiling as Sandy came inside. She ran the kitchen shop down the street, a popular store with tourists and locals alike.

"Hey, Sandy," I said, getting to my feet.

"Hi, Lyla." She swept a lock of gray hair out of her face. "I'm freezing. Something is wrong with the furnace at the store, so I'm here for one of your magical lattes to chase away the cold."

"A magical latte." I laughed. "I can do that. Vanilla, like usual?"

"It's my favorite."

"Mom's in the kitchen if you want to go say hi."

"Oh, good. I haven't seen her in weeks, so I'd love to catch up."

"I'll bring your coffee back in a few."

She nodded, her gaze darting to Vance, but she didn't introduce herself. She just wandered through the shop and ducked into the kitchen.

Vance's chair legs scraped on the floor as he stood and grabbed his coat. "I'm going to head to my room. Take a shower."

"Okay." I never asked if he was coming to my house later. Granted, he came over each night, but still, I never asked. I didn't want him to think I was clingy. I didn't want to hear him say no.

We weren't a couple. We didn't make plans. We didn't date. It was better that way, right?

I turned for the counter, about to leave, but stopped. Wait. Why couldn't we make plans?

"Do you want to go to the ranch on Friday for dinner?" I blurted before thinking it through. It sounded so eerily like my mother's voice that I cringed.

She'd put the idea in my head and it had just snuck out. *Damn it.*

"No pressure." My face began to flame. "Mom is planning a family dinner at the ranch on Friday and mentioned it. If you're sick of eating at restaurants every night and want something homemade . . ."

It was official. I hated the word homemade. And just like my mother, I was now insulting my own business. *Nice, Lyla.*

"Sorry. This is weird." I waved it off. "Ignore me. My family is a lot, and I just wanted to offer in case—"

"Blue."

Oh God. Here came the polite decline. And I probably wouldn't see him tonight either.

I couldn't meet his gaze. I didn't want to know what color his eyes turned when they were full of pity. So I stared at the floor instead. "Yeah?"

"What time is dinner Friday?"

CHAPTER FOURTEEN

VANCE

The Edens were loud.

Not just in volume—though Lyla's family laughed like there was a decibel quota to meet over dinner. They were loud in other ways. Their smiles. Their hugs. Their love.

It had been a long time since I'd been to a Sutter family dinner. Maybe my memory was failing me, but the only time I recalled my family being loud was the very last dinner. The one where everything had fallen apart. Not a good loud.

The Edens were a good loud.

Anne and Harrison sat on opposite ends of the dining room table and, between them, their children and grandchildren.

The table itself, a smooth, black walnut piece with matching chairs, was new. It lacked the dents and dings of furniture that had seen more than a handful of family functions. It was slightly too large for the space, but that was likely because it had been bought with this crush of people in mind.

A large family needed a large table. Even if it was crowded, Anne and Harrison probably wanted each person here to have a seat. They'd even made space for the little ones and their high chairs.

No surprise, Lyla's parents were good people. Anne had welcomed me with a hug. Harrison with a firm handshake. And then Lyla's siblings had descended, nosy but not intrusive.

They'd asked questions but hadn't pried into my personal life. Instead, they'd learned tonight that I preferred whiskey over beer. That I liked my steaks medium rare. And that my favorite color was blue.

Lyla's blue.

Though I hadn't been that specific when Eloise had asked a few moments ago.

"Blue would have been a good color choice," Knox said.

"I didn't want blue." Anne jutted up her chin. "I wanted yellow."

"But it's not yellow, Mom."

"Of course it's yellow." Anne had recently painted the powder room down the hall. Tonight was the first anyone but Harrison had seen it. "The color is called mustard. Mustard is yellow."

"It looks like baby poop," Griffin said.

"Griff," Winn scolded.

"What? It does."

"It's not the color of baby poop." Anne harrumphed, then adjusted Griff and Winn's daughter, Emma, on her lap. "Change your daughter's diaper once in a while and you'll know the difference."

Griffin just laughed and shook his head, making a face at

his two-year-old son, Hudson, who was making a hell of a mess in his booster seat with some Play-Doh.

Some dads didn't change diapers, but I suspected that none of the men here shied away from a loaded Pampers.

"It's sort of baby poop, Mom," Talia said, her hand splayed on her pregnant belly.

She and her husband, Foster, were having a boy. Current name options were Kaiden or Jude. I'd voted for Jude.

"Are all of my children color-blind?" Anne asked the room. "It's yellow."

Harrison hid his laughter in the beer bottle pressed to his lips.

"It's not that bad." Jasper's arm was draped around the back of Eloise's chair, his hand on her shoulder. He was rarely far from her side, and if she was close, he touched her in some small way.

I'd seen that sort of constant touch before. Jasper's obsession with Eloise had taken me off guard at first. Maybe just from my own personal history, but the hairs on the back of my neck had stood on end as I'd watched them from the corner of my eye almost constantly.

But after hours of seeing them together, I realized it was different than Andrea and Brandon.

Jasper didn't touch Eloise to possess her, to control her. He touched her like she was his tether to the earth. Like without her, he'd drift away on a breeze. He loved her.

There was a lot of love at this table.

Lucky table.

"Thank you, Jasper." Anne gave him a proud smile.

"Kiss ass," Knox teased. "It's hideous."

"It's not hideous." Memphis, Knox's wife, gave Anne a sweet smile. "I like it too."

Knox and Memphis each had a kid in their arms. Memphis was feeding their baby boy, Harrison Eden, a bottle. Knox stroked their oldest son's back.

Drake had fallen asleep about an hour ago, even with all this noise. We'd finished dessert. The dirty plates were still scattered across the table. He'd had his last bite of brownies and ice cream, then crawled into Knox's arms. He'd rested his head on his dad's shoulder, and five minutes later, he'd conked out.

"We're taking a poll." Anne aimed her gaze at Foster seated next to her. "What do you think?"

"I like it," he said, sharing a quick look with Jasper.

I'd learned tonight that the two of them had worked together for years while Foster had been in the UFC. Jasper had been Foster's trainer until he'd retired, and both had moved to Quincy about the same time.

They'd shared a few looks tonight, unspoken messages flying across this table.

Once upon a time, I'd had that sort of friendship. Brotherhood.

With Cormac.

Lyla put her hand on my thigh beneath the table, her delicate touch chasing away the past.

I covered her knuckles with my palm, drawing circles on her skin with my thumb.

"Lyla?" Anne arched her eyebrows at her daughter, waiting for her vote.

"I don't think it's the color of baby poop, Mom. More like split-pea soup."

Anne's jaw dropped. "It's not green."

"It's got a green tint."

I clamped my teeth together, fighting the laugh that

Lyla's brothers couldn't hide.

"Vance?" Anne asked, her eyes pleading.

"Yellow," I lied. "It's definitely yellow." It was split-pea, baby-poop green.

Her entire face lit up.

So did Lyla's. She smiled, knowing I'd lied for her mother's sake.

"Do we really need to vote?" Mateo asked. "I'll just tell you how it's going to go. Your kids hate the color. Your kids-in-law also hate the color, but they love you too much to tell you the truth."

"So not only are you criticizing my taste, now you're saying you don't love me." Anne picked up her cloth napkin and threw it at his head. "Get out. You're no son of mine."

Mateo caught the napkin and laughed, a deep, hearty laugh that was the same as his father's and brothers'.

I needed two hands to count the similarities between the Eden men. And the same was true for Lyla and her mother and sisters.

As twins, Lyla and Talia had the same shape to their face, nose and mouth. Cormac's twins had been almost impossible to tell apart for most people. It had taken me months to know which was Hadley or Elsie. But even though Lyla and Talia had the same features, I'd know Lyla anywhere.

Talia's eyes were blue, but not Lyla's blue.

And when it came to kindred spirits and personalities, Lyla was very much like Anne.

"How about I repaint the bathroom for you this weekend?" Lyla asked. "We could pick out a pretty gray or forest green."

"No." Anne sighed. "You're busy. I'll do it. Maybe. Or

maybe I'll just make you all suffer with the baby-poop yellow."

"Speaking of baby poop." Memphis stood with the baby in her arm. "Be right back."

She bent and kissed Knox's forehead, then ducked out of the room.

"Okay, cowboy." Griffin picked up a ball of Hudson's Play-Doh and put it in its yellow container. "Time for us to go home and get in the tub, then head to bed."

"No." Hudson's mouth turned down at the corners, then he crumpled, falling forward as he began to cry.

"Oh, my son." Winn was out of her chair in a flash, picking up Hudson for a hug.

He wrapped his legs around her waist and his small arms around her shoulders, like she was his saving angel. She probably was. Though Winn would likely still make her son take a bath.

"Let's go home." She kissed Hudson's cheek, then carried him with her as she moved to collect the diaper bag.

The rest of us stood, clearing plates and glasses to the kitchen.

Talia and Foster were the first to take off, followed closely by Jasper and Eloise. Then Knox and Memphis loaded up their boys and headed home. Mateo waved goodbye as he climbed into his truck, heading to the cabin where he lived in the mountains.

Griffin and Winn didn't have a long drive to their house on the ranch, so they stuck around the longest to say goodbye.

"Good to see you, Vance," Winn said as we stood beside the door.

"You too." Before dinner, I'd had a lot of respect for

Winslow Eden as a cop. After dinner, that respect had only grown, seeing her as a wife and mother, loyal and loving.

As far as I could tell, she was the only person who knew about my situation in Coeur d'Alene. The clusterfuck that was my job. The shooting. That she'd let that stay between us, well . . . I didn't have much to offer her as thanks, but if she ever needed a favor, I'd move mountains to make it happen.

"Glad you could make it out." Griffin shook my hand, then pulled Lyla into a hug, kissing the top of her hair. "Mom said there were a few things in the shop that need fixing. The paper towel holder in the bathroom and your office door isn't closing quite right. Dad and I are going to come in tomorrow and take a look."

"It's nothing major," Lyla said.

"Then it won't take us long." He let her go, then opened the door, ushering his family outside, leaving me and Lyla with her parents.

"Thank you for having me." I took Harrison's outstretched hand, then bent to kiss Anne's cheek. "Dinner was delicious."

"It was so wonderful meeting you." Anne smiled to me, then her daughter. "Love you."

"Love you too, Mom." Lyla hugged her parents. "Bye, Dad."

"See you tomorrow, sweetheart." Harrison held the door open for us, standing in the threshold as we crossed his porch. Then with a wave, he disappeared inside with his wife.

The air smelled like snow. It was coming, sooner rather than later. But I drew in a long breath, catching the scent of hay and animals and earth. A man could live a damn good life smelling that combination every day. I envied the Edens who called this home.

"When I was a kid, I wanted to be a cowboy," I told Lyla.

Lyla laughed as we walked down the porch stairs. "You did?"

"Yeah. Ten-year-old me would be in heaven right now."

Though thirty-four-year-old me was close to heaven at the moment too.

Stars coated the onyx sky. The moon cast a silver hue across the jagged mountains in the distance. And while it was a breathtaking night, its beauty paled in comparison to the woman at my side.

"Come on." Lyla snagged my hand, interlacing our fingers, then tugged me away from where we'd parked my truck.

I wasn't sure where she was leading me, but I fell in step beside her, keeping her hand in mine as we crossed the open gravel lot beside Anne and Harrison's house.

Three large buildings sat opposite their home—a barn, a shop and the stables. Lyla had pointed them out when we'd arrived earlier. The yard lights illuminated each of their fronts. Beyond them, past the fences and corrals, it was pitch black.

But when Lyla and I had come out before dinner, we'd made it before dark. It had given me the chance to see her family's ranch. It was a magnificent setting, with meadows and untamed evergreen forests and mountain ranges in every direction.

Paradise.

"Want to meet our newest horse?" she asked, leading me to the stables.

"Sure."

She let go of my hand to open a sliding door and step inside.

I joined her, squinting as she flipped on the lights. Then when my eyes adjusted, I took in the huge space, breathing in the scents of horses and leather and straw. A wide lane took up the center of the building. On each side was a row of stables.

She walked to a stall, peering over a gate.

I took the spot beside her. Inside the stall, a black colt stood with a white star on his head. His mother came over, nudging Lyla's arm.

"Isn't he cute?" Lyla petted the horse's smooth, round cheek, then moved away, heading deeper into the building. She strolled past empty stalls, her pace unhurried. "My horse, Mercury, and most of the others are out in the pasture. But if you want to live out your childhood dreams, we could come back another day. Go riding."

God, that sounded fun. I'd ridden a few times over the years, though never often. When I went out into the mountains, it was usually on foot. And as much as I'd love to spend a day with Lyla here, exploring the Eden ranch, that wasn't why I was in Montana.

And time was running out.

Soon the mountains would be covered in snow, making any attempt to search for Cormac more difficult than it already was. If he'd planned to spend the winter in these mountains, then he'd gathered enough supplies to stay in whatever hole he'd dug for himself. He'd limit movement, hiding away until spring.

If he was even here.

"Maybe," I told Lyla.

She heard the *no* and gave me a sad smile as we reached

the far end of the stables.

"Hey." I snagged her hand, missing it in my own. With a tug, I hauled her close. "Thanks for bringing me here tonight."

"You're welcome." Her free hand slid up my chest, her index finger skimming each of the buttons on the Henley beneath my flannel jacket.

"I like your family. I like how loud they are."

Her face softened. "I like it too."

"I have a big family." The words tumbled free before I could swallow them down.

Lyla's gaze shot to mine. Maybe she expected me to pull away, to change the subject. Normally, I would.

Not tonight.

"Do you ever feel lost in the crowd?" I asked.

"Sometimes," she whispered. "Is that how it is with your family?"

"Not lost. Just outside."

Her hand came to my beard, stroking along my jaw with her knuckles. "Does your family know you're here?"

"My dad does. My mother and I haven't spoken for . . . a while."

"Sorry."

"Me too."

There was more to explain. A story to tell. And goddamn it, I wanted to lay it on her. I wanted to unburden my heart again.

She had no idea how much it had helped, sharing my history with Cormac. Unloading it for the first time in years. Maybe it would help make sense of my family's bullshit too if I told her about it. The way Lyla listened, the way she absorbed my every word, made it so tempting.

But we'd had such a good night. Maybe if there wasn't an expiration date, maybe if the snow wasn't coming, I'd give in.

Instead, I closed my other hand over hers, taking it away from my face and twisting it behind her back, pinning it just above her ass. Then I pressed in closer, holding her to me as I bent and took her mouth.

She opened for me instantly, and when I slid my tongue inside, stroking hers, the past disappeared. There was nothing but this woman and the sweet taste of her lips.

My cock swelled, my body craving hers.

Lyla whimpered as I pressed my arousal against her hip.

How many times did we have left? Five. Ten. It wasn't enough. I already knew, no matter the number, it wouldn't be enough. So I shuffled us toward the nearest surface, pressing Lyla against a wide, wooden beam.

I tore my mouth from hers, trailing it along her jaw to an earlobe. "Have you ever been fucked out here?"

"No," she panted, reaching between us. Her palm pressed hard against my erection, earning a groan. "Vance."

Fuck, but I loved how she said my name.

Almost as much as I liked that she'd worn a dress tonight. It was a caramel turtleneck, the cable knit thick and soft. The boxy shape shouldn't have been sexy, but it was short, hitting her midthigh so a hint of those toned, smooth legs could taunt me all night. Her sexy boots came almost to her knees.

"I've wanted to hike up this dress all night." I bunched the fabric in my hands, dragging it up her hips. Exactly what I'd wanted to do since the moment I'd watched her come out of her bedroom, her hair curled in long, loose waves and a shimmer on her eyelids.

My hand slid beneath the dress's hem, diving for the center of her panties.

"You're already soaked," I growled against her neck as I slipped the fabric aside, sliding my fingers through her slit to tease at her clit.

"Yes," she purred, arching into my touch.

"You want my fingers? Or my cock?"

"Both."

"What do you say?"

She leaned in for a quick kiss and whispered the magic word. "Please."

I fisted the panties and, with a single, quick tug, tore them off her body.

Lyla gasped, her eyes popping open and shooting me a glare. "Vance."

She could pretend to be pissed all she wanted. We both knew she got wet as fuck when I tore her panties. Maybe she'd realize before I left there was no point in wearing them at all.

"Mine." I smirked and tucked the ruined lace in my coat pocket. Then with one hand palming her ass, I dipped a finger into her tight heat.

She melted against me, whimpering as I toyed with her, working her higher and higher. "I love your fingers."

"My fingers love your pussy." I added a second finger, stroking her deep until her legs began to tremble.

She'd come on my hand plenty of times, but tonight, I wanted to feel her explode on my cock, so I pulled away, earning another glare.

I quickly unzipped my jeans, fisting my shaft and giving it a few strokes. Then I hoisted Lyla up higher against the post, gripping her thighs as I pinned her with my hips.

"Mouth," I ordered.

She kissed me immediately, her tongue tangling with

mine. I lined up at her entrance, and with one thrust, I buried myself inside her, my jaw clenching as I fought to keep control. "Fuck. You feel so good, Blue."

Her inner walls fluttered. "Hurry."

One thrust, and she was ready to come.

I pulled out, slammed inside. Then I reached between us and pressed my wet fingers to her clit.

"Vance." Her cry echoed through the rafters as she came apart, pulsing around me as I rocked us together, over and over.

It didn't take long for me to follow her over the edge, my body collapsing over hers, both of us boneless and limp against the post.

A horse whinnied from the other side of the building.

Lyla giggled, that musical laugh right in my ear.

"You okay?" I asked.

"Yes. Are you?"

"More than okay."

She hummed, sleepy and sweet. She'd probably crash on the drive back to town. So I set her on her feet, and with my come leaking down her bare thigh, I led her from the stables and took her home.

Lyla was out before we even reached the highway.

And while she slept, I took in the star-marked skies, praying this weather would hold for just a couple more weeks.

Not just so I had a chance at finding Cormac, but because I needed the time with Lyla.

Except when I woke the next morning, alone in Lyla's bed because she'd already gone to work, beyond her bedroom windows was a thin layer of icy snow.

CHAPTER FIFTEEN

LYLA

Vance had me pinned against the shower wall. Steam billowed around us, and a drop of water clung to his lower lip as he pounded inside me, his breathing as ragged as my own.

My hands gripped his shoulders, holding tight. The harder I dug in my nails, the harder he fucked me.

"Oh, God." Every muscle in my body shook as my orgasm rushed toward me like an avalanche. My hands clung to his shoulders, my nails like claws in his slippery skin.

"Lyla." The way he moaned my name sent a shiver down my spine. It was erotic. Desperate. He was close, on the verge of his own release, but wouldn't dare stop until I came first.

His strong hands cupped my ass, holding me in place. He squeezed, his fingertips digging into my flesh, and that little bit of pain was the trigger.

"Vance." I shattered into a thousand pieces as he roared my name.

My body pulsed around his length. White stars consumed my vision.

He poured inside me, a string of incoherent sounds escaping his throat.

My heart thundered as I came down from the orgasm, my arms and legs wrapped so tightly around him he'd have to pry me loose. Not that he seemed in any hurry to let me go.

His large body enveloped mine as his arms snaked around my waist, his forehead falling forward to the tile at my back. Vance kept me trapped against the wall until the water changed from hot to lukewarm.

It was four o'clock in the morning, and I'd be late getting to the coffee shop. I'd just finished rinsing out my hair when the shower door had opened and Vance had stepped inside.

His days of staying in bed while I slipped out before dawn were over. Something had shifted in the past four days, ever since that night at the stables.

Sex with Vance had always been powerful, but now, there was an edge. This frantic desire. It was like we both knew time was running out, so neither of us squandered a chance to be together.

He eased away, dropping a kiss to my pulse as he set me on my feet. Then he pushed the wet hair away from my temples, holding my face in his hands as his eyes searched mine.

This was new too. He stared at me like he was trying to memorize every detail. My eyes. My nose. My lips. Standing still, letting his gaze rake over my features as I tried to hide the sorrow in my heart, was torture.

"I'm going to be late for work."

He sighed, taking one last long look, then nodded and let me go.

I slipped out of the shower, toweling off as the scent of his shampoo filled the bathroom.

This weekend, he'd shown up with his suitcase from the hotel. His reservation had ended. Rather than extend it, he'd just brought his belongings here.

I stared at his toothbrush in the holder beside mine. At the leather toiletry case on the counter next to the sink. There was a razor inside that he clearly hadn't touched in weeks. Not that I minded. I loved Vance's beard and how thick it felt beneath my fingertips.

What would he look like without it?

I'd never know.

My heart twisted. Vance would live forever in my memory exactly as he was today.

Another woman would get to watch him age. She'd get to witness gray thread his dark, chocolate hair. She'd get to see the laugh lines at the sides of his mouth deepen over the next decade. She'd get to sleep on his broad chest and make him coffee in the morning.

The idea of coffee snapped me out of my thoughts, and I hurried through the rest of my morning routine.

When Vance came out of the shower, he wrapped a towel around his waist and dragged his hands through his damp hair. Then he wiped his palm across the steamy mirror. Droplets raced down its surface, and when I returned home tonight, I'd have to use glass cleaner to erase the streaks.

Another woman would get to complain about the streaks. Maybe she'd try to break him of that habit.

"Lyla."

I jumped, tearing my eyes away from the mirror. "Yeah?"

"What's wrong?"

"Nothing." I forced a smile, then leaned in to swipe on a coat of mascara. "Will you come in to the shop when you get back to town?"

"Yeah."

"Be safe." I kissed the center of his chest, then left the bathroom for my adjoining closet.

Dressed in a pair of jeans and a soft crewneck, I stopped in the kitchen to turn on the coffee pot for Vance. Then I snagged my keys and hustled to the garage, driving across town and parking in my usual space in the alley behind the shop.

Every day, it was harder and harder to come to work. Vance didn't need me tagging along in the mountains as a distraction while he was searching, but the hours spent at Eden Coffee were hours I could have spent with him.

I stepped out of the car, my foot landing on the damp gravel. I dodged a puddle on the way to the coffee shop's door.

The snow from Friday had melted. *Thank God.* When I'd woken up on Saturday to see the ground covered in white, I'd cried in the shower before Vance had joined me.

Of course, the one year when I desperately needed a long, extended fall, winter's icy breath was cascading down my neck. But the weather had warmed enough to turn snow into slush.

The first couple of hours were quiet, like usual, so I spent them in the kitchen, baking whatever suited my fancy.

Today's choices were blueberry scones and chocolate croissants. Partially because Vance loved them. Partially because the dark, almost black chocolate suited my mood.

With the baking and breakfast prep finished, I went about my normal tasks to open the shop. I made lattes and cappuccinos for the regular customers who came in each morning. I warmed breakfast burritos and served yogurt parfaits. I dished cinnamon rolls and wild huckleberry muffins, all with an unwavering smile.

I'd just finished wiping down a table when Winn walked in.

She was dressed in a pair of dark-wash jeans and a white button-down shirt. She had on a black blazer today, its length mostly concealing her badge and gun.

"Hi." I gave her a quick hug before I went behind the counter, making her a latte. "Want breakfast?"

"Pops said you had chocolate croissants."

"I do." I laughed.

Winn's grandfather was the reason I had to save three croissants for Vance in the back. Covie would tell anyone he saw today that I had croissants. He was retired now, but when he'd been the mayor, I'd have sold out within an hour. Today, they might last until noon.

"I'm also here on official business," Winn said as I handed over her coffee and pastry.

I swallowed a groan. "Okay?"

"Can we talk in the kitchen?"

"Um, sure." I scanned the space, making sure the few people at tables were taken care of for now, then headed for the back. "What's up?"

"When I got to the station this morning, I had a message from an FBI agent. He was returning a call I made last week."

My pulse quickened. Was it a good thing for Vance if the FBI was now involved? Or a bad thing? "Okay," I drawled.

"The agent I spoke to is assigned the Cormac Gallagher

case. I told him about you and that I have reason to believe Cormac is who attacked you."

"And did you tell him about Vance?"

"No." Winn shook her head. "Vance has enough problems with his superiors since the shooting. I didn't want him to catch any flack for being here. As far as I'm concerned, he's in Montana on vacation and doing a lot of hiking."

Shooting. What shooting? What was Winn talking about? Vance hadn't mentioned a shooting.

"I'll call Vance later," Winn said, sipping her coffee. "I assume he's out in the mountains today."

I managed a nod, still trying to slow my mind from spinning. *What shooting?*

"I called the FBI because it's their case. If this really is Cormac Gallagher, then it's federal. They have jurisdiction."

"So does that mean they're coming here?"

"No." She shook her head. "The agent assured me that if it was Cormac—I'm not sure he actually believed me—he'd be long gone from Quincy by now. That without a trail or lead, there'd be nothing to find. The agent was, um . . . not exactly happy that I hadn't notified them immediately after the incident at the river."

I scoffed. "We didn't even know who he was at that point. We might never have known if not for Vance."

"Well, the agent made it clear that the reason Cormac was still at-large was because of me and the shortcomings of the local authorities."

"That's not fair."

Her shoulders fell. "Maybe. But I'm sorry we didn't find him."

"It's not your fault. You tried."

"Maybe we should have tried harder."

"Even then. I don't think it would have mattered." It was the harsh reality I didn't want to face.

Cormac was gone.

He'd left this area after the river, taking with him not only my chance for justice, but Vance's chance for closure.

"He's gone, isn't he? Cormac?" I couldn't ask Vance. I wouldn't make him answer.

"Most likely."

"Is that why you let Vance keep searching?"

"Yes and no. Given his experience, if there was something to find, he would have been the one to find it. But I also think he needed this search to take his mind off everything else."

The shooting?

"After something so awful, sometimes, you just need to remember why you're a cop." Winn's gaze was unfocused as she stared at an invisible spot on the floor. "To do something good. I wasn't going to take that from him."

For that, I would always be grateful. "I love you, Winn."

"I love you, Lyla." Her eyes softened. "You're falling for Vance, aren't you?"

There was no point in lying, but I was going to dodge. "He's leaving."

Maybe another friend, another sister, would have urged me to ask him to stay. Maybe suggested we try long distance. But Winn simply gave me a hug, whispering, "I'm sorry," before she slipped out of the kitchen and returned to work at the station.

The moment she was gone, I took my phone from my pocket and typed in a search.

vance sutter shooting

But before I could add *idaho* to the criteria, my fingers

stopped. I stared at the screen for a long moment, then deleted everything and returned the phone to my jeans.

There was a reason Vance changed the subject so often. There was a reason he'd avoided telling me about his job or his family.

He didn't want me to know.

I wasn't his girlfriend.

I was simply his escape.

Why was I always the person in a relationship who fell too far? Who cared too much? Who forgot the rules?

Who let her heart lead the way?

I didn't regret it. Not a minute. Not with Vance.

Maybe that would come, after he left Quincy. But for today, if he needed an escape, I'd be that refuge. So I squared my shoulders, shoved my curiosity down deep and returned to the counter to smile and serve my customers.

Vance came in around four, dressed like he was most days in Carhartt pants and a long-sleeved thermal layered beneath that thick flannel coat. Both his beanie and gloves were stuffed in the coat's pockets.

What kind of clothes did he wear in the summers? During his next trip to the barber, how short would he cut his hair? Besides fuck a woman senseless, what did he do for fun?

What shooting?

Questions I didn't ask.

"Hey, Blue."

"Hi." Did all his lovers get nicknames? Or just me? "Did you talk to Winn?"

He sighed. "Yeah. Got her message. Called her on the drive back. Can't say I'm surprised or disappointed. It's better this way."

"How was it? Find anything?"

"Cold. And no."

No. He used to say *not yet.*

I swallowed my disappointment. "Coffee?"

"Yeah. That would be great."

"I'll bring it over."

"Thanks." He dipped his chin, then turned, heading for his regular seat.

That chair was his. The table too, but mostly that chair. For the rest of my days, I wouldn't be able to look in that corner and not think of Vance.

Would he remember me too?

Of all the questions floating in my head, that one terrified me the most. So instead of wondering, I filled a cup of coffee. I plated a chocolate croissant.

And when I took them both to Vance, I reminded myself of the simple truth.

He was all but gone.

CHAPTER SIXTEEN

VANCE

I wasn't the type of man who got lost. North. South. East. West. My internal compass had always read true.

But damn if I couldn't let myself get lost in Montana.

As I stood on top of a rock outcropping, the view in front of me was nothing less than magnificent. Far in the distance was an indigo mountain range. Between us, the foothills were a spectacular mix of greens and golds. Snow dusted the treetops a sparkling white. Miles away, the river meandered through the valley, cutting its winding path through the landscape.

I filled my lungs with the cold, fresh air, holding it until it burned. Until it chased away any doubt.

This was it.

The last day.

Beneath the tree trunks, three inches of snow blanketed needles and fallen leaves. It was different than last weekend's snow. It was here to stay. Even if the weather warmed in town, the temperatures wouldn't change much out here.

The flakes that had fallen last night were here until spring. They were here to stay.

There'd be no hiding my presence anymore. There'd be no covering my tracks. If Cormac was out here, he'd likely know about me long before I knew about him.

And if I was being honest with myself, there was probably nothing to find.

There'd probably been nothing to find all month.

I'd only scoured a fraction of these mountains. The area was so vast, so untamed, I could have spent a year searching and still missed Cormac. It was time to face the truth.

He wins. He'd beaten me, time after time.

It burned. It fucking burned. The leather of my gloves squeaked as my hands balled into tight fists. Admitting defeat wasn't in my nature, but goddamn, he'd beaten me.

It was a strange mix of emotions, the frustration that came with even thinking Cormac's name and the way I felt so at peace staring out at the Montana landscape. In the end, the rage won.

"Fuck you, Cormac." The words vanished on a breeze.

With them, justice. With them, resolution. With them, hope.

It wasn't fucking fair.

He wins.

"I'm sorry, Norah. Goddamn it, I'm sorry, girls."

My throat started to close, thinking about their bright faces. About the lives they should have lived. Their father, their flesh and blood, had robbed them blind.

"Fuck you, Cormac!" My scream bounced off the cliffs at my back, echoing in the distance for no one to hear.

The pain in my chest was crippling.

I'm sorry.

I squeezed my eyes shut, the failure so heavy on my shoulders it sent me to a knee.

I'm sorry, Lyla.

How did I tell her that I was giving up? How did I crush her hope?

How did I say goodbye?

I shifted, falling to a seat, then propped my forearms on my knees. The snow beneath me began to melt and soak through the thick canvas of my pants. But even as my ass got wet, I kept my eye on the view, clinging to its peace. Its silence.

This used to be my dream, spending my days in the mountains in solitude.

When had it gotten so lonely? When had it gotten so . . . cold?

The best day I'd had in these mountains was the day I'd brought Lyla to her waterfall. The day I'd remembered how nice it was to have someone else on the trail.

That someone used to be Cormac. We'd spent countless hours together. Talking about nothing. Talking about everything.

God, I missed my friend. I hated that I missed him. His absence had left a jagged hole.

What would happen when I left Quincy? How big of a piece would I leave here with Lyla?

I sighed and hung my head.

The past week had been equally incredible and agonizing. In the midnight hours, we clung to each other, savoring every moment. Every touch. If we were alone, then I was inside her.

Lyla Eden.

Blue.

The surprise of my life.

I huffed a laugh. That son of a bitch Cormac. If not for him, I wouldn't have met her. I hated him for what he'd done to her. For the marks he'd left, both physical and mental. But damn, I was glad to have found her.

Even if it was only for a month.

"Fuck you, Cormac," I whispered.

He won.

But maybe I won too.

Maybe it was time to take a look at the baggage I'd been carrying. Maybe it was time to make some changes.

I kept my seat, staring into the distance until my ass was soaking wet and starting to go numb. It was only when the sun started to sink that I stood, put one foot in front of the other and made my way off this mountain to my truck.

The moment I was behind the wheel, the door closed, the silence might as well have been the lid closing on a coffin.

Done. It was done.

The next time a tip or lead came in about Cormac, I wasn't chasing it.

So I started the truck and put my foot on the gas pedal, keeping my eyes glued to the road as the mountains and trees streaked past my windshield.

With every mile, the pressure in my chest loosened, but it took the entire drive to Quincy for my shoulders to relax. And I didn't take my first deep breath until I was parked outside Eden Coffee.

Lyla was inside. She had her back to the windows, her hip leaned against the counter. Her hair was swept into a ponytail, the silky strands falling down her spine.

Fuck, but I'd miss that hair draped across my chest as we slept.

She was talking to Crystal, who was making something at the espresso machine. Lyla shoved off the counter, smiling as she disappeared into the kitchen.

I climbed out of the truck and walked inside, not bothering to stop at the counter.

"Um . . ." Crystal's wide-eyed look got ignored as I headed for the kitchen.

When I walked through the open doorway, Lyla looked up from her place beside a large, stainless steel table in the center of the room. Her face lit up like a supermoon against an inky night sky. "Hey."

Yeah, I'd won too.

I crossed the distance between us, taking her face in my hands.

"Are you ok—"

I crushed my mouth to hers.

It took her a heartbeat to relax, but then her hands came to my coat, gripping the lapels as she rose up on her toes.

I licked the seam of her lips, demanding entry, and when she opened for me, I devoured, tasting every sweet inch of this woman's mouth while I still had the chance.

She hummed, sinking deeper into the kiss. Her hands shifted, roaming my chest and trailing down my ribs. She pressed her palms against my back, flattening them against my muscles as she slid them to my pants. Then she tucked her hands into my back pockets and gave my ass a hard knead as I nipped at the corner of her mouth.

We kissed like we were in her bedroom, not a kitchen. We kissed like there was no tomorrow, sucking and licking until our mouths were swollen and wet. Until she was breathless and I was rock hard, aching to feel her pulse around my cock.

I tore my mouth away, chest heaving, and drowned in her sapphire eyes. "Hey, Blue."

My Blue. For a little while longer.

"Hi," she whispered.

I leaned my forehead against hers. "It will be hard to walk away from you."

Her eyes closed as she sighed. "It will be hard to watch you walk away."

But she would. She'd let me go.

She wouldn't ask me to stay.

There was so much she still didn't know. So much I wasn't sure how to explain.

Yet somehow, she knew I couldn't stay in Quincy.

The best part about her? She wouldn't ask, because she wouldn't make me tell her no.

Fuck, but I loved that about her.

The emotions from today, from this trip, swirled like a violent storm. So I blocked out the noise, I silenced it all by kissing Lyla again. The moment my mouth was on hers, the world went quiet. The only emotion that mattered was desire.

"Oh, um . . . sorry."

Lyla broke away at Crystal's voice.

Busted.

She giggled.

The sound was so pure and innocent, so happy, that I closed my eyes, bottling it up for the dark days ahead.

Lyla's hand came to her mouth as she leaned to the side and glanced past my arm. "It's fine, Crystal. We were just, uh . . ."

Making out. When it came to Lyla, I was like a randy teenager, desperate to have her beneath my hands.

Lyla cleared her throat, stepping around me. "I don't think you two have officially met. Vance, this is Crystal. Crystal, this is Vance."

I turned enough to give her a nod but not enough to reveal the bulge straining my zipper. "Nice to meet you."

"You too. Sorry. I was going to get the broom and dust-pan, but I'll just . . ." Crystal disappeared as her sentence trailed off.

"Oh my God." Lyla laughed again, then wiped her lips dry. "That was arguably worse than the time my dad caught me kissing my boyfriend in the back seat of his car my senior year of high school."

I held up a finger. "No more talk about the high school boyfriend."

She laughed, those pretty eyes dancing. "How was your hike?"

"Fine." I'd tell her later it was the last. Later, after I'd braced myself to see that light dim in her eyes. "I'll let you get back to work."

"Are you leaving?"

Not yet. "I'm going to get some coffee. Eat something."

"Crystal is leaving in about an hour. She has a family thing tonight, so I'll have to close. But since it's Sunday, it will be earlier than normal."

"I'll hang out until you're done." Just like last night. And all the nights this past week. When I drove to her house, it would be to follow her home and carry her to bed.

"Okay." Her shoulders fell, relief washing over her expression. "I'll make us dinner later."

"Or I can cook."

She arched an eyebrow.

"I do know how to cook."

"All right, Sutter." She came over and tugged on my coat, my sign to bend so she could have her kiss. "You're on."

I chuckled and left her in the kitchen, knowing I'd just truly fucked myself. Compared to Lyla, I was a shit cook. But I'd make her grilled cheese or scrambled eggs.

After an orgasm.

My table was empty, like it always was. It was colder by the windows, probably why most chose to sit deeper in the café. Fine by me.

I swung by the counter, ordered a coffee and almond poppy seed muffin, then retreated to my chair to stare out the front windows.

The maps were in my backpack, locked in my truck. I didn't need them anymore.

My phone vibrated in my pocket with a text. I took it out. Alec.

Are you back home?

I typed out my reply.

Not quite

Alec had sent me a few texts in the past weeks, checking to see if I'd found any trail of Cormac. Our exchanges had been brief.

Once I got home, we'd go out for a beer. I'd fill him in on what had happened here. Well, most of what had happened.

Lyla, I'd keep to myself. She'd be mine and mine alone.

I was just putting my phone down on the table when a flash of red out the window caught my eye. Like I had for four years, that ginger hair snared my attention.

A woman passed the window. The curtain of her hair hid most of her features. Most, but not all. It didn't hide the high cheekbones. The straight nose. The familiar chin and unsmiling mouth.

"What the . . ."

I knew that face.

I flew out of my chair, standing so fast that the backs of my knees sent it scraping across the floor.

The woman outside was gone in a blink. So fast it was like she hadn't been there to begin with.

No. No, it couldn't be her. She was dead. In my mind, I knew she was dead. But fuck, the resemblance was uncanny.

"Vance?" Lyla rushed over, a coffee pot in hand.

"One sec." I held up a finger, rounding the table.

Curiosity, that red hair, got the better of me, like it had for four years. So I walked to the door, ripping it open as I hurried outside.

I needed a closer look. I needed to get that face out of my damn mind.

Except there was no redheaded woman on the sidewalk. Whoever she was, she was gone.

I jogged to the nearest corner, searching the side street. *Empty.* I spun in a slow circle, looking everywhere, for a hint of that red. By the jewelry store. The hotel. The bank. *Nothing.*

There was no redhead. The only woman on the sidewalk was Lyla.

"Vance." She jogged my way from the coffee shop, her breath billowing. She wasn't wearing a coat, so I shrugged out of mine, draping it around her shoulders.

"Wear this."

"What is it? What's wrong?"

"Nothing. It's nothing." Just me losing my fucking mind. I scrubbed a hand over my face, then sighed. "I'm just . . . seeing ghosts."

CHAPTER SEVENTEEN

LYLA

The dead bolt flipped with a *thunk.* With that sound, my shoulders dropped from my ears.

I'd wanted to shut down the shop for hours so I could talk to Vance about what had happened earlier, what had sent him racing out the door. But I'd had to bide my time until closing. Finally, we were alone.

I turned off the lights, not bothering to mop the floors or wipe down tables—I'd do it in the morning. The work could wait.

Vance strode out of the kitchen, his broad frame limned by the dim light. "What about cleaning?"

A few nights spent working with me here and he'd already learned my routine.

"I'll do it tomorrow." I met him behind the counter, walking right into his space to put my hands on his hips. "Hey."

"Hey." He tucked a lock of hair behind my ear, his gaze tracing down my nose before he dropped his lips to mine.

The moment I opened for him, he sucked my tongue into his mouth.

I'd expected a chaste kiss, and his urgency took me off guard.

His hands raked down my back, sliding to cup my ass.

With a hand planted on his heart, I gave him a small shove, enough that he tore his mouth away. But he just moved his kiss from my lips to my pulse.

"We should talk," I breathed, threading my hands into his hair.

He ignored me and swept me off my feet with a quick hoist into his arms. With a spin, he turned and walked us to the counter, setting me on its surface. Then he licked the seam of my lips, eliciting a low moan in my chest as desire pooled in my core.

This was just another tactic for changing the subject. "Vance."

"Lyla," he murmured, trailing his mouth along my jaw, that beard leaving a delicious scrape against my smooth skin.

My head lolled to the side as my fingers continued to tug and pull at his thick, unruly strands. "Talk to me."

"Not yet, Blue." He pulled my earlobe between his teeth.

My breath hitched.

Goddamn it, I was going to cave. I always caved.

I'd let him have his way with my body and the important conversations would go unspoken. Like the shooting Winn had mentioned. Like whatever had happened today. Like whoever he'd thought he'd seen on the sidewalk.

"Have you ever been fucked on this counter?" His gravelly voice was thick with want.

I gulped. "No."

"Then I'm taking it. When you come to work every day, I want you thinking about me inside you."

He'd leave his mark, and I'd never recover. He'd change this place forever.

And I was going to let him.

Maybe I'd regret it someday. Maybe when I met the man I'd marry—if I met that man—I'd regret letting Vance claim this space.

But tonight, I just wanted to have something from him I'd never forget. So I reached between us and unfastened the button on his jeans, working the zipper free so I could dive into his boxer briefs. The moment I fisted his shaft, a hiss escaped his lips.

"No going back," he warned.

I loved him for knowing I'd remember him. I loved him for giving me a chance to stop and save this for someone else.

I hated him for expecting there'd even be a someone else.

With my free hand, I fisted his shirt, gripping it as hard as I had his cock. Then I hauled his mouth to mine. Now it was my turn to shut him up.

I delved inside, exploring every corner of his mouth. Leaving my own mark and memory. I kissed him with every bit of love and hate that coursed through my veins.

Good luck to the woman who came next. She'd have her work cut out for her to erase me from his mind.

His tongue tangled with mine as he tore at my jeans, somehow working them off my hips while keeping me from falling off the counter. Then when yet another pair of panties were shredded on the floor, he positioned himself at my entrance and thrust home.

"Vance," I cried out, my voice filling the dark space.

"Fuck," he gritted out.

I was already trembling, my inner walls fluttering.

His gaze drifted over my shoulder, so I followed it, looking to the windows that overlooked the street.

We were shrouded in darkness, hidden from anyone passing by. But if someone stopped, if they looked close enough, they'd see us together. My pussy clenched.

"You want someone to see us, Blue?"

My eyes whipped to his.

"You want someone to walk by, stop at the glass and lean in, just a bit, don't you? Maybe they cup their hands over their eyes to see inside." He pulled out, then pistoned his hips forward again. "You want someone to watch me fuck you."

I moaned.

"Say it, Lyla."

"Yes," I whispered.

"Close your eyes."

I obeyed, losing myself in the feel of him slide in and out.

"This is mine." He reached between us, his finger finding my clit.

"Oh, God." Those slow, perfect circles he alone knew how to draw would be my undoing.

"You can think about some stranger watching us together, but you're mine, Lyla. To kiss. To fuck."

I whimpered as his finger moved faster, my orgasm building faster and faster.

"Say it. Say you're mine."

"No." How did I promise myself to him when he was leaving?

"Say it, Lyla."

I shook my head.

Vance let out a frustrated groan. "Blue."

I opened my eyes, his gaze waiting.

He rocked forward, his cock finding that spot so deep inside it made me feel like I'd been put on this earth for him and him alone. "Please."

All these weeks and he'd made me say please. To beg for an orgasm. Each time, it had been driven by desire. But this please, his please, was different. Desperate.

This please made tears well in my eyes.

So I cupped his cheek. "Yours. Only yours."

He slammed his mouth on mine, swallowing my gasp. Then he moved faster, bringing us together until the only sound was our bodies colliding, our breaths ragged.

I came on a cry, my shout echoing off the walls. He was close to follow, pouring long and hot inside my body. And as I collapsed, boneless against his chest, his arms wrapped around me like chains.

God, I wanted to cry. Why did he have to leave? Why did he have to have this life beyond Quincy? This life I knew nothing about?

Tears threatened again but I squeezed my eyes closed, refusing to cry. Not yet. I'd cry when he was gone. It seemed silly, wasting the little time we had left on tears.

So I clung to him, my face buried in the crook of his neck to drag in that fresh, earthy scent. I held tight until we'd both regained our breath and he pulled back, tucking himself away before helping me off the counter and into my jeans.

"You okay?" he asked.

"Are you?"

He didn't answer.

"Vance?" I whispered. "Talk to me. What happened earlier?"

"I'm losing my fucking mind." He sighed, dragging a

hand through his hair. Then he hoisted me up again, putting me on the counter. He paced the length of the counter. Twice. "I thought I saw Cormac's daughter."

His daughter? Hadn't he killed her?

Vance stopped moving, giving me a sad smile. "She's dead. I know she's dead."

The way his voice cracked on that awful word. *Dead.* My hand came to my chest.

"Sometimes I see red hair and it makes me think it's one of his girls. I know it's not, but the grief is . . . it just never goes away." He rubbed a hand over his heart, like he was trying to erase the pain. "His oldest would have been twenty-one. I could have taken her out for a beer. Maybe she'd be in college. The twins would have been fourteen."

At fourteen, Talia and I would have been freshmen in high school. We would have been worried about acne and which boy would ask us to winter formal.

Vance didn't tell me their names. Was that because they were too hard to speak?

"What were they like?" I asked.

"They were lights." He swallowed hard, his Adam's apple bobbing. "The twins were a personality. Individually. Together. They owned every room they entered. It was impossible not to smile when they were around. They were dramatic and had these imaginations. You've never seen such imagination. They'd make up these stories and act them out over dinners, complete with costumes and makeup."

A tear dripped down my cheek. How was it possible to cry over kids I'd never met? But the love, the loss, in Vance's voice was overwhelming.

"Cormac's oldest was my favorite." He met my gaze and the grief in his eyes broke my heart into a thousand pieces.

"You would have loved her, Blue. She had this energy. It was contagious. She was always on the move. Always ready for the next thing, like if she sat still, she'd perish. And God, she was sweet. Whenever I saw her, she'd run forward and throw her arms wide, yelling, 'Uncle Vance,' at the top of her lungs. She loved her people. I was one of her people."

Uncle Vance.

He'd be a good uncle. "I don't know what to say," I whispered. "I'm so sorry."

"You don't have to say anything. You're listening."

Of course I was listening. Why did he say that like it was some big deal? Did people in his life not listen to him? Or was this the first time he'd shared?

"They were my family," he said.

And Cormac had stolen them away. The motherfucker.

"He drowned them, Lyla." Vance raked his hands through his hair. "He snuffed out the lights. How could he do that? How could he take away my family?"

The tears were constant now, impossible to catch. "What about *your* family?"

He started pacing again, back and forth. He followed the same path I'd walked a million times, from the espresso machine to the shelf where I kept extra coffee mugs. Back and forth. Back and forth. With every step, every turn, my hopes sank further.

This was when he'd change the subject. This was when he'd take my clothes off again, anything to escape sharing.

So I glanced around my dark coffee shop, taking in the walls as he walked.

This place was special. When people stepped inside my building, they shared secrets. They confided struggles with friends and family. They celebrated achievements or engagements. I'd overheard more than one pregnancy announcement.

The only person who seemed immune to the magic of Eden Coffee was Vance Sutter.

I was about to hop off the counter, to call this night over, when he stopped so suddenly I froze.

His shoulders fell. His chin dropped. Then he walked over to the counter and took a seat in the space beside mine. His legs were so long he didn't have to hop up. He just sat beside me, our thighs touching.

"I have three sisters. I haven't spoken to them in six years."

Six years? My jaw dropped. The idea of not talking to my siblings was unfathomable. Sure, we'd argue, but we always made amends. Always. "What happened?"

"I'm the oldest. Andrea is a year younger. Rochelle is six years younger, and Jacie is eight. Because of the age gap, Andrea and I were always the closest. As kids, we'd go on adventures together, building forts and hideouts in our backyard. We stayed tight, all through high school. She was my little sister. All the guys knew if they fucked with her, they fucked with me. I'm guessing Griffin and Knox were the same way."

"Protective? Yeah, they were. Mateo too." Even though he was the little brother, everyone in Quincy knew that if you messed with Talia, Eloise or Lyla Eden, there'd be hell to pay.

"Andrea went to college in Arizona," he said. "We didn't lose touch, but we lost that closeness. She met a guy, Brandon, and came home her senior year engaged. They got married right after graduation and moved home to Idaho."

"You didn't like him," I guessed.

"He wasn't who I'd pick for her, but I kept my mouth shut."

"What didn't you like?"

"At first, it was little things. He'd tell her what not to wear. What not to eat. Then instead of what *not* to do, exactly what to do. He dictates her entire life. How she styles her hair. Where she goes each day. And he's got her convinced it's for her own good. That he loves her so much it's okay when he punches her and cracks her ribs."

I gasped, my eyes closing. "Oh my God."

"She hid it well for a long time. That, or he didn't start beating her until they'd been married for a while. But we'd plan to meet for coffee or lunch and she'd be sick. She'd hide herself away until the bruises faded."

"How'd you find out?"

"Six years ago, at Christmas, they showed up at Mom and Dad's. She had a black eye. Did her best to cover it up but . . ."

"Some bruises are hard to hide." I knew from recent experience that a tube of concealer only went so far.

"I lost my ever-loving mind and beat the shit out of Brandon." Vance's voice dripped with venom as he spoke that asshole's name. "That fucker called the cops. He was abusing my sister and he had *me* arrested for assault."

"Shit."

"Pretty much," he muttered. "Needless to say, that didn't bode well for my career. But Cormac stepped in. Talked to the captain. Asked a lawyer friend for a favor. Helped me get it worked out. I earned a black mark on my record, but I kept my job. And Andrea convinced Brandon to drop it."

"Did she leave him?"

"Nope." Vance shook his head. "I thought she would.

After everyone learned about what he'd been doing, I was sure she'd get away. But she stayed. He told her how much he loved her. He promised he'd change and get help."

"Did he?"

"No. Three months after that we had a birthday dinner for my niece at Mom and Dad's. Andrea was limping. When I asked her about it, she said she twisted her ankle on a jog. Then fifteen minutes later, I overheard her talking to Jacie. Said she slipped on a wet spot in the kitchen."

So that bastard was still abusing her. "What about your parents?"

"Andrea has chosen Brandon. And like the abuser he is, he's done everything he can to alienate her from her friends and our family. To isolate her. But somehow, Mom, Dad, Jacie and Rochelle have clung to her. They've stood beside her so that she's not alone. They'll kiss Brandon's ass. In a way, I think they've convinced themselves he's not so bad. That he's not hurting her. Maybe that part is true. I hope it is, at least. They did what they needed to do to keep Andrea close so that if she ever does decide to leave him, she's got support. It's not that I don't want to be a lifeline for her, but it's not an option right now."

"Why?" I asked.

"It was part of the deal Andrea made with Brandon to get him to drop the assault charges. I'm not a part of her life. He gave Andrea an ultimatum. The assault charges or she cut me out."

So Andrea had chosen to stand up for Vance. Yet in doing so, he'd lost his family.

"I never should have gone after that son of a bitch." Vance shook his head. "I fucked up."

"I think a lot of older brothers would have done the same." Mine included.

Vance shook his head, like he couldn't believe this was the outcome. I couldn't quite either. "I argued against it for a long time. Tried to convince everyone that what really needed to happen was for Andrea to leave Brandon. Eventually, that arguing created a rift, especially with Mom and my sisters."

"What about your dad?"

"He supports my mother and my sisters. We text. Talk every now and then, but it's shallow. I let him know where I'm at. Check in. But he doesn't like being in the middle, and push comes to shove, he's on Mom's side. They won't cut ties with Andrea. She needs them more than I do. I've made peace with that. I haven't actually seen Dad in over a year."

A year? I couldn't imagine not seeing my father in over a year.

"Andrea and Brandon have a daughter. Rochelle has two girls. Jacie has two boys. I send birthday presents even though I don't get invites to the parties anymore. Same with Christmas. Andrea's daughter is into dance. Dad used to email me her recital times and I'd go, sneak in, sit alone and watch. But about a year ago, Brandon saw me. Must not have liked it because that was the last time I knew about a recital."

I leaned into his side, letting my head fall to his shoulder. "For the record, I don't think you fucked up by kicking that bastard's ass. But I'm sorry it's turned out this way."

"Thanks." Vance put his hand on my knee.

It was so unfair. He'd lost his actual family, then he'd lost Cormac's.

God, I wanted to hold him. To haul him into the Eden

family fold, because while we weren't perfect, my parents and siblings believed in family. To the end.

Instead, he'd leave and go back to Idaho.

Stupid Idaho.

Vance shifted, hooking his finger beneath my chin, tilting up my face until we were staring at each other. "Lyla, I have a fucking mess at home. As much as I want to ignore it . . ."

"You can't." I sighed.

So he'd leave to face it. To clean up that mess. Alone.

"It's more than just my family," he said.

It was also the shooting, wasn't it? "What happened?"

"How many stories do you want tonight?"

I put my hand in his and laced our fingers together. "As many as you'll tell me."

CHAPTER EIGHTEEN

VANCE

Where did I even start?

Everyone at home knew what had happened at the gas station, even my family. Not because I'd told them myself. No, they'd been like every other person in Coeur d'Alene. They'd read about the shooting in the newspaper.

Tiff included. She'd been pissed as hell at me for not telling her myself. But the only people I'd spoken to were in the sheriff's department: the captain and the deputy he'd put in charge of the investigation.

The idea of explaining it all made my gut churn. Part of me wanted to sweep Lyla off this counter, load her into my truck and drive her home, spend the rest of the night worshiping her body. But she deserved to know the whole truth. She deserved to know why I had to go home and face whatever fate was waiting.

She deserved to know why I was walking away.

"You asked me a while ago if I've ever shot someone."

Lyla nodded. "Twice, you said."

"I'll tell you about it. But I also know what happened at the hotel. With Eloise. With Winn. If you'd rather—"

"I'd like to know."

So she'd know. She'd hear it from my lips.

"About two weeks before I came to Quincy, I was out on a run one morning. It was probably five. Dark. Quiet. On days when I'm not working, I try to go for a run or hit the gym."

"To stay in shape for work?"

I lifted a shoulder. "Partly. And if I'm being totally honest, the early morning workouts were a good excuse to avoid Tiff."

"Tiff is your ex?"

"Yeah. She's a good woman. But things between us have been rough for a while." Rather than talk, it had been easier to just avoid her. There'd been no urgent need to just be in her company, not like there was with Lyla.

So I'd find excuses to avoid the house. I'd take extra shifts. I'd go fishing or hiking. And the mornings when I wasn't working, I'd go for a long run, making sure to stay gone long enough that she'd have already left for work by the time I returned home.

It wasn't shocking that Tiff had left.

What surprised me most was how long she'd stayed.

Though maybe if I hadn't been such a fucking coward, avoiding my girlfriend, I wouldn't have been at that gas station.

"How long were you together?" Lyla asked.

"Three years."

"Oh." Lyla stiffened. Maybe from jealousy. Maybe from fear that I was using her to get over an ex.

"I cared for Tiff, like I said, she's a good woman. But I

never loved her, not the way she loved me. And I should have called it off sooner. We weren't good together."

Tiff had moved in with me a year ago, and I'd known within two months that it had been a mistake.

"She doesn't understand why I'd rather spend my days in the mountains than working in an office job with the department so I could keep an eight-to-five schedule. She loves getting dressed up and going out on Friday nights while I'm content to stay home and read a book. We are just very different people. And she hates that I've kept trying to find Cormac after all these years. She thinks I should let it go."

Lyla looked up, waiting until our eyes locked. Then she gave me a small smile. No words, just a smile. She understood. She knew why I needed to find Cormac.

Closure. Vengeance. Justice.

Lyla would never ask me to stop, would she?

"So you were out for a run," she said.

"I was out for a run." Maybe I should quit running. Sex with Lyla seemed like a much better alternative for cardio.

"There's a gas station about five miles from my place. It's small. So old that the pumps don't have credit card readers. It's not in the best area of town, but I met the owner years ago. He had an older model Ford Ranger for sale. Cormac bought it for his oldest when she turned sixteen. I went with him to pick it up so he could surprise her for her birthday."

I'd never forget the way she'd shrieked for joy when Cormac had given her the keys to that old truck.

After she'd died, I'd been the person to sell that pickup. It had been one of the worst days of my life.

"The man haggled with Cormac for twenty minutes before they agreed on a price. Meanwhile, I spent those twenty minutes inside the gas station, picking out candy for the twins."

Elsie had been all about the chocolate. Hadley, anything cinnamon.

"I met the guy's wife while I was shopping. She was working the cash register. Never in my life have I met a person who could fill five minutes with so many words. She and her husband had owned the gas station for fifteen years. Their daughter had just dropped out of college and was working there too. She was a Scorpio, and an only child to parents who'd moved to Idaho from Atlanta. She was allergic to shellfish and had a thyroid condition. By the time I walked out the door, I had her whole life story."

Lyla leaned her head on my shoulder again. She fit so perfectly against me it made talking easier. Not easy, but easier. "You liked her."

"Immediately. A few days later, when I got up early for a run, I headed that direction. It's been my route for years now. Some mornings, she's working. Other times, it's her husband or her daughter, Celeste."

Celeste wasn't chatty like her mother. She wasn't as cheerful either, especially at five in the morning. But she was a nice person. And after years of running to that gas station, I'd learned plenty about her too. Like the reason why she'd dropped out of college.

It wasn't that Celeste hadn't enjoyed school. She'd quit to help her parents run the business after her father's second heart attack.

"She'd been working more often than not. Her dad's health was on the decline. Normally, that time of day, I was the only person in the store. The day of the shooting, I was against the back wall, hidden from the front door by display shelves. I'd just picked out a bottle of water from the cooler when I heard the door open. Then this guy started screaming at Celeste to give him the money from the cash register."

"She got robbed?"

"That was the plan."

"You stopped him?"

The way she said it made me sound like a hero. I was no hero. Just a guy out for a run who knew how to fire a weapon.

"I snuck up behind the guy. He was young. Too young to be holding a gun. He had it aimed right in Celeste's face. She was shaking, trying to take the money from the register. And he just kept screaming at her. Every time he yelled, she'd flinch and drop money on the floor."

His own noise was the only reason I'd been able to make it up an aisle. He'd been yelling and cursing and calling her a dumb fucking cunt whenever she'd drop something. When she'd bend to pick up the money he wanted, he'd shout even louder for her to keep her hands up.

"Celeste saw me coming. She looked over the guy's shoulder, and when she did, he tracked her gaze and spun around. By that point, I was close enough to tackle him to the floor. The gun went off, but the bullet went through a wall."

Lyla let out a long breath. "And Celeste?"

"Unharmed," I said. "Physically."

Emotionally and financially, who knew how they'd recover. Before I'd come to Montana, I'd heard that they'd closed the gas station. According to Google, it was currently listed for sale. I wasn't sure if anyone would buy it, not now, not in that neighborhood. But for Celeste and her parents' sake, I hoped it would sell.

"I got the gun out of the guy's hand. Tucked it in the waistband of my pants. Then I told Celeste to call 9-1-1."

Each time I replayed that morning, I still wasn't sure when everything had gone so wrong. How I'd missed the shout from outside until it was too late.

"The guy wasn't alone," I told Lyla. "There were two of them. One to come inside. The other to drive. I was still on a knee, holding the first guy down, when the door flew open. His friend from outside must have noticed something was wrong, and he came in with his own gun, aimed for Celeste. I just . . . reacted."

One moment, that guy's gun was tucked against my spine. The next, it was in my hands.

"I shot the other guy in the chest, and he just dropped"—I snapped my fingers—"like that. The gun he had wasn't even loaded."

"But you couldn't have known that. You did what you thought was best."

No, I'd reacted solely on training and instinct. Not a lot of thought had gone into my reaction. "He's alive."

Lyla sat straight. "He lived?"

"I missed his heart. It was an odd angle from where I was on the floor. The bullet went through his chest and into his spine. He'll spend the rest of his life in a wheelchair as a quadriplegic."

Paralyzed from the neck down.

"He's sixteen, Lyla. He was the other guy's younger brother. And I stole any chance he has at a normal life."

"You made the right choice," she said.

"Did I?" If it had been right, everything else had gone wrong. "The kids' parents have a lawyer. They're planning on suing me or the sheriff's department or Celeste. Hell, maybe they'll sue us all. It's a fucking cluster."

Lyla scoffed. "They want to sue you? That's bullshit. What were you supposed to do? Let them rob Celeste? Shoot her? Shoot you?"

"I don't know." I sighed. "But I'm being investigated."

"What?" Lyla jumped off the counter, turning to face me with her eyes wide and jaw slackened. "You're kidding."

"Wish I was, Blue."

"I don't understand. How is this your fault?" She began pacing, her path the same as mine earlier.

"My boss is a captain who wants to become undersheriff."

"Okay," she drawled. "What does that mean?"

"He needs deputies who don't make waves."

And I did nothing but churn the waters.

"The captain loved Cormac. It's the reason I didn't lose my badge after all that shit that happened with Brandon. Cormac went to bat for me and the captain helped smooth it out."

"But then Cormac . . ." Lyla didn't need to finish that sentence.

Cormac went off the goddamn rails. "Things between me and the captain have been strained ever since. When he looks at me, he sees Cormac's best friend. Cormac's partner. He sees the trust he shouldn't have given. It's strange. We both hate Cormac for what he did. You'd think that would bring us together. But it's been the opposite."

With Cormac gone, I was the only guy for the captain to blame.

"I haven't exactly been the most reliable deputy," I admitted. "If I got wind of a lead on Cormac, I'd drop everything and take off, usually without giving any notice. I've used every minute of vacation time. I've got no sick days left. So I wasn't on great terms to begin with. Then the shooting happened."

"He can't blame you for that, Vance."

"No, he blames me for the trouble that came afterward." The media attention. The potential lawsuits.

My temper.

"When I got the news that the kid was paralyzed, I didn't exactly take it well. I was at the station. Captain called me into his office. Told me to take a few days off. So I went to grab a few things from my locker. Another deputy was in there. Made a comment about me being trigger happy."

"Asshole," Lyla muttered.

"That's what I said. Then I broke his nose."

"Ooh." She winced. "I'm guessing that didn't go over well with your boss."

"Instead of a few days off, he told me to take a break until the investigation for the shooting is over. I'm not officially fired. I still have my badge. But I'm not welcome either."

Lyla stopped pacing, planting her hands on her hips. "You did what you had to do."

Any other cop would have done the same thing, regardless if they were on duty or out for a run. There'd been no way to know that the kid's gun had been empty. "But I still regret pulling the trigger."

"So what happens now?"

"I wait for the outcome of the investigation," I said. "More than likely, I'll be cleared. But if the captain wants me gone, he'll find a way to make that happen. Either by sitting me at a desk, knowing I'd hate every minute of it. Or by making some excuse to let me go, like he's downsizing the department."

"Then he's an asshole too," she muttered. She wasn't wrong. "What if that family sues you?"

"With any luck, that won't happen. But if it does, I hire a lawyer. Go from there."

I'd fight for my reputation. For my name.

Lyla's molars ground together so hard I could hear them clenching. Then with a huff, she started pacing again. "This is a fucking mess."

Yes. Yes, it was.

And now she knew why I had to go back to Idaho.

"It's not fair." She threw an arm in the air, her anger palpable. Fuck, but I liked that. That she'd get wound up on my behalf.

Tiff hadn't. Not once. She'd been upset, worried. But never angry.

Lyla had a right to be angry. And goddamn it, so did I.

For weeks, I'd kept it hidden. I'd lashed out once, in that locker room, and it had basically cost me my job. So I'd kept it in. I'd tucked those feelings away. I'd refused to talk about the shooting because I was angry.

Or I had been. Something about the fury on Lyla's face, her seething, made a lot of my frustration fade. She gave me the outlet I hadn't realized I'd desperately needed.

"Come here, Blue."

She kept pacing. "Your captain should be standing behind you. Singing your praises."

"To be fair, the asshole I punched, the other deputy? It's his son."

Lyla giggled. It came so freely she slapped a hand over her mouth.

I chuckled. How was it we could finish this conversation in laughter?

Fuck, but I was going to miss her.

"Thank you."

She dropped her hand from her mouth and shrugged. "I didn't do anything."

"You did."

She didn't even realize how much she meant to me, did she? How much I appreciated her standing in my corner?

"I hate how this happened, Lyla. I hate that Cormac hurt you and that's why I came to Quincy. But I'm also glad I came here. I *needed* to come here."

To find her.

Lyla changed course, walking over to stand between my knees. Then she rose up on her toes, taking my face in her hands to kiss my lower lip. "I'm glad you came too. You'll find him. I know it."

I wasn't talking about Cormac, but I didn't correct her. Because that felt too much like a goodbye.

So I kissed her instead.

And tomorrow, I'd say goodbye.

Tomorrow, I'd tell her it was time for me to go home.

CHAPTER NINETEEN

LYLA

Vance's heart was beeping. Short, quick beeps like the sound of my microwave when its timer went off.

We were in the coffee shop, sitting at his table. He was talking, gesturing to the maps spread open between us, but all I could hear was his heart.

Beep. Beep. Beep.

I jolted awake, lifting off his chest. A dream. It was just a dream. Except I could still hear the beep, only not from his heart. It was coming from his phone.

"Vance." I patted his shoulder.

He hummed, his hand drifting down my naked spine. He slipped past the waistband of my panties to cup my ass.

"Your phone."

His eyelids cracked open, sluggish with sleep. But the moment he registered the beeping, his body stilled. Then he was gone, flying out of bed and racing from the room wearing only the boxer briefs he'd pulled on before we'd crashed last night.

He'd left his phone in the kitchen, plugged into the

charger beside mine. I didn't like the distraction of having it in my room, and Vance was more than willing to give me his undivided attention in bed.

I whipped the covers from my legs and stood, snagging Vance's thermal from the floor and tugging it on as I hustled after him.

Moonlight streamed through the kitchen windows, casting us in silvers and grays. The clock on the oven read 3:23.

"What is it?" I asked, rushing to his side.

The glow from his phone lit up his face as he swept his finger across the screen.

The beeping stopped.

"Fuck."

"What?" I stood on my toes, peering past his arm.

The video he pulled up was grainy black and white. It was from one of the game cameras he'd left in the mountains. He must have hidden it in a tree, because the lower left corner of the video was a close-up of pine needles.

Still, there was no mistaking the location. It was the stream where Vance and I had hiked. The place where I'd slipped and fallen in the mud. The spot where he'd found that fish trap.

Beside the water, crouched low, was a man.

"Oh my God," I gasped. "Is it him?"

The man's back was to the camera. It was too dark and fuzzy for me to make out his face.

Vance stared at the screen, unblinking, like he couldn't believe his eyes. Then he cocked his head to the side, his gaze narrowing. "He's still here."

My heart tumbled. "You're sure?"

"I'm sure." He didn't look away from the screen. Neither of us did.

On camera, Cormac didn't make a move to take the trap from the water. Instead, he stayed low. The area was lit by the moon. It had to be why he'd gone to check the trap. It was bright enough.

One second he was crouched, the next he stood and twisted. Only his torso moved as he scanned an entire circle. Then his gaze shifted to the trees surrounding him, like he was searching. Like he could feel us watching him.

Whatever tracks we'd left behind had to be covered by the snow. There was no way he could tell we'd been there, right?

Except Cormac was so eerily still. So deliberate in every movement. The ground around him was covered in white, but I couldn't make out any footprints. How had he gotten there without leaving a trail?

He stepped and I had my answer. His feet were in the water, where the stream rushed over his boots. With a quick grab, he took the trap and tucked it under an arm. Then he moved from one clear rock to the next, carefully picking his way out of the camera's view.

"Damn it." Vance set his phone aside, then raked a hand through his hair.

"Could he have seen the camera?"

"I don't know." His nostrils flared. "I doubt it, but something spooked him."

"Now what? Will you go after him?"

Vance faced the window over the sink, staring at my dark backyard with his hands braced on the counter. The muscles in his shoulders flexed. His jaw ticked as the silence stretched. Then he stood tall and, with a nod, swept up his phone.

Whoever he called, the tone was loud enough in my quiet kitchen I could hear it ring. Then came a voice, muted but familiar.

"Winn," Vance said. "Sorry to wake you. I found Cormac."

I found Cormac.

A single sentence. How long had I hoped for those words? How many times had I prayed he'd be caught?

Except there was no relief in hearing them. That single sentence sounded a lot like a breaking heart.

Mine.

This was the end. Would I see Vance again? Would he come back?

I studied his profile as he spoke to Winn, taking in every line. Every detail. The straight, masculine line of his nose. The pout of his lips. The angle of his cheekbones. The sweep of his dark eyelashes. That one lock of hair that always seemed to fall against his forehead.

He reached for me, his free arm slinging around my shoulders to haul me close. "Yeah, I'm with Lyla," he told Winn, waiting for her response. "We're on our way."

He ended the call and set his phone aside, wrapping me in those strong arms.

My hands snaked around his narrow waist, and I burrowed deep into his chest, dragging in the scent of his skin, holding it in my lungs until it burned.

His lips came to my hair. "We have to go, Blue."

I nodded but couldn't seem to let go. Instead, I pulled him impossibly close, like maybe if I was strong enough, I could crawl inside his heart and stay forever. "I'm not ready," I whispered.

"Neither am I." His hold tightened, just for a second. Then he brought his hands to my face, cupping my cheeks and forcing me back. The kiss he gave me was slow. Tender. Sad.

And much, much too short.

But it disarmed me enough that he was able to slip away. He took me by the shoulders, turning me toward the hall that led to my bedroom. "Get dressed. Winn wants us to come to her place."

"Okay." I hurried back to the bedroom.

There'd be time to mourn Vance later.

Right now, it was time to catch that son of a bitch Cormac Gallagher.

THERE WAS a line of trucks at Griff and Winn's house at the ranch. They each belonged to an Eden—Dad, Griffin, Knox and Mateo.

Vance's Dodge took its place in the row, and the moment it was parked, we both jumped out, hurrying to the porch.

Griff opened the door before we could knock. "Hey."

"Hi." I let him pull me into a hug, then slipped past him as he shook Vance's hand.

The scent of coffee greeted me as I made my way past the open-concept living room to the kitchen.

Mom, leaning against the stove, was sipping from a steaming mug. She was wearing a pair of flannel pajama pants, a faded Eden Ranch sweatshirt and her favorite slippers.

Mateo, Knox and Dad were at the island, both bent over a map.

Winn emerged from the hallway, rolling up the sleeves of a flannel she'd obviously stolen from Griffin. "Hey. You're quick."

"We drove fast." I gave her a hug, then went to the kitchen and pulled out two coffee mugs from the cupboard, filling one for me and the other for Vance. "Here."

"Thanks." He brushed his thumb across my cheek, then joined my dad and brothers at the island.

"Hi, honey." Mom put her arm around my shoulders when I stood at her side.

"Hey, Mom."

The room buzzed with energy and anticipation. The hope we'd all but lost had surged to new life.

"Sheriff Zalinski is on his way over with two deputies and a search and rescue dog," Winn told the room as she went to stand beside Griff. "He's called in the county team, but neither of us wanted to waste too much time. So we'll head out with a smaller team, fanning out from the starting point."

A smaller team, meaning my family. That was why everyone here was dressed in thick base layers that we'd cover with coats and boots. The only person who'd stay behind was Mom to watch Griff and Winn's kids.

"Let's go through everything while we wait," Mateo said, nodding to Vance.

"All right." Vance leaned over the map to draw invisible circles with his fingers as he explained where he'd put his game cameras and where he suspected Cormac would go.

I rested my head on Mom's shoulder, listening to Vance's deep voice as he briefed my family.

Dad and my brothers were here for me. To find the bastard who'd almost killed me.

But I was here for Vance.

He hadn't spoken much on the drive out to the ranch. He'd focused on the road, following my directions to Griff's as I rattled them off. But when I'd asked why he'd called Winn first, he'd told me that he wasn't messing this up. That when Cormac was brought in, he wanted no mistakes. No holes.

Vance wanted Cormac to spend the rest of his life in prison and wouldn't risk a technicality.

So here we were, following the rules.

I only hoped it didn't mean we'd missed our chance. That this time around, Cormac really would disappear.

Car doors slammed outside.

Winn breezed toward the entryway, opening the door as Sheriff Zalinski came inside and shook her hand.

"Lyla." Vance jerked his chin for me to join him in a quiet corner of the kitchen. "Do you want to go?"

"I don't want to slow you down."

"You won't."

I would. We both knew I would. But if I wanted to go, he'd slow his pace. "Are you sure?"

He answered by looking over my head at Mateo, standing behind us. "Lyla's coming."

"Sounds good." Mateo nodded. "I'll stick with you two."

That made us all members of search and rescue, didn't it?

"Wait." My heart stopped. *Damn it.* "The coffee shop."

"Don't worry about it," Mom said. "I'll talk to Talia and Eloise. They'll take care of it and call Crystal if they need help."

I really loved my family. "Thanks."

Mom gave me a sure nod, like she was proud of me for going today.

Winn walked to a cabinet in the kitchen, one tall enough the kids couldn't touch. Inside was her gun safe. She keyed in the code, taking out her pistol and badge. With the gun holstered and her badge clipped to her belt, she hugged Mom. "Thanks for babysitting."

"Always."

"Thanks, Mom." Griff kissed her cheek, then followed Winn to the coat hooks, each of them gearing up.

One by one, we shuffled out the door and to our respective vehicles.

"Ready?" Vance asked when my seat belt clicked into its latch.

I stared at him across the truck's cab, taking in those clear eyes. Was I ready for today? Was I ready for this to be over? *No.*

But I said, "Yes."

CHAPTER TWENTY

LYLA

"Now what?" Winn asked Sheriff Zalinski.

"I don't know." He ripped open the door to his cruiser. Frustration and sweat steamed off his head as he huffed.

We were all upset, though unlike Zalinski, we were trying to hide it.

His two deputies and the search dog had already left the parking lot. Knox had taken off too, needing to get back to town and the restaurant.

Dad, Griff and Mateo all stood in similar stances—legs planted wide, arms crossed—waiting for the sheriff to give them the go-ahead to come back tomorrow.

"If someone is up here, why didn't the dog pick up on the scent at the stream?" Zalinski asked.

"*If* someone was up here?" Mateo held up a hand. "You watched that footage, just like the rest of us. He's up here."

"I don't know who that man was, Mateo." Zalinski shot my brother a scowl. "Could have been anyone."

"It wasn't just anyone," Griff said. "It was him."

"You can't know that." Zalinski looked to Vance. "Are you sure about that camera's location?"

"I'm sure." Vance's jaw clenched.

Zalinski had questioned anything and everything today, from the moment we'd parked in this lot to the moment we'd returned after a long, miserable and deflating day.

"Cormac doesn't want to be found. He's not going to make it easy and broadcast his location. And somehow, he knows he's being hunted. He either saw a camera or a footprint."

"One of your footprints." The sheriff pointed to Vance's boots.

"Yeah." Vance looked him straight in the eyes. "It would have been one of mine since I've been the only one out here searching."

The sheriff's mouth pursed in a thin line. Doubt was etched on his weathered face.

"No local would take the time to mask his scent or hide a trail," Dad said. "If this was just anyone, then the dogs should have picked up a scent. The man we're after is experienced. He's not hiking these mountains for recreation. It's him. He's living here, and he's dangerous. He tried to murder my daughter, Zalinski. So are you going to just stand there or do something about it?"

"Harrison, calm—"

"He's gone." Vance silenced the group. "It's done. If we didn't find Cormac today, we won't tomorrow or the next day or the next day."

The defeat in his voice was physically painful to hear.

"Sheriff Zalinski." Winn took a step away from Griffin, shifting to interrupt our circle and positioning herself between the sheriff and Dad. "There's nothing more we can do today. You and I can regroup tomorrow and formulate a plan."

He nodded, letting out another huffed breath. "I'm not happy there's a criminal on the loose in my county."

"I know that," Winn said.

"If I could put a deputy out here, I would. But I'm short staffed and have limited resources."

"Understood." Winn stepped closer, holding out her hand to shake his. Then she gave him a warm smile that didn't quite reach her eyes as he climbed in his cruiser and drove away.

"Fucking Zalinski," Griffin muttered.

"What an asshole." Mateo shook his head. "When's he up for re-election?"

"Two years," Dad said absently, his gaze aimed to the mountainsides we'd combed today.

We'd split up into three groups this morning, starting at this point and slowly making our way toward the stream where Vance had put the game camera that had captured Cormac.

The dog had been with us—Vance, Zalinski, Mateo and me. When we'd reached the stream, he seemed to have caught a scent. He took off into the trees, moving slow enough that we could follow. Even at that pace, I'd pushed hard to keep up, trudging through the snow and careful not to slip on a patch of ice.

My legs felt like limp noodles despite the stiffness settling into my muscles. But I refused to let the ache show.

Not when my heart hurt much, much worse.

The dog lost Cormac's scent about a hundred yards away from the stream. How, I still wasn't sure. I'd hoped we'd come across a trail of footprints in the snow, anything to keep going. Instead, the dog looped us in circles, nose to the ground, running all along the stream, not finding anything to carry us forward.

We'd kept searching, our groups fanning out to look for tracks. When none had been found, we'd all regrouped at the stream again. Then Vance had led us to his other cameras, checking their respective areas one by one, ruling out any sign of a man hiding in the woods.

By early afternoon, Sheriff Zalinski had insisted we return to the parking lot so as to not risk anyone getting lost or injured.

There were still hours of daylight remaining. Hours we could be searching.

"I'm coming back tomorrow." Mateo's declaration didn't surprise me.

Neither did Griffin's response. "Let's all meet at the ranch by seven. You good with that, baby?"

Winn nodded. "As far as I'm concerned, you're hiking with Vance. I'm done listening to Zalinski's excuses. Find Gallagher. Bring him in. Hit him over the head with a rock and call it a rescue attempt of an unknown hiker for all I care. But I'm not missing this chance. Not again."

"I call dibs on the rock." Mateo jerked his chin toward his truck. "See you in the morning."

Dad gave me a quick hug, then walked to his own rig.

Winn and Griff did the same before heading to theirs.

All while Vance stood unmoving, staring off into the distance, his eyes unfocused.

I waited until we were alone, until the taillights had disappeared beyond a bend in the road. "You okay?"

"Fuck." He shook his head, then tipped his head to the sky and roared. His hands fisted at his sides as the frustration poured from his throat. He yelled for us both. And when he stopped and looked to me, the apology in his eyes broke me into a hundred pieces, like the gravel beneath our boots. "I'm sorry, Lyla."

"I'm sorry too." I swallowed past the lump in my throat.

I was sorry he wouldn't get closure today. That he might never have the chance to find out why Cormac had murdered his wife and children.

What did it say about us that we cared more about finding Cormac for the other person than ourselves? Maybe that was what true, selfless love really meant.

"Don't give up," I whispered. If Cormac wasn't here, that didn't mean all hope was lost. It just meant the next time Vance got a lead, it probably wouldn't bring him to Montana.

"I almost did," he admitted. "Yesterday, I decided it was time to call it off. For good."

Was that why he'd confessed so much at the coffee shop last night? Because he'd already made the decision to leave?

"He's still here." Vance's gaze shifted to the mountains.

"How did he hide from the dog? How could he walk without leaving any kind of trail?" My footprints were all over now, frozen in the snow. And they weren't alone.

"I don't know," Vance said. "He taught me a lot about survivalist skills, but this? We never had to hide our tracks. We were the ones finding them."

"Now what?"

His expression hardened. "I found him once. I'll find him again. Even if it takes me another four years."

Even if it meant sacrificing his own life, his own job and happiness.

He'd do that for the family he'd lost. For the girls he'd loved.

For me.

"You'll find him." Down to my bones, I believed in Vance. He would find Cormac. Maybe tomorrow, when he went hiking with my brothers. Maybe weeks from now, when he had no one to slow him down.

"Come on." He unglued his feet, taking my elbow and escorting me to the truck. Then he drove us back to town, straight to the coffee shop. He didn't have to ask if I wanted to check in, he just knew I would.

Talia was at the espresso machine when we walked through the front door. The moment she spotted us, her entire frame relaxed. "Did you find him?" she asked when I reached the counter.

"Not yet." I chose those words deliberately. "Thanks for helping today."

"Anytime. Foster's in the kitchen. He found a recipe book and is attempting your quiche Lorraine."

"He didn't need to do that."

She waved it off. "He can't be stopped. He's on a mission because I told him I was craving quiche."

And since Foster worshiped the ground beneath my twin sister's feet, he'd do everything in his power to satisfy those pregnancy cravings.

"Did Crystal come in?" I asked.

"Yeah, but it's been slow, so we sent her home. Foster's loving this. He might ask you for a part-time job."

I laughed, glancing over my shoulder at Vance.

I expected him to be close, but he'd wandered to his chair. Not that he was sitting. He stood at the window, hands stuffed in his pockets, and stared outside.

"Thank you," I told Talia. "I know this isn't how you wanted to spend your day off."

"Helping my sister? That's exactly how I want to be spending my day off." She glanced at Vance. "You guys should go. We've got this."

"Are you sure?"

"Positive." There was a softness in her eyes. A sadness. Like she wanted me to spend as much time with Vance as possible because he was leaving.

"I'll call you tomorrow," I told her, then joined Vance, hugging his arm. "Let's go for a walk."

We'd walked all day, but I worried what would happen when we stopped moving. I worried that he'd tell me he was leaving. So we set off along Main, strolling at an easy pace.

Vance took my hand, threading our fingers together. It took three blocks until his shoulders relaxed. Another four until his jaw unclenched. By that point, we'd almost reached the grocery store that acted as a bookend on one side of Main.

"Are you hungry?" It wasn't even close to dinner time, but all we'd had to eat today were the smooshed granola bars Vance kept in his backpack. "We could go shopping. Find something for dinner."

"Sure," he said, looking both ways before crossing the street.

But just as we'd stepped onto the curb of the opposite sidewalk, Vance froze.

"What?" I asked, following his gaze.

It was locked on a young woman walking through the grocery store's parking lot. Her red hair was in a long and stringy ponytail.

Vance's hand dropped mine. He took a single step.

The girl rounded a car, then turned, walking straight

toward us. She had her eyes aimed on the concrete, chin tucked like she was trying to be invisible.

A car rolled past on Main. It caught her attention and she glanced up, watching it pass. But before she could focus on the sidewalk again, her gaze shifted and landed on Vance.

Like him, she froze. Her eyes widened, so big I could see every bit of recognition. Every ounce of fear. The color drained from her already pale face.

She had two plastic bags looped over her forearm. In a single swoop, she swung them into her chest, clutching them tight.

"Stop!" he shouted.

The woman took a backward step. Then she tore across the street and ran away.

Vance chased her.

CHAPTER TWENTY-ONE

VANCE

Fuck, she was fast. She'd always been fast.

"Stop!" I shouted again, my boots pounding on the sidewalk.

She kept running.

So I gritted my teeth and found the next gear.

We crossed a side street, her red ponytail lashing across her face as she scanned for cars before darting across the asphalt. She risked a glance over her shoulder, and when she saw me, those eyes held sheer terror.

Of me.

She was scared *of me*. Why?

That question only made me push harder. My lungs were on fire. My legs were tired from the hike today, but I ran.

We raced through a residential neighborhood, the charming homes streaking by as we tore down the sidewalk.

She was fast. But not fast enough to outpace my longer stride. It took almost two blocks from Main for me to get within reach.

On the street ahead, a yellow school bus was stopped, its red lights flashing, as a line of children hopped out.

A mother came walking down the sidewalk from her house, probably to meet her kid. When she saw us running, her jaw dropped and she blinked, like she wasn't sure what was happening.

Shit. I didn't need a parent calling the cops. Not yet. Not until I had answers.

"Stop running," I barked. "Goddamn it, Vera. Stop."

Maybe it was me saying her name or maybe she was getting winded, but she slowed enough that I could wrap her up.

"No." She struggled, throwing her elbows toward my ribs. The plastic bags she had clutched to her chest whipped against us but didn't fall.

"Vera." How was this possible? How was I saying her name? How was she in my arms?

"Let me go."

"No." I held her tighter, the world spinning beneath my feet.

Vera. This was Vera. She was alive. She was here in Montana.

A cry escaped her mouth but she kept throwing those elbows, something Cormac had taught her in their garage self-defense sessions. He'd always wanted his girls to be safe.

Before he'd killed them.

Except he hadn't. Not Vera.

I clamped down harder, pinning her to me. "Stop. Please."

"Vance," Lyla panted, stopping at our side. Her eyes were wide and her chest heaved from chasing after us. Her gaze darted to Vera, who kept fighting me. Then she glanced around, no doubt taking in that mother who'd spotted us earlier.

Lyla held up her hand, signaling it was okay. The woman nodded, then steered her little boy toward their house.

The distraction gave Vera an opening. She picked up a foot and slammed her heel into my shin.

Pain spread through my leg, but I swallowed it down, my hold on her as strong as ever.

"Vera." My voice was low. Steady. I pulled her even closer, my heart racing as I put my cheek on her hair. "Vera. It's me."

She stilled. Completely.

Then her entire body went limp. The grocery bags she'd been carrying fell to the ground. If not for my arms, she would have crumpled into a heap on the sidewalk beside them.

Her chest started to shake as she cried. "Y-you have to go! You can't be here. You can't see me."

"Why?"

"Because I'm dead." She cried harder, whole-body sobs that wracked her shoulders and broke my heart. "Uncle Vance, I'm dead."

Uncle Vance.

Words I hadn't thought I'd hear Vera say ever again. Words that cracked me in two.

She spun in my arms and buried her face in my chest. "Uncle Vance."

"Hey, kiddo," I whispered, dropping my cheek to her hair as I held her tight, blinking away my own tears. "I'm here."

"I'm so tired."

"I got you." This time, I wasn't letting her go.

Vera collapsed against me, soaking the front of my coat with her tears. Like she'd held them back for four years.

And I just breathed her in, feeling her shoulders and ribs. She wasn't a teenager anymore. Four years and she'd finished growing up. She was taller, lean, but strong.

"I missed you, Vera."

She nodded, her hands fisting my coat as she kept crying.

Alive. She was alive.

This was why they hadn't found her body in the lake. The divers had recovered the twins. I'd been the one to identify their bodies. But not Vera.

Her body had never been found. With the size and depth of Lake Coeur d'Alene, everyone had assumed she'd just been lost.

But there was no body to find. She was alive.

What did that mean? What was happening? I looked at Lyla. The shock written on her face probably matched my own.

"Vera," she mouthed.

I nodded. *Vera.*

Cormac's daughter.

The child he'd murdered.

Or not.

CHAPTER TWENTY-TWO

LYLA

This girl needed a hot shower. She needed a warm meal. She needed a bottle of shampoo and a soft bed. Maybe if she slept for a few days, those dark circles beneath her eyes would fade.

But there'd be no shower or food or bed. Vera kept glancing to the door, looking more like a caged animal ready to escape than the vibrant, happy girl Vance had described. She was going to bolt and break his heart, wasn't she?

Well, she'd have to get through me first. Until she explained, I'd be a human blockade at that door.

"I have to go," she told Vance from her seat beside him on my couch. "I can't be late."

"Not until you tell me what's going on." His hand was on her knee. It was likely a gentle touch, but I had no doubt that if she tried to get up, he'd clamp tight and sit her ass right back down.

Vera clutched the bags from the grocery store against her chest.

The label on her blue box of tampons showed through

the thin, white plastic. She'd also bought batteries, Tylenol, first-aid ointment and a few different sizes of bandages. I'd been the one to pick everything up off the sidewalk and return it to the bags while Vance had lifted a bawling Vera into his arms, cradled her to his chest and carried her to his truck.

She'd pulled herself together on the drive to my house. The crying had stopped, though her cheeks were still splotchy and her eyes red-rimmed.

She hadn't wanted to come inside, but Vance had pointed to the house, his face so stern. So fatherly. It was a look I hadn't seen on him before. One from his life before Quincy, when he'd been *Uncle Vance.*

It was a look Vera must have known because she'd followed me inside, and after he'd done quick introductions, he'd told her to take a seat on the couch. She'd done just that.

While I'd been in the kitchen, getting her a glass of ice water, she'd collected those bags to hold close. Was she afraid we'd take them from her? Was someone hurt? Cormac, maybe?

"Here." I handed her the water.

"Thank you." She took it, staring at it for a long moment. "I haven't seen an ice cube in a while."

Vance tensed. Not enough for Vera to notice, but those broad shoulders inched ever so slightly toward his ears. There was a storm of questions raging inside that man, but he'd keep it in. Keep it hidden.

He'd stay strong for the young woman at his side who couldn't stop shaking.

She looked up at him, her big brown eyes swimming with tears. The same brown eyes I'd stared into weeks ago when I'd thought Cormac Gallagher was going to kill me.

"Dad is waiting for me," she said. "I have to go or else he'll come looking for me. He can't come to town, but he will if he's worried. I've got to get to our meeting point so we can go home."

"Home?" Vance asked.

"To our shelter."

Vance's eyebrows came together. "You have a shelter? Where?"

"In the mountains."

"You're living in the mountains." He kept repeating everything like he still couldn't believe it.

"Yeah."

Where in the mountains? How long had they been there? How was she alive? There were so many questions, but I kept quiet, standing aside and watching as Vance sat with her.

"Vera, what happened? You've been gone for four years. Everyone thinks you're dead."

Her hand trembled as she lifted the glass of water to her lips for a sip. Then she sniffled, sitting a little straighter. Squaring those shoulders. "I'm okay with that."

"You're okay with the world thinking you're dead?"

"If that's what it takes to keep Dad safe."

Vance shook his head, blinking too many times. He'd spent four years hating Cormac for killing his family. But *had* Cormac murdered them? What about the twins? What about Cormac's wife? If Vera was alive, what the hell had actually happened four years ago?

"I'm all he has left," Vera whispered, her voice cracking. "We're all either of us has left."

So her mother, her sisters, were gone. My hand flattened over my heart, pressing at the ache.

"You have me." Vance hooked his finger under her chin, his gaze softening as he took in her sweet face. "Talk to me, kiddo."

"I can't." Her chin started to quiver. "I really have to go."

He stared at her for a long moment, then in a flash, he was on his feet. "Then let's go."

"You can't come." She shot to her feet too.

"Oh, I'm coming." Vance stood, looking down at her as he crossed his arms over his chest. The dad glare. I'd been on the receiving end of that one plenty of times from my own father and uncle. "Your dad and I have a lot to talk about."

"He won't talk to you."

"He will." Vance's voice gentled.

"I won't let you come, not if it means he'll go to jail."

"He's not going to jail."

But Cormac belonged in jail, didn't he? My head was spinning, my emotions swirling. I hated that asshole for what he'd done to me. For the pain he'd caused. But Vera's beating heart changed everything.

If she was alive, what did that mean?

The bastard had still strangled me. But what if he'd done it to protect his daughter? What if everything I'd assumed was wrong?

"Where are we meeting him?" Vance asked her.

"Uncle Vance—"

"No arguments." Spoken like a man who'd given her orders before. Orders she'd obeyed. He was her uncle, maybe not by blood, but practice. He jerked his chin down the hall. "Want to use the bathroom before we go?"

A strange look flashed across Vera's face. It was a combination of relief and exhaustion and elation, like using a bathroom, with running water and a flushing toilet, was a luxury she rarely got to experience.

"First door on your left," I said, offering her a small smile.

"Thanks," she murmured, then slipped past Vance and walked down the hall.

The moment the door clicked shut, he blew out a long breath. Both of his hands dove into his hair, pulling at the strands. "What the fuck? How is this real?"

"I don't know."

"She's alive." He stared at a spot on the wall, his gaze unfocused. "He kept her hidden for four years. We all thought he'd killed her. If he didn't . . . what else did we get wrong?"

"The twins?"

Vance shook his head. "I was the one who identified their bodies. Norah's too."

So it was just Vera.

"Why would he hide her?" I asked.

"I don't know. Nothing about this makes sense." He let out a frustrated groan, then held out an arm. An invitation.

So I moved to him, wrapping my arms around his waist as he hauled me close.

"I mourned her, Lyla. I cried for her. But she's here. She's in the bathroom, isn't she? Am I dreaming this?"

"She's here."

"I don't know what to think, Blue."

"You have to go with her. You have to talk to Cormac." I tilted my chin back to meet his gaze. "And I'm coming with you."

"Lyla—"

"No arguments." I stole his own words. "There's more to this story. I have the right to know the truth."

Vance wasn't the only one who wanted answers. I needed to know if the man who'd tried to kill me, who hadn't killed me when he'd had the chance, was truly the villain.

I needed to know why he'd let me go.

"It's too dangerous. I have no idea how he'll react. He was violent with you once."

"His daughter will be there." I was counting on Vera acting as a buffer.

"No."

"Please? What if you need a witness?"

"Lyla. I won't risk something happening to you."

"I need this, Vance. To face him." And to be there when Vance faced Cormac too. "We're stronger together."

Vance sighed, tucking a lock of hair behind my ear. "I don't know what's going to happen."

"There's a chance you'll let him walk away, isn't there?"

"I don't know," he murmured.

"You'll keep me safe. And I trust you." Depending on what Cormac had to say, Vance would do what he thought was right. And if he let Cormac go, it wouldn't be because he didn't want the man to pay for what he'd done to me. It would be because whatever truths we learned today would dictate Cormac's fate.

"I can't ask you to keep this a secret," he said.

From my family. From Winn. "You don't have to."

"Lyla." His eyes searched mine. His fingers threaded through the hair at my temple. There was something in his gaze, something big and powerful and something I desperately wanted him to say. "I—"

The bathroom door opened.

And just like that, we were out of time.

CHAPTER TWENTY-THREE

VANCE

The way Vera walked through the forest was so similar to how Cormac moved it was uncanny. She picked her steps deliberately. There was no hiding our tracks in the snow, but still, she stepped carefully, the only sound the crunch of ice beneath her boots.

Her pace was quick but not rushed. Her gaze swept back and forth through the trees, searching for threats and noting landmarks.

He'd taught her a lot these past four years, hadn't he?

"You've been living out here," I said.

"Yes." Vera glanced over her shoulder, keeping her voice low as she spoke. Habit, no doubt. Cormac had taught her to live out here undetected, and he'd done a damn fine job.

"For how long?"

"We've been in Montana for two years, I think? I lost track. Dad knows."

I hummed.

Behind me, Lyla stayed close. Her cheeks were flushed as she followed my steps. She had to be tired from earlier, but she marched on, her strength and resilience as breathtaking as her beauty.

"Good?" I asked, stretching a hand for hers.

She took it and nodded. "Good."

"We can slow down." Vera stopped ahead of us, turning to face us. "I'm always the one trying to keep up, so I know how it feels. Sorry."

"I'm okay," Lyla said.

I tightened my grip on hers, then waved for Vera to continue.

She'd slow down. I knew before she even took a single step that she'd slow down for Lyla. That sweet heart of hers was still there, despite everything that had happened.

Everything she wouldn't tell me.

"How often do you come to town?" I asked.

Maybe the two times I'd seen that red hair in Quincy hadn't been my imagination or a stranger. Maybe it really had been Vera.

"Usually once a month," she said.

"For tampons," Lyla whispered so quietly only I could hear. There was a box in those bags she carried.

"Does your dad come along?"

"Never," Vera said.

Lyla and I shared a look. So that was part of how he'd survived out here. He'd had Vera sneak into Quincy, where she'd just be any normal face.

Only not to me. Had I not come to Montana, no one would ever have suspected she was the link to a killer.

Was he a killer?

"How do you pay for things?" Lyla asked.

"Cash. Dad took as much as he could when we left Idaho. That ran out a while back so he, um . . ."

"Robbed a gas station in Oregon," I finished.

Vera cringed. "How did you know?"

"I went to Oregon."

She stopped, turning to face us again. "He said there'd always be people chasing us. I didn't believe him. I figured after this long, we'd be forgotten. But Dad is always careful, just in case. I guess he was right. That was you, wasn't it? You left the game camera by the stream where we put a fish trap."

Fuck. "He saw the camera."

"This morning." She nodded. "He said he felt like someone was watching him, so he circled back once the sun came up. Found it."

He must have come up on the back side, otherwise my alarm would have gone off again.

"Yeah," I told her. "That was me."

Vera's shoulders slumped. "We're leaving because of it. Today was my last trip to town."

Damn. How fucking lucky was it that Lyla had wanted to walk along Main?

"Dad's been strange lately," Vera said. "He wouldn't tell me why, but he's kept us close to the shelter. He's sent me to town more often than usual for supplies. I've had to take different, longer routes to make sure no one would be able to follow me back. I thought it was just normal prep for winter. Stocking up on food and batteries and first-aid supplies. But he went out to check the trap this morning and came back panicked. Said we had to leave. I think he's been preparing for it for weeks but didn't want to tell me."

Cormac had been acting strange because of Lyla, hadn't he? But he hadn't told Vera what he'd done. About the river.

Maybe he'd expected the local teams to give up their search. To be fair, he'd been right.

Except he hadn't counted on me.

"We're almost there." Vera looked right, then left. "I think it would be best if you gave me a minute."

"I'm not letting you out of my sight." I loved Vera, but this entire situation was fucked up.

For all I knew, she'd been leading us nowhere. We'd parked nearly a mile away from where I'd been searching. As much as I loved her, I didn't trust her. There was a very real chance that the minute she was out of sight, she'd disappear again.

Cormac would have taught her how to hide.

Even from me.

"Figured you'd say that." She blew out a long breath, then cupped her hands over her mouth, letting out a piercing whistle.

The sound bounced off trees and rocks, until the wilderness swallowed it whole. We stood in silence, the only sound my pounding heart.

Then it came, faint and almost inaudible. Another whistle.

"He's coming," Vera said, giving me a pleading look. "Just hide behind a tree or something. Let me warn him first. Please?"

"Vera," I warned.

"I'm not going to run off, Uncle Vance. I promise."

For fuck's sake. "Fine," I clipped, leading Lyla to a large pine tree. I positioned her back to its trunk, standing in front of her, both as a shield and so I could keep an eye on Vera.

"You can stay right here," I told Lyla. "You don't have to see him."

"Yes, I do." Her response didn't surprise me in the least.

"Okay." I pressed a kiss to her forehead, then adjusted my grip on her hand. No matter what, I wouldn't let it go.

"You're late." Cormac's voice filled the air.

My frame locked. That voice was the same as I remembered, yet different. Panicked. Haggard.

"Are you okay?" he asked Vera. "What happened? I was getting worried."

"I'm okay," Vera said.

"We gotta go. It'll be dark soon. Give me those bags. I'll carry them."

"Dad, wait."

"What?"

I didn't wait for Vera to make a big announcement. I took one sideways step, coming out from behind the tree, and facing the man—my friend, my brother, the one I'd prayed to find for four years.

"Vance." Cormac stiffened, but otherwise, he didn't look shocked. That changed when Lyla stepped out from behind the tree. That was when Cormac's face paled.

I clutched Lyla's hand, watching as she raised her chin. Watching as she leveled him with a cool glare.

That's my girl. I was so goddamn proud of her.

He'd beaten me. I'd let him win.

Not Lyla. Right here, right now, she was taking back her power. She was taking back what he'd stolen.

Fuck, but I loved her.

I was in love with Lyla Eden.

I had been for weeks.

Cormac snapped out of his trance, reaching for Vera. He took her by the arm, pulling her behind him and the pack strapped to his back. "Get out of here, Vera. Run. Now."

"No." She shook her head.

"Go." He shoved her so hard she nearly stumbled.

"Dad, stop!"

"Wait." I took a step, holding up my free hand. "I just want to talk."

"Vera, run!" Cormac's bellow was pained and frantic.

Tears sprang to Vera's eyes as her hands balled into fists, her head shaking. "No. No more running."

"You have to leave."

She didn't move. "We can't keep doing this."

"We have to, love." Cormac was just as broad and tall as he had been years ago. But he looked smaller now. Broken by guilt and sorrow.

"I won't say anything." Lyla's voice was steady. "If that's what you're worried about, I won't tell anyone that I saw you or Vera. But you owe Vance the truth."

Here she was, fighting for me, not herself.

How was I supposed to walk away from her now?

I squeezed her hand tighter.

Cormac stared at Lyla, apology written on his scarred face. He turned that same apology to his daughter. "I just want to keep you safe."

"I know, Daddy." She reached out and clutched his hand. "But I'm so tired. Please. Talk to Uncle Vance."

The faith she had in me to fix this was staggering. I clung to Lyla's hand, borrowing a bit of her strength, as I faced Cormac.

How long had I hoped for this? To come face to face with him?

It was nothing like I'd expected. Nothing like I'd planned for. I stared at him and didn't see a cold-blooded killer. I didn't see a man who'd betrayed my friendship. I didn't see a liar or manipulator.

I saw a desperate father.

"Please," Vera whispered.

I knew before he nodded that he'd say yes. It was impossible to say no to that girl sometimes.

He cupped her cheek. "Okay."

She leaned into him, her eyes closing.

He took the plastic bags from her, putting them in his pack. Then with it slung on his shoulders again, he turned and led his daughter through the trees, ordering, "Follow me."

I took a step, expecting Lyla to stay beside me, but her feet seemed glued to the snow. Maybe I'd stolen too much of her strength. "Hey."

Her eyes shifted to mine. "I should hate him. Why don't I hate him?"

"Why don't I?"

Lyla looked behind us. "Can you find our way back to the truck at night?"

"Yeah, Blue." I bent to kiss the top of her head. "We won't get lost."

We walked hand in hand, following Cormac and Vera until the forest got thicker and thicker, forcing us into a single-file line.

Not wanting Lyla to be last, I put her in front of me, one eye trained constantly on Cormac. There were a lot of unknowns here, but without a doubt, he'd hurt her once. I wouldn't let him do it again.

The sun was sinking toward the horizon, the light dimming. Yet we walked and walked, pushing hard to wherever Cormac and Vera were taking us.

Lyla slipped on a patch of ice, her foot sliding out from beneath her.

I rushed to catch her and help her to her feet. "You okay?"

She was out of breath but nodded. "I'm good."

Vera, who walked behind Cormac, turned back, offering Lyla a kind smile. She'd slowed earlier but wouldn't ask her dad to take it easy now. So we hiked at a punishing pace up the steep terrain.

The trees were so thick that there were patches where the snow hadn't reached yet. They'd get covered as winter progressed, but for now, the dirt and pinecones and needles were only covered in a thick frost.

"Stay off the snow," Cormac said. "Follow only where I step."

Lyla glanced back, and when I nodded, she did as he'd ordered. A few stretches were so wide that both she and Vera had to jump.

We continued for another quarter of a mile like that until we reached an outcropping of rocks that broke through the trees.

Cormac stopped, shifting the pack off a shoulder to dig out a spray bottle. Inside was a clear liquid.

"What's he doing?" Lyla asked, panting as we stopped.

"It's bleach and water," he said. "Up you go, love."

Vera nodded, then slipped past him to scale a section of the rock that was about eight feet tall, using a few notches and footholds to climb its flat face. When she reached the top, she lay on her stomach, stretching for the pack he hoisted up.

"You're next." Cormac jerked his chin for Lyla to follow, but that would mean passing him. Being within arm's reach.

"Lyla." I shifted in front of her. "Her name is Lyla Eden."

Cormac met my gaze, cowering slightly. Then he dipped his chin. "Lyla Eden. I'm sorry for what I did at the river."

"What are you talking about?" Vera asked. "What happened at the river?"

He looked up at her. "I'll explain later. We're running out of light and need to hurry."

"We won't be going home tonight, will we?" Lyla asked me.

"Not likely."

She shuffled closer to my backpack.

"You guys climb up. Vera, keep going. I'll catch up." Cormac walked past us, giving Lyla a wide berth. He descended the slope about twenty yards, then began spraying the bleach water over the ground before he jogged even further away.

"What's he doing?" Lyla asked Vera.

"He'll go run in a loop to leave his scent in a circle. If a dog comes up here, it won't know exactly what direction to choose."

"And the bleach?"

"He says it can mess with a dog's nose. Overpower their senses."

"Damn." So that was how he'd masked his scent with the dogs. And on top of that, he'd chosen a path no dog could follow up that rock face.

"Come on." I nudged Lyla forward. "I'll help you up."

Beyond the rock face was nothing but steep, wet rocks. There were no trees here, just jagged terrain that would be hell to descend.

Yeah, not a chance we'd be leaving tonight. Not in the dark.

Vera climbed, somehow finding a path between the rocks, probably because she'd done this a hundred times. And about fifteen minutes later, Cormac cleared his throat behind me.

I wasn't sure what else he'd done to mask our scents but I suspected that if anyone came looking for us tonight or tomorrow morning, they'd find a trail of prints in the snow that just . . . stopped.

Lyla's breathing became labored as we climbed. She pushed a lock of sweaty hair off her temple.

"Want a break?" I asked.

She shook her head.

"We're almost there," Vera told us.

The scent of snow and rock and wind filled the air. I breathed in the cold air, hovering close to Lyla with my hands at the ready in case she slipped.

When I glanced back at Cormac, his gaze was glued on Lyla. On my hands. "You're together."

"Yeah." And if he came near her, if he so much as looked at her the wrong way or made her uncomfortable, I'd slit his fucking throat.

Cormac nodded and backed off, giving us more space.

We hiked for another ten minutes until the ground leveled off into a canyon between cliffs. Clusters of trees and bushes grew on the canyon's floor. I scanned the area, assuming we'd keep going, but did a double take when I spotted a shelter tucked against a massive rock.

The hut was larger than I'd expected. It had four walls all made from small tree trunks. The roof was covered in moss and foliage to keep the heat inside.

Cormac had built his daughter a home.

It was far from any known trail. No one would see it from an aerial view. And given the winding, miserable path to get here, it was unlikely any random hiker or hunter would make it this far.

No wonder they'd lived here undetected for two years.

Vera's frame relaxed as we strode toward the shelter. She opened the door, holding it open for Lyla. "Come on in."

Lyla ducked past her, stepping inside. Vera followed.

I hung back, and when Cormac was close enough, I struck so fast he never saw it coming. My fist slammed into his nose.

Blood gushed from his nostrils, dripping down his chin.

"Fuck," he hissed, pinching it with both hands.

"That was for Lyla, you motherfucker."

CHAPTER TWENTY-FOUR

VANCE

"Dad!" Vera gasped when we walked into their shelter. Home. Hut. Whatever the fuck I was supposed to call this place. "Oh my God."

"I'm fine." Cormac held up a hand streaked with blood. The bleeding had stopped and he'd done his best to wipe his nose and face clean outside before resetting the bone I'd broken, but he still looked like shit. "I, um . . . tripped."

"You tripped?" Vera looked between us.

Cormac didn't trip.

"Yeah," he muttered, going to a small bowl positioned against the wall. It was full of fresh water. They must have a supply somewhere close. He picked up a dingy cloth that had seen better days, then washed his face clean. But even with the blood gone, his skin was pink and swollen.

I'd hit him with everything I had, and tomorrow, his eyes would be as black as Lyla's had been the day we'd met. It served the asshole right. My knuckles were beginning to ache, but damn, that had felt good.

Lyla moved to my side, positioning herself as far away from Cormac as the cramped space would allow.

I put my arm around her shoulders, pinning her close, as I surveyed the single room.

Against the back wall were two bedrolls. They each rested on a wooden platform that lifted the blankets about a foot off the ground. The cots, similar to the shelter's walls, were made from neatly cut and trimmed branches about three to four inches thick. They were held together with parachute cord. No doubt something Vera had bought during her trips into various towns.

The knots keeping the branches together were familiar and clean.

In our years together on the force, Cormac had taught me a lot, but the one area where I'd always had more knowledge was with tying knots. Square. Bowline. Prusik. Double fisherman's. I had the Scouts to thank for that skill. As a kid, I'd practiced tying knots for hours and hours. Then I'd taught Cormac.

Then he'd used those knots to make this home for his daughter. He'd built a place to keep her from the world. From me.

"Time to explain," I said, crossing my arms over my chest.

Cormac folded the bloody rag and set it aside. He looked to Vera, arching his eyebrows.

A silent conversation passed between them. They'd had that before too, like they could read each other's thoughts.

Whatever passed between them made her shake her head. "I'll get fresh water for dinner."

She grabbed a flashlight from a small, handmade shelf beside her bedroll, then went outside.

Cormac watched Vera leave, then exhaled. When he looked up, it wasn't at me, but Lyla. "I'm sorry for what I did to you. Vera doesn't know."

Lyla stiffened. "And I'm guessing you'd like to keep it that way?"

"I don't have many secrets from my daughter. She knows who I am. You're welcome to tell her."

"Why didn't you?" Lyla asked.

He swallowed hard. "I'm not exactly proud—"

"That you tried to kill me."

"I had no intention of killing you. I panicked. I came down lower than usual to hunt. We've been stocking up for winter, and it's been stressful. When you walked up on me like that . . . not many people can sneak up on me. And besides Vera, I haven't seen another person in a long time. Needed to make sure you'd stay quiet long enough for me to get the hell out of there." Cormac juddered and a strange, faraway look flashed over his face. It was almost like he couldn't believe what he'd done. "I got spooked."

"So you choked me until I nearly passed out and left me beside a gut pile, where any other predator could have come along and finished the job you'd started."

She wasn't going to make this easy on him. *Good for you, Blue.*

"I watched you get up," he said. "I made sure you were okay. Then I followed you back to your car."

Lyla's eyes narrowed. "How do I know that's true?"

"You drive a navy-blue Honda."

"Oh," she muttered.

So Cormac had hurt her, then followed her to make sure she was okay. That was something, I guess. I sure as fuck wasn't going to thank him, but maybe I shouldn't have hit him quite so hard.

Nah. He deserved to be punched again for what he'd done.

To all of us.

Lyla blew out a long breath and went quiet. Apparently she was done talking about the river. Time to move on to a different discussion.

"Should we wait for Vera?" I jerked my chin at the door.

Cormac walked to his bedroll and sat down on its end, leaning his elbows on his knees. "She won't talk about it. Four years and I still don't know everything that happened that night."

"What?" Four years and she hadn't spoken about it. "Why?"

"I used to ask. I'd beg her to tell me. She'd just stop talking entirely. After a while, I decided it didn't really matter. Hadley and Elsie are gone." His voice cracked. "I wasn't going to risk losing Vera too."

So he didn't know what had happened? What the fuck was happening? What about Norah? The evidence was indisputable. He'd killed her, right? Why was Vera the only one who knew what had happened?

"You might want to sit down." Cormac gestured to the packed dirt floor. "Vera won't come back inside until we're done talking. I'll be quick because I don't want her outside in the dark alone too long. But there's a lot that happened. A lot I never told you."

No shit. I kept that comment to myself and took a seat on the floor. This would probably be the spot where we'd sleep tonight. I'd take the ground and let Lyla sleep on my chest.

There was no way I'd risk taking her down the mountain, not on such a steep climb after nightfall.

Lyla claimed the space beside me, her body tucked close. Then we waited, both watching as Cormac stared at the door, like he wanted to be anywhere but this hut.

"Best way to do this is to start at the beginning. The very beginning," he said. "Did I ever tell you that Norah and I met in a bar?"

"Yes." Once. "You were there with friends. She was alone. You took one look at her and ditched your crowd. Then you proposed the next day."

He huffed. "Not exactly how it happened. That was the story she invented for the girls. The real truth was that I was there with friends. She was alone. I went to the men's bathroom and found her passed out in a stall with a heroin needle stuck in her arm."

I flinched so violently Lyla gasped. "What the fuck?"

"I didn't propose the next day," Cormac said, dragging a palm over his stubbled cheek. He had more gray hair now than years ago. The white strands blended with the red. "I went to visit her in the hospital I took her to from the bar. Day after that, went back again. I told her that once she got out of rehab to call me. I'd buy her a cookies-and-cream milkshake from my favorite diner."

His voice was flat. Dead. Nothing akin to the way he used to talk about his wife.

The love of his life.

This man had loved Norah with every fiber of his being. How could he talk about her without a hint of emotion?

"She got clean. And when she left rehab, she found me. I bought her that milkshake." His jaw clenched like he was holding back a curse.

"We took it slow," he said. "Or, we'd planned to take it slow. Until we got pregnant with Vera. That changed everything. Norah and I got married. She stayed home with the baby while I worked. And for a while, everything was perfect. Too fucking perfect, I guess. When Vera was about nine months old, I came home to find Norah passed out drunk in the bathtub. Vera was in her crib, dirty diaper, screaming. Starving. Because her mother had decided instead of eating a normal breakfast, she'd down a liter of vodka instead."

This was a joke. This had to be a joke, right? A lie? Except I knew Cormac. Even after four years of hating him, I knew this was the truth. "You never told me any of this."

"No one really knew. It all happened when we were living in Alaska. Norah promised it would never happen again. She said it was postpartum depression. That and the long, dark winters. So we got her on some medication. I started searching for jobs in the lower forty-eight. Landed in Idaho."

Cormac was ten years older than me, and I'd always looked up to him like a brother. Clearly, a brother I knew fuck all about. It was like he'd had this whole other life that he'd never shared.

"Norah was better after we moved. Normal seasons, sunshine, helped. Being away from her family helped. They were as toxic as those drugs she'd been hooked on when I'd found her. But there's a reason I waited so long to have more kids. I needed to make sure Norah was solid. Stable."

Norah had been solid. She had been stable. She'd loved her daughters. She'd doted on them just like the rest of us. The most I'd ever seen her drink were a couple glasses of red wine with the occasional dinner. Maybe a beer if we were all out on the boat in the heat of summer.

She'd been a good mother. She'd always made sure the girls brushed their teeth and did their homework. She'd braided their hair and made them eat at least two bites of vegetables before they could have a treat.

My world was tipping upside down again, like I was living in an hourglass and couldn't figure out which way the sand was flowing. Who was the bad guy here?

Cormac? Norah?

Everything I'd thought, everything I'd believed, was bullshit. I'd been living in a world of smoke and mirrors.

These people I'd loved had omitted so much of the truth. I wasn't sure what to think. I couldn't trust them. I couldn't trust my own memories.

Lyla's hand slipped into mine.

One touch. The dizzying thoughts stopped. The frustration ebbed.

I looked down into those dazzling blue eyes and found steady.

Lyla held my hand, and I held hers. And we listened as Cormac continued to repaint the past with ugly colors.

"I watched her like a hawk after the twins were born. I rarely left her alone. If I was working, I'd have friends just randomly pop by. I'd call constantly. She was . . . great. Happy. We were great. We were happy." Cormac tossed out a hand. "Hell, why am I telling you this? You were there."

"Yeah." I'd been there. I'd witnessed this great happiness.

Until it had all gone up in flames.

"When my parents died, I used my inheritance to buy the place on the lake. Bought the boat because she wanted to teach the girls how to waterski. She got into scrapbooking because she was worried we wouldn't remember what the girls were like when they were little. Everything was good." Cormac closed his eyes. "That fucking bitch made me believe everything was good."

I jerked. Never, not once, had I heard Cormac call Norah a bitch. Even if they'd been in a squabble, he'd never tarnished her name.

"The girls were busy," he said. "*I* was busy. We had an activity every night. Basketball. Softball. Swimming. Hadley wanted to take acting lessons. Elsie decided she wanted to write a book." Cormac's eyes flooded and he sniffled, wiping away a tear. "It still hurts . . . to say their names."

Which was why I'd rarely spoken them myself.

He took a minute, breathing through the pain. There sat a father missing two beautiful daughters. Mourning two beautiful daughters.

Not a killer.

He hadn't killed them.

I'd believed he had, for four years. Maybe. Or maybe deep down, the reason I'd been so determined to find him was because I'd known in my soul he wouldn't have murdered the girls.

He sucked in a sharp breath, pulling himself together.

"A friend of Norah's from high school came to visit us in Idaho. I never knew the guy. He was in her life before I met her. Honestly, I didn't think much about it. They met up once for lunch, then he was gone. Guess that lunch was all it took."

"Took for what?"

"Took for her to spiral."

No. No way. We would have seen it.

Cormac met my gaze, those sad eyes boring into mine.

"You're thinking we should have noticed, right? If she was drinking or using, we should have seen the signs?"

"We should have."

"*I* should have." He slapped his chest, so hard it made Lyla jump. "I should have seen it. And I didn't have a *fucking* clue. Not until I came home that night. Not until I found her drunk. High. Alone."

Cormac buried his face in his hands, like if he physically shut out the world, he could make it go away, he could stop talking about that night.

Lyla's grip on my hand tightened as she peered at the door, like she could see Vera through the branches.

Vera had been there with Norah that night. With Hadley and Elsie. And whatever happened had likely scarred her for life.

Cormac hung his head, the tears uncatchable as they dripped to the dirt. "I kissed the girls that morning before they got on the bus, but I didn't tell them I loved them. Should have told them I loved them. But I was in a hurry, so I just kissed their heads and shuffled them out the door. Then I went to work."

With me.

He'd come to work with me.

"Normal day." He sniffled. "That thunderstorm had rolled in, but otherwise, just a normal day."

"Yeah." It had been a normal day. The last normal day.

"I had that meeting at the school after work, remember? All the volunteer coaches had to go in and do their concussion training. It was an off night for once. The girls didn't have anything. I texted Norah that I'd bring home a pizza for dinner after the meeting."

There'd been a pizza at their house—the crime scene. Half pepperoni, half veggie.

It had been on the coffee table in the living room, not the kitchen. The box had been unopened, the food untouched. Like he'd gotten distracted, so the pizza had been set aside.

"She was out of her mind." Cormac lowered his voice, either because it was hard to voice or because he worried Vera was within earshot. "She kept mumbling about swimming lessons. How the girls needed more swimming lessons. How they couldn't go out on the boat again until they had more practice swimming."

What the fuck? The girls had been great swimmers, especially Vera. She'd been on the high school's swim team. There weren't many summer weekends when Cormac and I hadn't taken the girls tubing or waterskiing.

"I got spooked," he said.

It was the same thing he'd told Lyla. Was that why he'd choked her at the river? Because it had reminded him too much of Norah? Maybe he'd been thinking about his wife in that moment. Maybe he'd been thinking about his daughters, and when Lyla had surprised him, he'd snapped.

"I kept asking Norah what she was talking about," he said. "I got close enough and smelled the booze. Saw how glassy her eyes were. She didn't even recognize me. She thought I was a lifeguard. She asked me if I could go get her kids from the pool because it was time for dinner."

They didn't have a pool.

Just the lake.

"I went outside. I screamed and screamed and screamed for the girls. The boat had been run up on the shore, not tied to the dock. The waves, they were . . ." A sob broke free from his mouth. "My girls were good swimmers. But not that good. Not in that kind of storm."

The hut was still for a few long minutes. The only sound came from Cormac as he cried and swiped at his tears.

"I went back inside and slapped her. I slapped her so fucking hard, Vance. Just so she'd snap out of it. Tell me what had happened."

The autopsy had shown an injury to her cheek. The cause of death, strangulation. There'd been alcohol in her bloodstream, but we'd all assumed she'd had one too many glasses of wine from the open bottle in the kitchen. There'd been no note of drugs. Though depending on what she'd been on, some substances like LSD metabolized quickly. Still, would the medical examiner have even thought to test for narcotics?

Small town. Well-known family. Tragic incident. Not a single person, including me, had thought to investigate *Norah*.

Not when Cormac had run and cemented his guilt in our minds.

"She said she took them out for swimming lessons." Cormac looked at the door.

My gaze tracked his.

Outside was the only person who knew what had happened on that boat.

"I killed her."

I whipped back to face him. There was no remorse in his voice. Just fact.

"She drowned them. She drowned my little girls." His eyes blazed behind more tears. "So I killed her."

This was why he'd run. All the evidence that had pointed to him was true. He'd killed Norah.

That fucking bitch.

Four years, I'd blamed Cormac for their deaths. I guess I'd get the next forty to hate Norah for it instead.

Lyla swiped at her own cheek, catching a few tears for kids she'd never known. I loved her for that too. She leaned deeper into my side, a silent hug, then held tight to my hand while we waited for Cormac to dry his face.

"Sorry." He shook his head, sitting taller. "I've never talked about this."

"Not with Vera?" I asked.

"No. We don't . . . it's easier."

Easier if they didn't mention that night. Easier if they didn't speak Hadley's or Elsie's names.

"I had the girls cremated," I blurted.

Norah and Cormac's will had requested they be buried in plots they'd purchased at a cemetery. But there hadn't been any specific wishes for the girls. Parents didn't plan for their children's deaths. There hadn't been two open spaces beside Norah in the cemetery, just the one for Cormac. And I hadn't wanted to separate the twins.

A blessing now that I knew the truth. So I'd had them cremated.

"Remember that trail we found ages ago, the one that led to that meadow with all the wildflowers?"

Cormac nodded.

"I took their ashes there." It had been the hardest day of my life.

He put a hand over his heart, like he was trying to keep it from breaking. "I knew you'd take care of them."

While he'd been taking care of Vera.

"How did you find Vera?" I asked.

"After Norah, I took the boat out. I didn't have a damn

clue where to look. It was dark. Pouring rain. Waves crashing over the hull. Stayed out until I was sure I'd drown with them. I only came back to shore because I needed more gas. Then there she was, lying on the dock. Soaking wet. Numb. She made it back. Her sisters didn't."

Lyla leaned into my arm, muffling the sound of her own crying in the sleeve of my coat.

Oh, God. My throat closed. My nose burned. My own eyes blurred with tears, one cascading down my cheek.

What horror had Vera survived? How scared had the twins been before they'd been pulled under?

I pinched the bridge of my nose, breathing from my mouth as my heart broke for what felt like the thousandth time.

Hadley and Elsie were gone. Killed by their mother, not father. And goddamn it, I missed them.

It wasn't fair. It wasn't fucking fair.

"I'm sorry," I whispered.

"Me too."

"Why'd you run?"

Cormac shrugged. "It was either run or go to prison. I wasn't leaving Vera, not after that."

So he'd found a way for them to stay together.

"Vera said you're leaving Montana," Lyla said.

Cormac nodded. "We can't stay. If Vance found me, it's only a matter of time before someone else stumbles upon us. We've been here too long anyway."

My stomach knotted at the idea of him taking her away. Of disappearing again.

"Where will you go?"

"The goal was always to get to Canada, but a couple

years ago, we were coming through this area and Vera got sick. Found this place. She didn't want to leave."

"I still don't want to leave." Vera pushed through the door, arms crossed over her chest.

How long had she been listening?

"It's not up for debate." Cormac stood, his hair nearly brushing the shelter's roof. He'd made this home just tall enough that he could walk without bumping his head.

"I'm not going this time," she said. "Not again."

"And what will you do? Live here? Alone?"

Vera sighed, dropping her chin. "You could stay."

He crossed the space, pulling her into his arms. "You know why I can't."

No, he couldn't stay. And this wasn't a life for a twenty-one-year-old young woman. She deserved more.

She deserved the world.

"She can come with me." I shoved to my feet, helping Lyla to hers. Maybe Cormac couldn't stay. Maybe he was okay living a life off the grid. But that wasn't a life for Vera.

"What?" Cormac whirled, a glare on his face.

"You really want this to be her life?" I circled a finger in the air.

His glare flicked to the roof he'd put over their heads. Then it vanished, faster than I could blink. He'd probably thought about this already. He'd likely looked into the future and known something would eventually have to give.

This was not the life he'd wanted for his daughter.

He faced her, giving her a sad smile. But when he spoke, his voice was firm. Absolute. "You're going with Vance."

Maybe he'd expected Vera to argue.

But she whispered, "Okay."

CHAPTER TWENTY-FIVE

LYLA

From the moment we'd awakened in the shelter this morning, I'd been ready to leave this mountain.

But for Vera, morning had come too soon.

"Maybe I should stay." Vera started to remove the backpack strapped to her shoulders, but Cormac's hands settled on hers, stopping her before she could take it off.

"No, love. You need to go with Vance."

"But, Dad—"

"You were right." He bent to kiss her forehead. "We can't do this forever. You can't live like this."

"What about you?" Her eyes swam with unshed tears. "Will you stay?"

He cupped her cheek, giving her a sad smile. But he didn't answer.

Vera's confidence in this decision had wavered since last night.

Cormac's had cemented.

It was dawn. The snowcapped mountain peaks high above our heads were tinged with canary yellow. It was barely light enough to see the dark forest we'd have to hike through to Vance's truck.

With any luck, we'd make it back in time for me to call my brothers and tell them we wouldn't be joining them on today's search so they wouldn't worry.

Instead, once we left these mountains, we'd be going immediately to my house to hide Vera and make a plan. And, hopefully, get some rest. My head felt fuzzy, the lack of sleep making my sore and tired limbs feel sluggish.

No one had slept well in that cramped hut. Cormac had volunteered to sleep on the dirt while Vera had taken his bedroll—I hadn't wanted to sleep on his bed. Vance must have sensed it, so he'd asked Vera to take it instead. Then we'd slept curled together on hers.

He'd held me all night, his heart pressed against my spine, our clothes and a thin blanket to keep us warm. That, and the small fire Cormac had stoked throughout the night. Sleep had come in minutes, rather than hours. Everyone in that shelter had been too anxious to truly shut down.

We'd all feared what this morning would bring.

Heartache.

Irrevocable change.

A gut-wrenching goodbye.

Vance stood at my side, his hand on the small of my back. He was at the ready in case I swayed on my feet.

It hurt to watch Vera and Cormac together, these two people who had counted on only each other for the past four years. They'd shared grief. They'd shared this unthinkable tragedy.

Cormac's story had replayed in my mind on a loop last night. The vivid picture he'd painted of Norah. Of that night.

I probably would have strangled her too.

My hand lifted to my throat. The bruises and tenderness were gone. I was fully healed, inside and out. All that remained was my hatred for Cormac. Except it was different this morning. Dull and fragile.

Would I ever like Cormac Gallagher? No. I'd always hold some anger, maybe a bit of fear, when I pictured his face and the scar that interrupted his cheek.

But I wouldn't hate him. Pity, yes. But not hate.

"Give me a hug," he told Vera, hauling her into his chest.

She began to cry, her body shaking against his. "I love you, Daddy."

"And I love you, Vera." He kissed her hair, swallowing hard. He was holding back tears but just barely. "Never forget how much I love you."

"Will I see you again?"

"Of course."

It sounded like a lie.

Vance dropped his chin, his jaw clenching as he worked to keep his own emotions in check.

There was no knowing if Cormac would ever see his daughter again. Another man might have refused Vance's offer. Might have insisted on keeping Vera close.

Maybe because I had such a good dad, I could appreciate Cormac as a father. I respected his sacrifice for his daughter.

"Okay." Cormac kissed her again, then let her go. "Let's go."

Vera stole a long, lasting look at the shelter that had been her home for the past two years. Tears streamed from her brown eyes. But she didn't move her feet. Instead, like she couldn't make herself take that first step, she held out her hand.

Cormac took it.

He took her hand because he'd been taking it for her entire life. He'd been the man who'd held it for her first step. Now he was taking it again, possibly for the last time, to help her walk into a better life.

My heart. I turned from them, hiding my tears.

Vance turned too, his jaw ticking. His eyes pained. But there was a surety in his gaze too. In his heart, he knew this was the right choice for Vera. So I chose to trust him, to give him that faith.

With a nod, he started away from the shelter. Somehow, he knew exactly the right path to take over the rocky ground even though we'd only been across it once.

The four of us walked in silence, a line of solemn hearts, until we reached the rock face that we'd have to scale down to then hike through the forest.

Vance went first, then stood at the bottom, arms outstretched to catch me as I jumped down.

"Thanks," I told him, breathless. How was it that hiking downhill was almost harder than up?

"You doing okay?" he asked, voice low.

No. "Are you?"

He cupped my face, his thumb stroking my cheek. "No."

Maybe today wasn't *our* goodbye, but it was coming. I shoved that thought aside and watched as Vera scaled the rock with practiced ease.

She reached the bottom and looked to Cormac, probably expecting him to come down next.

But at the top of the rock, where he'd been standing just a moment ago, there was nothing.

Cormac was gone.

CHAPTER TWENTY-SIX

LYLA

Nine hours. That was all Vance and I had left. *Nine hours.*

It wasn't enough.

Never in my life had two days passed so quickly. I kept wishing for time to slow down, but from the moment we'd hiked down that mountain with a weeping Vera, the seconds and minutes and hours had evaporated.

Monday was when Vance and I had woken up to that beeping alarm from the game camera. Now it was Thursday. How was it already Thursday?

They were leaving tomorrow. Friday.

In just nine hours.

As I stood at the kitchen sink, rinsing the dishes from dinner, I refused to look at the window in front of me. I refused to acknowledge that the sun had already set. That Friday was almost here. But even in my periphery, I could see the dark blue creep into my yard. I could see the glitter of those first brave stars.

I really needed a curtain to cover that fucking window.

Vance strode into the room, his bare feet heavy against the hardwood. He set his phone on the counter, leaning against it and crossing his arms. "Captain and I are meeting first thing Monday morning."

"Good." That was good, right? This was the plan. But my heart was in freefall, sinking deeper and faster. "Did you tell him about Vera?"

"No. I'll save that for Monday. He thinks I want to talk about the shooting. Probably hoping I'll quit."

Would he quit?

If Vance's job wasn't keeping him in Idaho, would he come back? I was terrified to ask. Terrified to learn that I wasn't enough for him to uproot his life. So I didn't ask.

"How do you think she's doing?" Vance asked, looking at the ceiling.

Upstairs was the guest bedroom. Vera had excused herself after dinner for a hot shower. She kept saying it was because she'd missed hot, running water. Really, I think she went in there so we wouldn't hear her cry.

For the past two mornings, I'd woken up wondering if I'd find the guest bedroom empty. If Vera would decide that becoming part of society was overrated and leave to track down Cormac. If anyone could find him again, it would be her.

Yet despite my fears, each day, she'd shuffled downstairs, half asleep, her eyes puffy and red from the tears she'd been crying into a pillow, and said good morning.

"She's still here. That's a good sign." I dried my hands on a towel, then moved into his side, pressing my nose to his chest and drawing in that Vance smell.

They were leaving soon. But for tonight, they were both here.

My phone rang on the counter, so Vance stretched to grab it and hand it over.

"Hey," I answered.

"How are you feeling?" Mateo asked.

"On the mend."

The lie tasted bitter on my tongue, but keeping Vera's secret was paramount. So I'd lied to my family and told them that I'd gotten sick after that hike with Sheriff Zalinski. My sudden illness was the reason why we hadn't met at Griff's the next morning. And it was the reason why I hadn't been to work in days.

Guilt for burdening my parents and siblings with the coffee shop crawled beneath my skin. But I'd endured it, knowing it would be short-lived. Tomorrow morning, I'd say goodbye to Vance and Vera, then go back to work. Go back to my life.

Eden Coffee would once again be my sanctuary.

"I'll be back tomorrow," I told Mateo. "How did it go today?"

"Crystal tried to teach me how to use the espresso machine."

I grimaced. "Please tell me it's not broken."

"Not broken." He chuckled. "But I'm never allowed to touch it again."

Mom had passed down her culinary skills to Knox and me. Talia wasn't helpless in the kitchen but cooking wasn't her preferred pastime. Mateo and Eloise, well . . . they were helpless.

"Thanks for being there, Matty," I told him.

"No problem. It was quiet. Crystal did most of the work."

I made a mental note to text her another *thank you.*

Without her, without all of them, I wouldn't have had this extra time with Vance.

"Griff needs a hand tomorrow at the ranch," he said. "But I can come to town if you need another day."

Mateo was a pilot, and he'd spent last year in Alaska, flying planes to deliver supplies to remote areas of the state. Mom had been convinced that Matty would never come home given how bad he'd been about visiting. This spring, he'd returned to Quincy for what I'd assumed was a vacation, except he hadn't left. We'd all been so happy he'd moved home that none of us had questioned why.

And he hadn't offered much of an explanation.

Since he'd moved back, Mateo had pitched in everywhere, including the coffee shop. Wherever he was needed, he came. Like the rest of us, he had spent his teenage years working on the ranch and at the hotel.

I'd figured this arrangement would last a month or two. That he'd get restless and move back to Alaska. Maybe he'd start flying around Montana. But as far as I knew, he hadn't spent much time at all in his plane.

And as a sucky big sister, I hadn't pressed.

Later, after Vance was gone, I'd find the right time to press. Just not tonight.

Besides, Mateo didn't seem ready to share. But I didn't want whatever he was feeling to fester, not the way Cormac and Vera's secrets had worsened from too many years of being kept inside.

Not that long ago, all I'd wanted was time. Time to think. Time to feel. Time to grieve. Maybe Mateo just needed more time. So for now, he had a reprieve.

"No, you don't need to come in tomorrow. I'm sure I'll be

fine." Another lie. Tomorrow, I would most definitely not be fine. "Thanks again."

"All good?" Vance asked as I ended the call and set my phone aside.

"Yeah. I'm lucky to have them."

He rested his cheek on the top of my head. "I'll understand if you want to tell them the truth."

"No." This was a secret I'd keep from everyone until the end of my days.

For Vera. For Vance.

Over the past two days, Vance had rarely left her side. He'd always been close by, ready to give her a hug when fresh tears appeared. If there was a person to get her through this rough patch, it was her uncle Vance.

He'd guide her back to life. He'd bear the secrets. He'd tell the lies.

We'd spent two days formulating a plan for Vera to become undead without sending the FBI chasing into the Montana mountains searching for her father.

Vance was going to leave Montana suddenly. I'd tell everyone here that he'd gotten a phone call about the shooting's investigation in Idaho. Even Winn wouldn't know the truth.

It would be best if the world believed Vera had never set foot in Quincy, Montana.

Vance would drive her to Idaho tomorrow and they'd spend the weekend getting her settled into his house. Luckily, she was close to my size, so I'd given her some clothes. The ones she'd been wearing for years were at the bottom of my garbage can.

On Monday, Vance would meet with his captain at the station. He might even take Vera along.

Their story would be as close to the truth as possible. Hopefully, that would ensure it was believable. And that if she was pushed hard for details, Vera wouldn't struggle answering questions. The truth. Just not the whole truth.

Cormac had taken Vera that night four years ago. Truth.

He had killed Norah. Truth.

He'd kept her in the remote wilderness ever since. Truth.

They'd leave out Norah's history. At this point, it would be too hard to convince the world that Cormac was mostly innocent. Besides, no one knew his current whereabouts, Vera included.

To the world, Norah would remain innocent. Cormac would remain the villain.

He'd always been the villain, right?

It didn't sit right. Not anymore.

As far as what had happened with her sisters, well . . . Vera hadn't told Cormac. She hadn't told Vance. Each time the subject was brought up, she'd leave the room. No way she'd tell the police. There wasn't a doubt in my mind.

That story was hers and hers alone. Maybe she'd share someday. I suspected that whoever earned that confession would likely earn her shattered heart too. But for now, it was locked away.

"Do you think this will work?" I asked Vance.

"I don't know." He sighed. "I hope so."

"Do you think the FBI will come here and look for Cormac?"

"It's doubtful, considering they didn't come when Winn called weeks ago. But there's a chance they'll visit after Vera reappears. They might make the rounds to everywhere she tells them they've been and scope it out. But if we do a good job of selling the lie, they'll focus on Idaho."

Where she'd claim to have parted ways with her father.

"Do you think they'll ever find him?"

Vance scoffed. "Not a damn chance."

Vera would tell the authorities each of the states where she and Cormac had traveled these past four years. She'd tell them where Cormac might go. She'd also tell them why she'd stayed with him. She'd share more truths.

She'd admit that she'd wanted to go with her father. That she'd stayed with him, never trying to escape or run away. But after four years, she no longer wanted to live that life. So she'd finally broken free.

When it came to the details that needed to be told, Vance would be the one to deliver the bigger lies.

What a coincidence that he'd been in Montana, trying to locate her father. Meanwhile, she'd been making her way to his doorstep in Idaho. It seemed easier to spin a coincidence than admit Vance had found Cormac and Vera, then let Cormac go.

Would his captain, would the authorities, believe this story?

God, I hoped so.

"Nine hours," Vance murmured.

"I thought I was the only one keeping track." I leaned back, rising up on my toes as he bent to take my mouth.

His tongue swept across my lower lip, but before we could deepen the kiss, footsteps descending the stairs broke us apart.

Vera walked into the kitchen with damp hair and sad eyes. "I think I'm going to go to bed. Will I see you in the morning?"

"Probably not." Tomorrow, I was heading to the shop at

four to catch up on baking before we opened. Vance and Vera were planning to leave Quincy around six.

Her chin quivered. "Thank you for everything, Lyla."

"You're welcome." I walked over and pulled her into a hug, then whispered in her ear, "Take care of him."

She nodded. "I will."

"Take care of yourself too."

Vera nodded, hugging me so tight it took me off guard. It was almost like she didn't realize her own strength. But damn, she was brave. Some might think that living off the grid, hiding in the Montana mountains would be a hard life. I think what she was doing now was the real challenge.

She could do it. Vance wouldn't let her fall.

I let her go and swallowed the lump in my throat. "Good night."

Goodbye. Would I see her again?

"Night, kiddo." Vance took my place, giving her a hug.

"Night." She sagged against him for a long moment, then with a wave, she retreated upstairs.

He waited until she was gone, then faced me. In our time together, I'd never seen him look so miserable. I'd never seen those stormy eyes so full of regret. "I don't know what's going to happen."

Other than planning Vera's reemergence, we hadn't talked about what would happen after tomorrow. We hadn't talked about us.

I didn't want to talk about us. I didn't want him to say he'd call, only to forget if he got busy. I didn't want him to say he'd make a visit, only for it to fall through.

"No promises." I wanted no promises that he might break.

"Lyla—"

"Please. Please don't make me any promises."

I loved him. I loved him so much it hurt in every cell of my being to know he'd be gone soon.

If he broke those promises, I'd resent him. My love would turn to hate.

I just wanted to love him.

He hung his head and nodded. "Okay, Blue."

"Thank you."

Vance snagged my hand and turned, tugging me behind him as he walked through the house, flipping off lights as we made our way toward the bedroom. "We have nine hours. We're not spending them in the kitchen."

It was thrilling. It was misery. This would be our last night unless—

No, Lyla. That was a road I wouldn't wander. If I let myself give in to the hope that Vance might come back, my entire life would stop. I'd wait and wait and wait for this man.

And in that waiting, I'd wither away, day by day. Dying just a little if he didn't return.

So this had to be our goodbye.

We reached the bedroom and Vance spun, slamming his mouth on mine as soon as we crossed the threshold.

The ache in my heart was brushed aside for now by the sweep of his tongue against the seam of my lips.

I opened for him, soaking in every moment of that kiss. The softness of his lips. The taste of his tongue. The heat from his delicious mouth. The scrape of that beard.

If this was the last night, then I wanted it to be a night neither of us would ever forget, so I gave him everything I had. My palms flattened on the iron plane of his chest, his heart thrumming beneath his shirt.

One of his hands stretched behind my back, shoving the door closed. Then he bent, swooped me up beneath my ass and carried me to the bed.

We crashed, a mess of tangled limbs and frantic kisses as we worked to strip away our clothes.

Heat radiated off his body, hot and liquifying against my bare skin. I melted into the mattress as he settled his weight on me, almost crushing and so powerful. God, I loved to be trapped beneath this man.

His tongue flicked against mine, sending a shiver down my spine. Then he broke away, trailing his wet mouth along my jaw to my ear. "Fuck, but I want you, Lyla."

"Then take me," I breathed, wrapping my legs around his hips.

He reached between us, fisting his cock as he dragged it through my drenched center. "This isn't going to be sweet or slow."

"Yes," I hissed.

"You'll feel me for days."

Days after he was gone.

I arched into him, my nipples hard and pebbled, zinging as they rubbed against the coarse hair on his chest.

He filled me with a single thrust.

"*Vance.*" His name was a mewl as my body stretched around his. My nails dug into the corded muscles bracketing his spine.

I'd leave my mark too.

Leaning up, I latched on to his pulse as I kissed and sucked against his collarbone. I nipped at him, my teeth leaving enough of a bite that he groaned.

"You want it harder?" He rammed his hips forward, sending his cock impossibly deep.

"Oh, God," I moaned. "Yes."

"Fuck, you feel good." He pulled out only to hammer inside again.

Stroke after stroke, he didn't give me a chance to catch my breath. Every time he drove us together, the air rushed from my lungs.

He growled as a sheen of sweat covered his body. Then he bent and took my throat in his mouth, sucking so hard I knew exactly what I'd find when I looked in the mirror. Red marks, peppered along the column of my neck.

For the rest of my life, I wouldn't see the invisible bruises from Cormac.

I'd see the hickeys Vance had given me instead.

I love you. I wouldn't say those words, but they ran in my mind as he kissed me.

He was thorough. He was deliberate.

Vance marked me as his.

Not that he needed to. I'd been his for weeks.

"Too much." My orgasm was racing toward me too fast, too hard. It would leave me in ruins. "It's too much."

"It's not enough." Vance didn't stop. If anything, my whimper only spurred him on faster. The upholstered headboard knocked against the wall in a muted *thump, thump, thump*.

My toes curled. My back arched as pleasure flooded my veins. And then I was gone, shattering into the oblivion. Stars exploded behind my eyelids as my pussy clenched around Vance's length.

He didn't stop or slow, not until he planted deep and came on a roar into the crook of my neck.

Vance's body shook with mine, his muscles taut and trembling. Then he collapsed on top of me, giving me his full weight for a few moments as our ragged breaths filled the room. With a quick flip, he shifted so I lay boneless on his chest.

My ear was pressed against his heart and I closed my eyes, memorizing that sound.

Vance's hand trailed down my spine. It wasn't an absent, mindless movement. There was too much pressure in his touch. He didn't draw random patterns. He touched me with intent. To memorize?

His other hand came to my throat, touching the marks I knew were blooming. "You still got your scarves?"

"Yes." A smile tugged on my lips.

"Good."

He propped up on an elbow, glancing at the clock on my nightstand. A frown marred his handsome face. "Eight hours."

Before my heart had a chance to sink, he rolled us again, once more trapping me as his hands found mine, clasping them while he gave me a tender, sweet kiss.

Eight hours.

We used them all. Every minute. Every second.

TOO SOON, I was sitting behind the wheel of my car, slowly backing out of the driveway.

Vance stood on the concrete, his hands tucked in his jeans pockets.

We hadn't said goodbye. We'd climbed out of bed thirty minutes ago, and while I'd showered, he'd begun packing clothes in his suitcase.

Then he'd walked me to the garage, kissing me before I'd

slid into the driver's seat. And now he was following me down the driveway.

I reversed into the street.

Vance stopped at the edge of the pavement.

It was dark, but I saw him as clearly as if it were broad daylight. And this was how I'd remember him.

Disheveled hair. A hand on his jaw, rubbing his beard. That tall, broad frame cast in the shadows of twilight with the brightest stars fighting the dawn. Gray-blue eyes locked with mine.

He raised a hand in the air.

I pressed one against the glass.

Then I aimed my eyes on the road.

And as I drove away, I didn't let myself look back.

CHAPTER TWENTY-SEVEN

LYLA

"Lyla?" Talia's voice rang through the kitchen at the coffee shop.

"One second," I called from the walk-in refrigerator. My voice was scratchy. I'd come in here hoping the cool air would quell the burning in my throat.

It was inevitable that I'd have to tell my family Vance was gone, that he'd left this morning. But I'd hoped it would be Mateo or Knox or Griffin who'd come to the shop first. It would be easier to tell one of them to disseminate the news.

Unlike my sisters, my brothers wouldn't want to talk about my feelings. *I* didn't want to talk about my feelings. They were too raw.

Maybe I'd get lucky and Talia would want to spend her lunch hour talking baby names. Fingers crossed.

Steeling my spine, I grabbed a block of muenster and the butter, then carried them to the prep table before setting them down to hug my sister. "Hi."

"Hey." Talia was dressed in blue scrubs, her pregnant belly round and adorable. We'd each pulled our dark hair into a ponytail today, and people always said that we were easier to tell apart when our hair was up.

"Want some lunch? I was just going to make myself a grilled cheese."

"Sure."

I was grateful for the task of cooking. It meant I didn't have to make eye contact. My sister would see too quickly that I was barely holding it together.

"Feeling better?" she asked.

"Much." I sliced two pieces of cheese.

"What was wrong?"

"I don't know. I just felt sick."

"Did you have a fever?"

"Um, no?"

"What were your symptoms?" This was the problem with having a doctor in the family. Doctors asked questions, and good doctors, like Talia, could tell the difference between a fake illness and an actual illness.

"I was kind of sore. Like body aches? I think I overdid it on the hiking."

Her stare burned into my profile. I didn't need to look at her to know her eyes were narrowed. That she could hear the lie in my voice.

"Lyla."

"Yeah?" I walked to the shelf and took down a loaf of bread.

"Vance is gone, isn't he?"

Shit. That didn't take her long to figure out, did it? My shoulders slumped. Then I nodded, keeping my back to my sister. If I said the words aloud, if I looked at her, I'd cry.

And by some miracle, I hadn't cried. Not yet.

Not from the time I'd left Vance in my driveway. Not

through my entire morning routine. I'd fought the tears like a warrior. But this was a battle I'd lose. It wasn't a matter of if, but when. The tears would come in a devastating wave.

Just not yet.

They'd have to wait. I had to get through my workday first. I had to make grilled cheese sandwiches.

"Are you all right?" Talia asked.

No. Not even a little bit.

I shrugged, returning to the table. I found a serrated knife and began slicing the loaf. "I always knew this would happen."

"Did he say anything about coming back? Maybe staying?"

I loved my sister, but God, did we have to talk about this right now? I shook my head, the fire in my throat blazing hotter than ever. "It's not like that. I'm not . . ."

"Not what?" Talia put her hand over mine, forcing me to stop cutting.

"I'm not the right shade of blue."

Deep down, I knew that the reason Vance left had nothing to do with me. But the doubts were creeping in, crippling and heartbreaking. Would he have stayed for another woman?

Talia's eyebrows knitted together. "Huh?"

"Never mind." I slid my hand free of hers and set the knife down, moving to turn on the cooktop.

"You don't want to talk about this right now, do you?"

I shook my head.

"Okay." She went to my office, wheeling out my desk chair. Then my beautiful, happy sister spent the next thirty minutes talking to me about baby names while she ate her sandwich before going back to work.

As the day wore on, the exhaustion from a sleepless night began to take its toll. My bones felt too heavy. My muscles weak. But somehow, I persevered, and when I finally turned the lock on the front door and flipped the sign to closed, I breathed a sigh.

I reached for the light switch, dousing the shop in shadows. The streetlamp outside cast its white hue through the front windows. Normally, that light would scatter, barely brightening the front third of the shop. Tonight, it was like a spotlight shone directly on the empty table and chair by the window.

Vance's chair.

A sob escaped my throat. I gave in to the burn in my throat. And tears began streaming down my face.

The war was over. So I stopped fighting.

Instead, I buried my face in my hands and cried for the man who'd changed my life. The man I loved.

The man who'd walked away.

CHAPTER TWENTY-EIGHT

VANCE

The drive from the station to my house was eleven minutes.

For the past eleven minutes, I'd felt like I'd forgotten something in the captain's office.

Not just something.

My badge.

Effective today, I was no longer a deputy with the Kootenai County Sheriff's Office. And even though I'd planned for this, eleven minutes hadn't been long enough for this new reality to sink in.

I wasn't a cop, not anymore.

There was a duffel bag in the back seat of my truck full of everything I'd had stuffed in my locker at work. Even though Christmas was still a few weeks away, Alec's wife had made me a tin of holiday cookies. They were in the passenger seat.

I hauled everything out of the truck but left it on a shelf in the garage, not having the energy to deal with it right now, then headed inside the house.

The moment I walked through the door to the laundry room, Vera came rushing around the corner. Her sock-covered feet slid like ice skates across the hardwood floor. "So? How'd it go? Did you quit?"

"It went. And yes, I quit." I sighed, setting my keys on top of the dryer.

There used to be a hook beside the door where I'd hang my keys. But when we'd arrived in Idaho six weeks ago, the hook had been missing along with a long list of other things that Tiff had taken when she'd moved out.

In the past six weeks, I hadn't bothered to find a new hook. Or new nightstands for my bedroom. Or a coffee table in the living room.

The furniture had been mine, though apparently Tiff hadn't cared. Vera didn't seem to mind that there were holes where pieces of furniture should be. And I didn't give a shit about, well . . . a lot. At least not much here in Idaho.

For the past month and a half, it had become glaringly obvious that I'd left far, far too much of myself in Montana.

With Lyla.

"Are you okay?" Vera asked.

"All good," I lied. "You got a haircut."

It was still long, the orange-red strands brushing against her heart, but it was six inches shorter than it had been when I'd left this morning.

"It was still scraggly." She plucked at a lock. "It needed to go shorter."

Which was exactly what the stylist had told her the first time we'd gone to the salon—it had taken Vera nearly a month before she'd leave the house without me, so I'd taken her to that first haircut. And despite the stylist's advice, Vera hadn't wanted to lose too much length.

She liked her long hair. And I think she'd feared that if there were too many changes, she'd lose herself. She'd lose the girl who'd spent those years in the wilderness with her father.

I was proud of her for going there today. For making another change.

"It looks really great."

"Thanks." She shrugged. "I like it."

"Then that's all that matters." I toed off my boots, then I took off my winter coat, glad I had nowhere else to go today, because the roads around town were slick and covered in snow. "Maybe it's time I got another haircut too."

The day I'd taken Vera, I'd had mine trimmed too, but that had been weeks ago and it was getting long again. Without Lyla around to run her fingers through it, there didn't seem like much point in letting it grow.

"We could walk to the salon tomorrow," Vera said.

"Or you could practice driving."

She shook her head.

Vera wasn't ready to drive again, not yet. Without any practice in the past four years, she had a lot of relearning to do. For now, wherever she needed to go, she walked. Even so, she rarely left the house.

"On my walk back, I picked up stuff at the store to make soup. It's ready and I set the table. Are you hungry?"

No. My stomach had been in a knot all day and would need a while to unravel. The idea of food only made the cramp worse.

But a week ago, Vera had declared that she wanted to contribute more around the house and that I needed to *let her* contribute more around the house. Apparently I'd been babying her. So in an effort to back off, I'd put her in charge of dinner every night.

If she'd made soup, then it was time to eat soup.

"Soup on a cold day sounds great."

"Okay." She stood a little taller. A tiny smile graced her mouth before she whirled around and slid-shuffled across the floor toward the kitchen.

That small smile was about as much joy as Vera showed these days. It was hard to remember what she looked like when she was actually happy. There was no laughter in her. No blinding, toothy smiles.

I missed that Vera. And I wasn't sure how to get her back.

So I'd focused on the practicalities instead.

Turns out . . . bringing a kid back to life was a clusterfuck of paperwork and skepticism.

Most people, like Alec, had needed an in-person visit to believe our story that Vera had shown up on my doorstep six weeks ago.

After I'd called to tell him, letting him be the dry run before my meeting with the captain, Alec had rushed over and stared at Vera, speechless, for almost thirty minutes.

Other people, like my captain, had required DNA tests to prove Vera was in fact Vera.

Was it strange not to feel the weight of my badge on my belt? Yep. But fuck, I was glad I'd never have to see that asshole's face again.

Sorting through the mess had been a nightmare, but we'd made it through. The world now knew that Vera Gallagher was alive—the local papers had plastered her photo on the front page for weeks. A few national news sources had picked up the story too.

But the story we'd spun in Quincy with Lyla's help had held up. As expected, Vera still refused to talk about that night with her mother. Since there wasn't a damn thing people could do to make her talk, they'd had to accept the rest of the details.

Cormac had taken Vera. They'd been living off the grid for four years. And finally, she'd left. She'd come home to a family friend. *Uncle Vance.*

The FBI had rushed to Idaho in hopes of finding Cormac, but also as expected, they hadn't found him. And just like before, they'd move on to other cases. Now that I wasn't searching for Cormac, the world would likely forget he even existed.

The media attention had dwindled, though not fast enough for my liking. Not only had they drudged up the details from that night years ago, but since I was linked to Cormac, the gas station shooting had made a resurgence too.

Thankfully, that investigation was over.

I'd been cleared of any wrongdoing, thank fuck. But the damage had already been done. The captain wanted me to keep a low profile, so he'd put me on desk work. The rumors about the family suing the department had faded—probably because they'd realized their chances of winning were slim to none. Still, he hadn't wanted to take any chances. Hadn't wanted to broadcast my face to the public.

Apparently, the attention I was getting with Vera was already too much.

So for the past six weeks, I'd been doing paperwork. A lot of fucking paperwork. It had just about sent me over the edge. But I'd stuck it out. For Vera.

I'd wanted to be at the station, in the department with a

few resources at my disposal, until she was a full-fledged member of society.

She had her social security card reinstated. She had a driver's license. She had a checking account and a credit card.

And since the FBI seemed to have run out of questions for her, well . . . I was thinking we were out of the woods. So today, I'd called it quits.

"Do you want milk or water?" Vera asked from the kitchen.

"Water, please," I answered, walking through the house as a shiver rolled over my shoulders. "Is it chilly in here?"

"Not really."

"Huh." Maybe it was just this house.

Had it always been this cold and sterile? *Yes.* Even when Tiff had lived here and I hadn't been missing furniture, this place hadn't had much of a personality. The walls were a dull gray that seemed to suck up the light. My lack of home décor skills meant there was no artwork to bring color into the space. No toss pillows or throw blankets or house plants.

It was nothing like the warm, inviting farmhouse on the outskirts of Quincy, Montana.

Goddamn it, I missed Lyla.

I should have made her promises, even when she'd asked me not to.

All I wanted was to pick up the phone and hear her voice. Every day, I fought the urge to drive to Montana for a glimpse of her beautiful face. It killed me to think of her moving on.

But I wouldn't tell her I was coming back, not until I knew it was true. I wouldn't call her, drag her along, and make promises that I might not manage to keep.

Was she okay? Did she miss me a fraction of how much I missed her?

"Big spoon or little spoon?" Vera asked.

"Big. I'll get napkins."

With them in hand, I went to the table and took my usual seat.

Vera carried over a bowl of soup made with golden broth, carrots, noodles and chicken.

"Looks delicious."

"I've never made chicken noodle soup before."

I stirred it for a minute, letting it cool, then took that first, steaming bite. Salt filled my mouth. It was like swallowing a gulp of ocean water, but I fought a grimace and choked it down. "Yum."

Vera took her own bite. And immediately spit it back into the bowl. "Oh my God. It's awful."

"It's not." I took another bite. Fuck, it was awful.

"I tasted it and it wasn't salty enough, so I added some but . . ." She set her spoon aside as the corners of her mouth turned down. "Sorry."

"Don't apologize. You're a good cook. One salty soup isn't the end of the world."

Her chin began to tremble.

"Vera." I covered her hand with mine as tears filled her eyes. "It's just soup."

"It's not even about the soup." She sniffled, wiping at her lashes. "The cashier at the store today asked me if I was that girl from the paper."

Shit. "What happened?"

"I lied and told her no."

Because otherwise, Vera would get bombarded with questions. People had no qualms about stepping past boundaries if it meant satisfying their curiosity. People were the worst.

"I'm tired of lying, Uncle Vance. I'm tired of being recognized everywhere I go." She caught another tear. "And I miss my dad."

"I know you do, kiddo."

"I thought . . . I thought it would feel different being here. I thought it would feel more like home. I thought . . ." Vera trailed off and dropped her gaze to the salty soup.

"Thought what?"

"Thought I would feel them."

Hadley and Elsie.

Maybe, if we could have visited the spot where I'd scattered their ashes, Vera would have felt that connection. But the snow was here to stay. If she wanted to visit, it would have to be this spring.

"What are we doing here?" She sniffled, drying both eyes. "You miss Lyla."

I missed her so much it was hard to breathe.

If Vera wanted to go back to Quincy, I'd start packing tonight. But I also needed her to say the words. To choose that path for herself.

The only reason I was in Idaho was for Vera. To give her whatever life she wanted. But if we went back to Montana, that was it. There wasn't a fucking chance I'd leave Lyla again.

"What are you saying, Vera?"

"I'm saying . . . I think we made a mistake. I think we should go back to Montana."

CHAPTER TWENTY-NINE

LYLA

Crystal walked into the kitchen with her mouth flapping open. "You painted snowflakes on the windows."

"Well, yeah. I do every year."

"But usually after Halloween. When you didn't do them by Thanksgiving, I figured you wouldn't do them at all."

I shrugged. "Just took me a little longer to get in the holiday spirit."

It was a lie. The only spirit currently occupying my body was misery.

But if I'd perfected anything in the past six weeks, it was faking happy. Faking normal.

Every year, I hand-painted snowflakes on the windows of Eden Coffee so that when tourists and locals came in for a cappuccino or pastry, they'd be greeted with charming, winter décor. So last night, after closing down the shop, I'd spent five hours adorning the glass with snowflakes of various shapes and sizes.

It had been well after midnight when I'd made it home

and crashed. Then I'd roused at four, returning to the shop to spend another day faking it.

"You're not wearing lipstick today," I said, taking in the soft pink of her mouth.

She shrugged. "I couldn't pick a color."

"Well, lipstick or not, you look pretty." I smiled. It was Sunday and her day off. Why had she come into the shop? "What are you up to today?"

"I came downtown to shop for Christmas presents. But it's busy, so I wanted to pop in and make sure you didn't need help."

"Thanks for checking, but I'll be okay."

I picked up the tray of muffins I'd pulled from the oven earlier and had set out to cool. With Crystal trailing behind me, I carried them to the counter, scanning the room to make sure no one new had wandered in while I'd been in the back.

Nearly every table was full. Every table but the one against the window.

Vance's table.

And the reason it wasn't full was because I'd taken away his chair. Both chairs, actually. Did it look ridiculous to have an empty table in the corner? Yes. But I couldn't bear to see another person in that spot. Not yet.

The minute I appeared with fresh muffins, three people came to the counter, each buying one to take to their seats. A man I'd never seen before asked for a refill on his coffee.

This time of year, there'd be a plethora of unfamiliar faces in Quincy. The weekends from now until New Year's would be slammed at the shop. Tourists would flock to our little town to shop or enjoy a winter getaway in the charming atmosphere.

The streetlamps along Main were all strung with white

twinkle lights. Mine wasn't the only shop window decorated for the season. And Eloise told me yesterday that the last open room at the hotel had just been booked. There were no vacancies until January.

"So I had this idea." Crystal propped her hip against the counter once the customers had all been served. "Let's join a dating app."

That was her idea? Hard pass. "Been there, done that. I don't think I'm the dating-app type."

Months ago, she might have convinced me to try again. But now?

Everything was different.

In the past six weeks, I hadn't heard from Vance. Not a word. Not that I'd expected a call or text. Not when I'd been the one to insist he make no promises.

But he hadn't truly disappeared either.

I'd read the news articles about Vera. About him. And beyond that, he was here. He was in this shop, a ghost at the table with no chairs. A phantom roaming the halls of my house, reminding me every morning and night that I was alone.

I missed him with every beat of my lonely, lonely heart.

It had been six weeks. He wasn't coming back, was he?

No. He wasn't coming back.

"What if I set up the profile for you?" Crystal asked. "Then all you'd have to do was swipe through any matches."

"Is there even a dating pool in Quincy?"

"Emily Nelsen was in yesterday, and she told me that she's been seeing a guy in Missoula. They met on an app."

"Crystal, I don't—"

"Just think about it." She held up a hand before I could protest. "That's all I'm asking."

I sighed. "Okay. I'll think about it."

Did I want to join a dating app? *Hell no.* There. Thought about it.

"Thank you." She smiled as the shop's front door opened and the bell jingled.

Mateo strode inside, his head covered in a black baseball cap that seemed to accentuate the sharp corners of his stubbled jaw. Gone was my lanky younger brother. He'd grown into a strong, handsome man, the resemblance to Griff and Knox almost uncanny.

Crystal's cheeks pinked, like she'd turned shy without a bold lip color. If Mateo showed even a hint of interest, this dating-app idea of hers would go sailing out my snowflake-adorned windows.

But his love life consisted of the occasional fling with a tourist he'd pick up at a bar. Not once in the time he'd been back from Alaska had he taken a woman out on a date. He was as allergic to relationships as he was shellfish.

"Hey," he said, placing his hands on the counter.

"Hi." I stood on my toes as he bent to kiss my cheek.

"Crystal." He dipped his chin, and her face turned from pink to bright red.

"Hey, Mateo." She looked everywhere but at his face, her hands fidgeting. Then she pushed off the counter and did a curtsey with a finger wave. "I'll see you later, Lyla."

"Bye."

She scurried around the counter, then rushed for the door.

"Did she just curtsey?" Mateo asked.

I giggled. "I think she's got a little crush on you."

"I thought she was into women."

"People."

"Ah." He nodded. "If she has a crush on me, is it going to get awkward?"

"I doubt it. It's a teensy, tiny crush. Mostly, I think she just finds you pretty to look at."

"Obviously." He smirked.

I flicked the tip of his nose like I used to do when we were kids. "What's up?"

"Nothing much. Came to town to pick up a few things Griff needs on the ranch. Thought I'd swing by and see if you needed anything."

Mateo was still focused on helping everyone out. Griffin on the ranch. Eloise at the hotel. Talia and Foster had just built a house on the ranch, and since she was due any day now, Mateo had spent weeks helping them pack and move.

He was a good uncle, always visiting his nieces and nephews. Just last night he'd babysat the boys so Knox and Memphis could go on a date. And whenever I needed help, Matty was only a phone call away.

"I'm good. Are you?"

He lifted a shoulder. "Yeah."

"Can I ask you something?" I jerked my chin for him to come around the counter.

Mateo took the spot where Crystal had been leaning. "Shoot."

"Why'd you leave Alaska?"

I'd wanted to ask him that question for weeks, but there'd never seemed a good time. We'd always been busy or working. But I'd realized last night as I painted snowflakes days late, I could lose my chance entirely.

If the past six weeks had taught me anything, it was that everything could change in a blink.

"I missed home," he said.

While I didn't doubt that answer was true, it felt . . . superficial. "Mateo."

"Lyla."

"I'm worried about you."

"That's my line."

I gave him a soft smile. "So it is."

Mateo had made that declaration countless times. So had every other member of my family.

As much as I tried to pretend I was happy, everyone knew that when Vance had left Quincy, he'd taken a piece of me with him.

"I was sleeping with this woman." Mateo's statement surprised me. Maybe he was sick of pretending too. "It was supposed to be casual."

"She caught feelings."

"*I* caught feelings."

"Oh."

He shrugged. "That's not what she wanted, so we broke it off. Kind of fucked with me though. I loved flying every day. I loved Alaska and made some decent friends. But . . ."

"It wasn't home."

"It wasn't Montana."

"For the record, I'm glad you're here."

"Me too."

"One more question." I held up a finger, earning me a teasing eye roll. "If you love flying every day, why'd you stop?"

His blue gaze, the same color as mine, shifted over my shoulder to a blank spot on the wall. "I guess . . . I went to Alaska, hoping I'd find what I needed. Didn't quite work out that way."

So he'd come home, and instead of exploring his own

passions, chasing his own dreams, he'd helped his siblings with theirs because it was easier. Familiar.

It required that he make no decisions about his own future. Take no risks. It was a temporary solution, but sooner rather than later, I hoped Mateo would find his own direction. His own purpose.

"Okay, enough with the heavy." I waved off that subject, sensing he was ready for a change too. "Want something to eat? I just made muffins."

"Sure."

We spent the next hour talking about nothing while I attended to my customers. After he left for the ranch, I made a fresh pot of coffee, helping myself to a steaming mug to fight the yawning that wouldn't stop.

Without Vance in my bed, sleep seemed elusive. Still, I kept my smile firmly fixed in place as the hours passed on another day.

The sun set so early this time of year that it was dark even before the dinner rush. While the days were hectic and busy, people tended to retreat to the warmth and safety of their homes once night fell.

Leaving me alone in a coffee shop for one more hour until I could go home.

And be alone there too.

The shop was empty, the tables clean, so I went to the kitchen and made myself a peanut butter, banana and honey sandwich. While I ate, I pulled out my phone from my pocket.

I'd missed six texts. Three from Eloise. One from Talia. The last from Mom.

Nothing from Vance.

A month ago, I'd gone through a period where I'd been

so angry at him. I'd been furious that he could just go back to his life. That he could forget about me so easily. But that anger had been short-lived.

I'd never been the type who could stay mad at someone I loved.

And, oh, how I loved Vance Sutter.

Even if we lived our lives apart. Even if I never saw his face again. I would love Vance for the rest of my life.

The door's bell jingled, so I shoved the last bite of sandwich in my mouth. Then I gulped a drink of water before wiping my lips dry and hurrying to the counter.

Three steps down the hallway, I froze.

A man stood just inside the doorway, his back turned toward me. His gaze was aimed at the table against the windows.

My hand pressed against my heart.

I'd know those broad shoulders and that dark, disheveled hair anywhere.

I closed my eyes, sure he'd be gone when they opened.

He wasn't.

Vance stood motionless, staring at the place where his chair had been.

I risked another step but stopped again. If I got too close, would he disappear in a puff of smoke?

He turned, took a step of his own, then twisted to look at the table again. His jaw ticked. When he faced forward, it was with a scowl. His gaze swept across the empty counter. Then it darted down the hallway, and when he spotted me, he stopped. His expression blanked.

My heart climbed into my throat as I unglued my feet and walked out, stopping when I was three feet away.

God, he looked good. Like a dream. Was I dreaming?

Vance's gray-blue eyes traced a line up and down my body, head to toe.

I was in a pair of jeans and a charcoal Henley. His Henley. It had gotten mixed in with my laundry, and when he'd packed, he'd left it behind. Even though I had to roll up the sleeves and tuck it in so it didn't look like a dress, I wore it at least twice a week.

"Hi." His voice was raspy, like his throat had gone dry.

"Hi."

Vance's frown deepened and he planted his hands on his hips. "Where the hell is my chair, Blue?"

Tears flooded. My knees wobbled. A laugh escaped, or maybe it was a sob.

Whatever the noise, it relaxed his frame. Then he surged, closing the gap between us, and hauled me into his arms.

I buried my face in his chest and inhaled. Soap and spice and earth and wind. Heaven. "Is this real? Are you here?"

"I'm here." He breathed in my hair. "Fuck, but I missed you."

"You did?"

"Every damn day."

I squeezed my eyes closed, balling his coat in my fists to keep him from moving. "I put your chair away. I couldn't look at it empty every day. I *can't* look at it empty every day."

If he was just going to leave again, he needed to go. Now. While I could still stand on my own.

He eased me back to frame my face in his large hands, his thumbs stroking my cheeks. "It won't be empty. Never again. That's a promise, Lyla."

A promise he'd keep. "I like promises."

The corner of his mouth turned up. Then he slammed

his mouth on mine. His tongue stroked my bottom lip, tender and slow, coaxing my mouth open. When he slid inside, it was slow. Torturous. He explored my mouth like this was the first kiss.

In a way, maybe it was.

I melted against him, the ache in my chest abating with every soft kiss until he broke away, his gaze colliding with mine.

"I love you, Lyla." Those gray-blue eyes were as bright as stars. It was a color I'd seen in them before. I just hadn't named it yet. *Love.*

"I love you too."

"I love you so fucking much." His hold on me tightened. "I couldn't breathe when we were apart."

"Don't ever leave me again."

"Not a chance." A growl escaped his throat as his mouth crushed mine once more, kissing me until I was breathless. Then we clung to each other, his arms banded around my back. His face buried in my hair.

I snaked my arms around his waist, pressing my cheek to his shoulder as I molded around his hard, broad frame.

We stood locked together until something vibrated between us. Vance's pocket. He shifted, letting me go just enough to dig out his phone.

"It's Vera," he said.

"Where is she?"

"At the hotel. She just texted to say she's tired from the drive and will just see us in the morning."

The last reservation at The Eloise. That was him.

I closed my eyes, leaning against his heart, listening to its beat and feeling the heat from his body radiate into mine.

Was he really done with Idaho? What about his job?

What had happened with the investigation into the shooting?

There'd be time for questions. There'd be time to talk about the future. But not yet. Tonight, I just wanted to take him home.

"I'm the only one here tonight and still need to close up."

"I'll wait until you're done." He took my face in his hands once more, his gaze full of love and something new.

Peace. He was at peace. And it was breathtaking.

"I'll get your chair."

EPILOGUE

LYLA

Three months later . . .

Four conversations floated around my parents' kitchen.

Dad was telling Griff and Knox about the flat tire he'd gotten on Wednesday.

Talia was lamenting to Mom and Winn about the upcoming end of her maternity leave.

Foster and Jasper were discussing some UFC fight.

Memphis, Eloise and Vera were huddled over a phone, shopping for Harrison's first birthday presents.

"We're getting married."

All four conversations came to a screeching halt.

Vance shook his head and chuckled. "So much for keeping it to ourselves until Mateo got here."

"He's late." I shrugged. "That's not my problem. Besides, someone would have noticed the ring."

And I refused to take it off.

My family, momentarily stunned, gaped at us, then everyone seemed to move at once. There were hugs and handshakes. Mom dabbed tears from the corner of her eyes. And when the overlapping conversations started again, this time the topic was our engagement and wedding plans.

The noise in the room spiked, excitement infusing the air. The kids, sensing the energy, chased in and out of the kitchen, racing along an invisible path that wound around legs and chairs and a few scattered toys, all while the adults talked.

The solitaire diamond ring on my finger still felt a bit foreign against my knuckle. But someday, after I'd worn it for decades, I hoped that whenever I slipped it off, I'd see its indentation in my skin.

Vance had taken me on a hike this morning. The weather had warmed over the past two weeks, enough that some of the snow had melted in the foothills. It was only March and we'd undoubtedly get another storm or two, but he'd wanted to take advantage of winter's reprieve and my day off.

The trail he'd found had taken us to a secluded meadow in the forest. Maybe he'd planned the hike. Maybe he'd scoped out the area in advance. Maybe he'd just gotten lucky to find such a picturesque clearing in the trees.

I wasn't sure and wasn't asking.

The minute we'd broken through the tree line, Vance had dropped to a knee and asked me to be his wife.

My cheeks flushed just thinking about how Vance had fucked me against the trunk of a nearby cottonwood after I'd said yes. Then we'd celebrated again in the back of his truck. And again when we'd gotten home. Twice.

Like he could read my thoughts, Vance's gaze met mine from across the room.

"I love you," I mouthed.

He winked.

"Where's Mateo?" Eloise asked, popping a carrot from the veggie tray into her mouth.

"I don't know." Mom checked her phone. "He said he was coming."

"Well, I'm getting hungry," Dad said. "I'll start the grill. We can cook his burger when he gets here."

A line of men, each carrying a cocktail, trailed from the kitchen to the deck. Apparently it took six males to turn on one barbeque.

"So where do you want the wedding?" Mom asked, taking the burger patties she'd prepped earlier from the fridge.

"I was thinking the barn. If that's okay with you guys."

"Of course." She clapped, giddy with excitement. "What about the ceremony?"

"The weather is always a risk, but maybe we could have it outside."

"We could set up tents just in case of rain," Winn said.

"Oh, I saw this amazing picture the other day of an altar." Memphis scrolled through the plethora of wedding inspiration pictures she'd saved on her phone as an event planner. She found the right one and held it out for us all to look at. "Isn't that pretty with the wood arches and flowers? We could easily add a roof or covering."

"I love it." I smiled. "Will you be my wedding planner?"

"Aww." She pressed a hand to her heart, then swept me into a hug. "I'd be honored."

"How are your classes going, Vera?" Talia asked.

Vera had become a regular at our family dinners these past three months. She'd actually become a regular at Mom and Dad's, period.

After Vance had come back to Quincy, he'd told me about the weeks we'd been apart. How miserable they'd been for Vera.

His place in Idaho had sold a few weeks ago, along with most of his furniture. We'd all gone back for a weekend to pack his remaining belongings and move them to my place.

The plan had been for Vera to keep living in the guest bedroom at our house. But then she'd declared she wanted her own place. She wanted to start living like a normal twenty-one-year-old woman.

Vance didn't think she was quite ready to be entirely on her own again. Maybe he was just being protective, but after four years of isolation, I agreed that easing her into things was probably the best bet.

So I'd called my parents.

There was a loft above the barn. Mateo had lived there for a time after college. Then my uncle Briggs had called it home when his dementia had become worse and Dad had wanted his brother closer. After the dementia had become too advanced, Briggs had gone into a nursing home.

The loft had been empty ever since.

It seemed like the perfect place for Vera to find her footing.

My parents adored her. They invited her over for dinner at least three times a week. Dad had taken it upon himself to help her refresh her driving skills. And Mom was teaching her how to cook.

Meanwhile, Vera had wanted to dive straight into a full-time job, but instead, we'd encouraged her to get her GED first. She'd aced her tests last month and had started two online courses since.

"I really like them," Vera said. "I still have no idea what I want to do, but for right now, I like having options."

She was enrolled in a nutrition class and a psychology course. Two wildly different topics but both seemed to pique her interest. For money, she'd been working at the coffee shop. Between her and Crystal, I was able to take Fridays and Saturdays off.

I wasn't sure how long I'd get to keep her at the shop. Mom and Dad had all but adopted Vera in the past three months, so if the day came when she wanted to move out for college or a career, they'd miss her terribly.

But for now, she seemed content. When she wasn't working, she spent a lot of her free time with Vance. And day by day, her sweet smile appeared more and more.

While I wanted to give Vance and my family and my coffee shop credit for her growing happiness, I suspected a part of it had everything to do with the hikes she took into the woods.

She was searching for her father.

Neither Vance nor I asked if she'd found him. We stayed quiet, letting her do whatever it was she needed to do.

Poor Dad though. The first time she'd gone on a hike alone, Dad had panicked, worrying she'd get lost or hurt. Vance had promised my parents that he'd talk to her. And he'd reassured them that if anyone was safe in the wilderness, it was Vera Gallagher.

No one beyond the three of us knew that we'd found Vera with Cormac. My parents, like the rest of the world, believed that Vera had just shown up on Vance's doorstep in Idaho.

And though I'd braced for it—and so had Winn—no one from the FBI had bothered to visit Quincy.

The door to the deck opened and the guys streamed back

into the kitchen. Vance came to my side, hauling me close. He smelled like soap and earth and wind and . . . mine.

"Zalinski came into the restaurant for lunch today." Knox pulled Memphis against his chest. "He mentioned retiring soon. I didn't realize he was considering it."

"News to me," Winn said.

"Same here." Dad nodded. "But I think it's time."

"Are you interested in running for sheriff?" Jasper asked Vance.

"Nah. Too much politics." He grinned at Winn. "Besides, I like my new boss."

"Thanks." Winn smiled back. "If you want to run for sheriff, you know I'll support you. But selfishly, please don't leave me."

Vance chuckled. "I'm not going anywhere."

Winn had told me not long ago that Vance was like a breath of fresh air at the station. Most of the cops that worked for her had grown up in or around Quincy. Vance brought a different perspective. Different experience. She appreciated his steady nature, his total aversion to gossip or drama. And she knew he was loyal. He'd have her back.

The front door opened and bootsteps came thudding down the hall before Mateo appeared.

"There you—" Mom's eyes widened. "What's wrong?"

The cheerful mood from just seconds ago vanished as we all took in his ashen face.

"I, um . . ." He blinked, shaking his head like it was in a fog. "I have to go to Alaska. Tonight."

"Tonight?" Dad asked. "Why? What's going on?"

Mateo swallowed hard. "I think . . . I think I have a daughter?"

The room erupted in questions that Mateo didn't

answer.

He was already out the door.

"YOU OKAY?" Vance asked as we drove home from the ranch.

"Yeah." I sighed. "Worried."

Dinner had taken an entirely different turn after Mateo's announcement. Mom had spent the rest of the night trying to call him—he hadn't answered. And I'd kept my mouth shut as everyone else had speculated about the possibility of Mateo being a father.

No one else seemed to know about the woman he'd told me about months ago. The woman from his not-so-casual fling. So I just assumed he hadn't wanted anyone to know. I'd let him explain to our parents and siblings.

But I was definitely telling my fiancé.

"A while ago, Mateo told me that he'd been seeing this woman in Alaska. He had hoped it would go somewhere but she wasn't interested. Do you think that's the mother? Of this baby?" I asked. Vance wouldn't know the answer, but I couldn't help thinking out loud.

"I don't know, Blue." He stretched an arm across the cab, taking my hand and bringing it to his lap.

"Ugh. I hate not knowing what's happening."

"He'll figure it out. Give him time." He brought my knuckles to his lips. "Your dad said he was cool with us having the wedding reception in the barn."

Vance always knew when it was time to change the subject. And he was right. All we could do was give Mateo time. When he knew what was happening, he'd tell us.

"I want a big wedding," I said, going along with the new topic. "The white dress. The cake. The party. I want a Lyla-and-Vance day." That was the wedding of my dreams.

"A Lyla-and-Vance day," he murmured, like he was tasting the idea to see if it was sweet.

"If you'd rather have something small—"

"I love you, Lyla. If you want a big wedding, then we'll have a big wedding."

"I love you too."

"Could I toss out one idea?"

"Of course."

He slowed the truck, easing to the side of the road. But there was nothing to see, just darkness and our headlights on the pavement ahead.

Vance unbuckled his seat belt, then bent over the console, crooking his finger until I was close enough to kiss. It was slow and lazy, the swirl of his tongue against mine causing a low ache to bloom in my center.

When he broke away, I unbuckled my own seat belt, ready to scramble into the back seat and have a repeat of our romp earlier. Me riding him, rocking the truck until we both cried out in ecstasy.

But before I could move, Vance held up a finger. "About this wedding."

"Yes," I drawled.

"You want it this summer."

"Preferably."

"Deal." His gray-blue eyes locked with mine as a smirk spread across that sexy mouth. "But you let me get you pregnant first."

Not at all what I'd expected him to say. It was the best idea I'd heard all night. "You're on, Sutter."

BONUS EPILOGUE

VANCE

"Daddy, look it." Trey held up a stick and waved it in the air. He swung it back and forth so fast it made a *whoosh.*

This was his fifth "sword" we'd come across so far on the hike. Its predecessor, and the three before it, had all been discarded on the trail because he'd found bigger, better versions.

"That's a good one, T." I flicked the brim of his hat, earning a giggle.

My son's laughter was about the most beautiful sound in the world. Although the same was true with Lyla's and Darcy's.

"Let's have some water." I took off my pack and dropped to my haunches, fishing out his water bottle.

While he guzzled, Lyla came up behind us on the trail.

"You want me to take her now?" I nodded to Darcy in the carrier strapped to Lyla's chest.

"No." Lyla kissed the baby's dark hair. "She's asleep."

Our daughter had just turned one, and though she was still tiny, hiking with the added weight of a baby and the pack was tiring. But no surprise, Lyla had kept up. Not that I was hiking fast. Not with Trey.

At four years old, he was a trooper, but still, I was giving it another fifteen minutes until he asked to ride on my shoulders. The hunt for stick swords had already pushed him thirty minutes longer than normal.

"It's so pretty out today." Lyla tipped her head to the sky, letting the sun warm her beautiful face.

The view was breathtaking. And it had nothing to do with the scenery.

We were on a trail bordered by trees, but the path itself was wide and open. It was a popular spot in the summers with tourists who wanted to get out and experience the Montana outdoors, but who didn't want to venture far from town or leave cell service. It was also an easy trail, nothing too strenuous for kids or seniors.

I loathed this spot in the summers because it was so damn crowded. But with the fall came the quiet season in Quincy, and we'd go on hikes closer to town, rather than drive out to the private property on the ranch to escape the tourists.

"Here, Daddy." Trey thrust the water into my chest, then skipped past me, swinging his stick around. He moved to a nearby tree and hit it with a *thwack*.

"Trey, if you want to see a deer, you have to be quiet," Lyla said.

"What, Mommy?" he yelled.

"Never mind." She laughed, shaking her head.

I chuckled and stood, brushing a lock of hair off her temple. "Ready to head back?"

"Not quite." She smiled up at me, rising to her toes, searching for a kiss.

So I bent and dropped my mouth to hers, stealing a taste of her sweet lips, until Trey came running over with a rock, stick abandoned.

"Watch me, Mommy." He wound up, arm bent and hand lifted by his ear, then sent the rock sailing through the air.

"Nice throw, buddy!" She was his personal cheerleader, always ready with a fist bump or high five. "Okay, follow Daddy."

"I need my stick." He spun in a circle, searching the ground, then remembered he'd left it by the tree.

As he raced to pick it up, I gave Lyla another quick kiss, then caught up to Trey, letting him be the leader for a few minutes.

My son had an independent streak that I loved. He'd come into this world with a brave scream six months after Lyla and I had gotten married, and he'd been blazing his own trail ever since. Even with his older cousins, Trey never followed for the sake of staying with the group.

So he marched along the path while I stayed close, ready to pick him up if he tripped or stumbled.

The fall air was crisp and clean this afternoon. The trees painted the mountain foothills in greens and golds and reds. Montana had become home.

In the years since I'd moved to Quincy, the distance between me and my family had only grown. My parents and sisters had all come to our wedding on the Eden ranch. Andrea had come alone since Brandon had chosen to stay in Idaho with their daughter. Mostly, I was just glad he'd let her come. And that I was able to see her on our annual trips to Coeur d'Alene.

Those visits to Idaho were Lyla's insistence. She wanted

our kids to know their grandparents, even if they weren't close. She just wanted that familiarity. So we took a yearly, awkward road trip.

It didn't matter as much as it had once. The people I considered family were hiking with me today.

"I need to go potty." Trey stopped on the trail, his hands immediately shooting to his pants. That boy pushed his tiny bladder to the limit, and whenever he declared he needed to pee, it was an emergency.

"Find a tree," I said.

He raced toward the closest, fumbling to shove down his pants.

I chuckled, watching him decorate a tree trunk, then checked over my shoulder for Lyla.

She'd veered off the path to pick up a stick that she'd probably give to Trey. When she looked over, she blew me a kiss.

I caught it and pressed it to my heart.

Years ago, back in the days when Lyla and I were new, I'd wondered if I should let myself get lost in Montana. Turns out, it had never been about getting lost. This was where I'd come to be found.

Lyla had found me.

Strange how a man could think he was happy and not even know what the hell he was missing.

I turned in a slow circle, taking in our surroundings. Breathing in the air.

Catching a figure in the corner of my eye.

I did a double take, staring into the distance at a mop of reddish-orange hair. And a familiar, scarred face.

Cormac emerged from behind a tree. He didn't step fully

on the path, nor did he move quickly, not drawing the others' attention.

Lyla walked over to Trey, bending to help him pull up his undies and pants.

While I kept my gaze locked on Cormac.

"Son of a bitch." So he was still here. After all this time. He hadn't left Montana.

I'd asked Vera on countless occasions if she'd seen her father, but she'd always avoided an answer. Guess it was *yes*.

Not that it was really surprising Cormac had stayed here. He wouldn't be far from his daughter.

Now that I had kids of my own, I wouldn't stray far from them either.

Cormac's gaze shifted to Lyla. To the kids. Even from a distance, I could see his face soften. Then he looked back at me and lifted a hand in the air.

I lifted mine in return.

He was gone by the time Lyla reached my side.

"Mom just texted. She invited us out to the ranch for dinner."

I gave her an absent nod, my gaze still tracking the trees for Cormac, but he was nowhere in sight.

"Hey." Lyla put her hand on my ribs. "You okay?"

Tearing my gaze from the trees, I looked down at her. At our son, thoroughly enamored with his new stick. At our daughter, sleeping peacefully with her ear pressed to her mother's heart.

"Yeah, Blue." I pulled Lyla into my arms. "More than okay."

SABLE PEAK

Vera Gallagher is chasing constant. For four years, her life was anything but normal. And the years before that she refuses to even remember. Dwelling on the past only hurts. Life is fragile, a lesson her mother taught her well. She's determined not to waste a moment of her newfound freedom.

Maybe some would consider her crush on Mateo Eden wasted time. Maybe some would call her a fool for loving a man who hasn't once dropped a crumb of interest her way. Still, to Vera, it's Mateo or nothing.

He's handsome. Charming. Witty. And he loves his family the way Vera loves—with her whole heart.

Maybe he'll never notice her. Maybe she's too damaged, too broken, to find that normal life she craves. Maybe her secrets will always keep them apart. But Vera will love him anyway. Whether Mateo realizes it or not.

ACKNOWLEDGMENTS

Thank you for reading *Crimson River*! Special thanks to Elizabeth Nover, my incredible editor. To Julie Deaton and Judy Zweifel for your proofreading expertise. Thank you to Sarah Hansen for the stunning cover. Thanks to Vicki for helping me keep my life in order. To Logan for the long phone calls and cinematic masterpieces and general awesomeness on a daily basis. Thanks to Monica, Marni and Valentine for being the best Vegas Party Bus companions I could wish for. To Bill, Will and Nash, thank you for the joy you bring me each and every day. And to Nina. I could fill a hundred pages with how much I adore and appreciate you. Thanks for all you do.

ABOUT THE AUTHOR

Devney Perry is a *Wall Street Journal*, *USA Today* and #1 *Amazon* bestselling author of over forty romance novels. After working in the technology industry for a decade, she abandoned conference calls and project schedules to pursue her passion for writing. She was born and raised in Montana and now lives in Washington with her husband and two sons.

Don't miss out on Devney's latest book news.
Subscribe to her newsletter!
www.devneyperry.com

Made in the USA
Las Vegas, NV
08 June 2024

90897797R00194